Obscured

Book One
The Obscured Series

C.M. Boers

ISBN-10:
0-9906452-6-6

ISBN-13:

978-0-9906452-6-9

DEDICATION

This book is dedicated to my family and friends, without them I would never have decided to dedicate my time and effort to write and publish this book.

CONTENTS

This is a work of fiction. Names, characters, places and incidents are either the product of the author's imagination or are used fictitiously. Any resemblance to actual events or locales or persons, living or dead, is entirely coincidental.

ACKNOWLEDGMENTS

I would like to thank all of my friends and family that had a hand in helping to make this book what it is today. I would also like to thank all of my readers. Thank you for taking time to read my book.

CHAPTER ONE

My breathing is ragged. The vast desert surrounds me the further I ran. Terror grips every ounce of my body. The slowly rising darkness does little to cool the sweltering heat—it only seems to add to my panic. Sweat pours down my back, and my T-shirt sticks to me. Darkened saguaros spring up on the horizon as the sun descends from its rightful place in the blackened sky, which has yet to reveal the twinkling gems of the night. I maneuver around the bushes and shrubs until a clearing appeared. I take the opportunity to sprint faster. As the dust from my footfalls envelopes me, a coughing fit ensues. My lungs involuntary attempt to clear themselves.

I shot straight out of bed, gasping for air. Each time the dream became more real than the last. It began shortly after I learned we were moving to Arizona, and it had grown increasingly more prevalent. The torment was always the same. I was in the desert, running and scared—but of what? I hoped the dreams would go away after we got settled in Arizona, but after a full week, nothing had changed.

We had moved from beautiful Los Angeles to the deadening heat of Phoenix. Why? Well, I could thank my mom for that one. After the divorce, she said we needed a change, a clean slate if you will. And of all places she could have chosen, she very well may have picked the hottest.

The first day at a new school is bad enough, but the first day at a new school in a new *town* is terrifying. On top of that, I had just turned sixteen and was starting high school. High school, for goodness sake!

My name is Abigail Martin, but everyone calls me Abby. *Tomorrow will be the first day of pure torture when I start at Kinsley*

High School. My stomach was a jumble of nerves just thinking about it.

"Abby, your dad is on the phone for you," my mom called up the stairs.

Rounding the corner, I saw my mom at the bottom of the landing. It was hard not to admire her beauty. My mom has exquisitely beautiful hair, which happens to be just like mine—long, brown, and curly. I get my looks from her. Most people say they can't see any of my dad's features in me. Mom and I share the same blue eyes, and she's short like me. However, thanks to my dad, I have a slight height advantage.

I knew my dad was calling to check in and make sure we were doing okay. I had to give him credit for being so tough throughout the whole ordeal. I mean, his only child had moved six hours away—that was sure to be hard on anyone. I wouldn't tell him, but things were a lot harder than I wanted to admit. I really missed him. I longed to move back to California and pretend that none of this ever happened.

I spent my last day of summer decorating my new room. The curtains on my window were pastel blue, which matched the rest of the chocolate brown and pastel blue décor. For the finishing touch, I hung a few pictures on the walls.

Preparing for school should have been my next priority. Instead, I was enjoying my last bit of freedom relaxing in my new bedroom. From my window, I could see the beautiful sunsets that Arizona is known for. The horizon was a magnificent orange, and the sky above it saturated like a pink, red, and purple watercolor painting. The sun had sunk halfway out of view, glowing orange in the midst of the bright sky. Even though these sunsets couldn't compare to a sunset on the beach, the rich colors made them glorious in their own way. Suddenly, the sun disappeared, leaving night to descend over the Valley.

As I climbed into bed, I grabbed a picture of my mom, my dad, and me on the beach. I fell asleep staring at my past, unsure of my future. My mom said it was time for me to move on and embrace this new life. But was I ready for that?

The next morning, I awoke drenched in sweat once again. My nightmares still hadn't subsided; in fact, it seemed like new details revealed themselves with each dream. This time, I was sure I had been running away from someone, but I was unable to see my assailant's identity. The last thing I remembered before waking up was the darkened figure trailing behind me. I briefly wondered if I would ever get to the end of the dream and discover what I was running from. I had my doubts.

After rummaging through the boxes on the floor, I found an acceptable outfit for my first day—a red tank top and dark denim shorts.

I hopped down the stairs to the kitchen, where my mom was cooking up eggs, bacon, and toast for breakfast. Mom always made a good breakfast in the morning. "Breakfast is the most important meal of the day," she would always say. I couldn't really complain—I loved breakfast.

"Mmm, that smells delicious!" I said.

"Good morning, honey! Sit down and pour yourself some orange juice. Breakfast is just about ready. How'd you sleep?"

My mom had no idea I had been enduring nightmares for the last six months, but I wasn't going to fill her in on that detail. She would probably drag me off to some therapist.

"Good." I tried not to sound too enthusiastic so she didn't think I was lying.

"Are you excited to start high school today?"

"No."

She glared at me. I didn't bother to respond. Instead, I sat in silent protest for the rest of the meal.

Mom drove me to school on her way to work. I flipped through the radio stations until I found a rock station that sounded good, but then Mom changed it back to classical music. I rolled my eyes. I wished I had an iPod. We typically agreed on most things, but music was a different story entirely. I had my likes, and she had hers, and under no circumstance did they cross paths.

I gave my mom a quick wave as my eyes darted around the school, taking in my new surroundings. The school didn't look much different than the high school I would have gone to in California.

I arrived earlier than anyone else and decided to take the extra time to find all of my classes. I didn't relish the idea of rushing around later in the day and walking into class late. Bringing attention to myself turned my stomach.

Even though the school looked about the same size as the high school in my district in California, it was still much bigger than the middle school I had attended the year before.

All my classes proved fairly easy to find and weren't far from each other—and for that I was grateful. I could only assume that I having to travel from one end of the school to the other in seven minutes would be a big challenge.

I still had an abundance of time before my first class began, so I found a picnic table in front of the school and sat down. I passed the time watching my fellow students arrive. Many of them looked around as if they were lost or felt just as strange as I. Then there were the relaxed ones who emanated popularity. For them, the first day of school was like a party thrown in their honor. They floated from friend to friend, catching up on the latest gossip. I had never been one of those people, and I doubted I would ever be. Not that I cared.

Realizing I had only five minutes until the bell rang, I hopped out of my seat. The walls in the hallway were plastered with posters and banners promoting all the clubs and events around the school. My eyes drifted from poster to poster, and I considered which groups looked the most enticing. Only Yearbook Club caught my eye. I loved to take pictures, though I didn't do it often.

My mind changed gears when I noticed a drop-dead gorgeous boy. He stood out in his khaki cargo pants, button-up blue plaid shirt, and stylish sneakers—although I think he would have looked amazing in anything. His backpack had a football patch pinned on it, and I wondered if he was on the football team. He had annoyingly perfect, wavy blond hair, and his eyes were the most interesting shade of green.

He looked right at me, and my heart skipped a beat. It was unlikely he would ever be interested in a plain girl like me, but I immediately began imagining what it would be like to date someone like him. As he casually walked over to me, my breath hitched in my throat.

He towered over me, making me feel like a child.

"Hi there." He grinned.

He was actually going to talk to me?

"Hi," I replied, almost in a whisper. I was unsure of what else to say.

"Are you new here? I don't remember seeing you before, and I think I'd remember that face." His voice was as smooth as silk.

I tightened my jaw, trying to push back a smile, and cleared my throat. "Yeah, I just moved here from California," I said, my voice a little stronger than before.

He chuckled. "Wow! You moved from the perfect weather of California to the insane heat of Arizona? Your parents must be nuts!"

"Yeah, I don't know what my mom was thinking."

"What's your name? I'm Pete. Pete Denali."

"Abby," I said just as the bell rang.

I realized we were alone in the hallway, and I cringed. *So much for getting to class on time.*

"Late on the first day. Not the ideal start to the school year," he said with a hint of sarcasm.

"Yeah, no kidding!" I laughed. "I'd better get going."

We both turned to stride down the hall in the same direction. I shuffled my feet in time with his without even trying. I waited for him to turn and leave me, but when we walked into the same class, I was shocked.

I hoped the excitement wasn't written all over my face. *We have a class together!* Algebra, my least favorite subject, wasn't looking so bad after all.

When we walked into class and everyone turned to stare, my face blushed red hot. I hadn't realized we were that late. I took the first open seat I came to, willing the embarrassing redness to subside from my cheeks. Pete followed suit, sitting in the seat directly in front of me. *Perfect.* I could stare at him the whole class period, and he wouldn't have a clue. I felt a tinge of exasperation as I realized I was blushing again.

Pete and I didn't talk the rest of the period. Instead, we listened to Mr. Robbins go over the class syllabus. Feeling bored, I alternated between staring at the back of Pete's head and doodling in my notebook. When the bell rang, everyone gathered their belongings and headed out of class. All except Pete, who waited for me.

"What's your next class?" he asked as we meandered out of the classroom together.

"English. You?" I asked.

"Darn, I have reading."

He walked me to my next class, and it felt like my heart would beat out of my chest. Never had someone so attractive appeared interested in me before. You could call my dating life less than mediocre. I went on a few dates in California but nothing to brag about.

It was obvious that Pete was pretty popular just from our walk through the halls together. My self-consciousness started to get the better of me, and I found myself wondering if he had a girlfriend. Maybe he was just nice because I was new, not because he was interested in being anything more than friends. I chastised myself for jumping to conclusions.

Before I knew it, we were standing in front of my next class.

"Well, I guess I'll see you later," Pete said.

"Okay. Thanks for walking with me to class."

Out of the corner of my eye, I noticed an attractive boy staring at us. I found myself drawn to his frigid gaze. He seemed to be glaring at Pete, and I couldn't help but wonder why.

His spiked black hair and piercing blue eyes captivated me for a moment. He was tall, though not quite as tall as Pete.

"Abby? Are you okay?"

Oops! Pete had been talking to me while I was in my daze. I didn't have a clue what he had said.

"I'm sorry. What did you say?" I asked, embarrassed that I hadn't been paying attention.

"Would you like to sit with me at lunch?" he asked a little sheepishly.

I was ashamed I had made him repeat it.

"Sure, that would be nice!" I probably sounded overly enthusiastic.

"I'll meet you by the cafeteria after third period. See ya!" he called over his shoulder.

I was on cloud nine as I walked into the classroom until a glare from the same boy I had seen in the hall shattered my euphoria. He stood next to the teacher's desk, and I noticed how well his baby blue shirt complemented his icy eyes. I wasn't sure why he was glaring at me. *Maybe he didn't like Pete, but why would he dislike me if he didn't even know me?* I picked a seat in the center of the room. He sat down as the bell rang. Right. Next. To. Me.

I tried to ignore him, but I couldn't. I peered at him out of the corner of my eye. He was looking right at me, and he caught me glancing at him. Something in his hand was coming toward me: a folded piece of paper. It surprised me, but I took it anyway. His handwriting was a little sloppy but not terrible for a boy. The contents took me by surprise.

> You're new here, and you're already talking to the wrong
> people. Not the best way to start out a new school year.
> Take my advice and ditch the dumb jock.
>   -Eli

I was right. He did have a problem with Pete.

> Yes, I am new here. Isn't making new friends a
> good thing? Why not Pete?
>   -Abby

I waited for the opportune time to pass the note back. Itcame quicker than I expected. I put it in his hand as fast as I could so that Mrs. Mosebee didn't catch me. As my hand brushed his, a tingle shot up my arm. I snatched my hand back from him, looking down at it as if I had been bitten. I wondered if he felt itbecause he didn't seem disturbed. Maybe I had imagined it.

Anxiously, I waited for hisreply. It never came.

The bell rang, and everyone filed out of the room except Eli. He waited at the doorway for me.

Once we left the classroom, he finally spoke. "Where are you headed right now?"

"Science."

"Same for me," he said as he started to walk in the direction of our next class. "That's good. We'll have more time to talk."

"What is it?" I asked, sounding somewhat annoyed.

"I don't really know how to say what I want to say without sounding . . . jealous," he admitted. "I just don't think you should be friends with Pete Denali. Can we leave it at that? Can you just trust me?"

I laughed. "Let me get this straight. You want me to stop talking to Pete, but you won't tell me why? You want me to trust you and just leave it at that, even though we just met? You must be crazy! I don't know you any better than I know him. What makes you more trustworthy?"

I couldn't believe what he was suggesting—after all, it was my first day. I had only made one friend so far, and he was already insisting that I was messing up my chances of fitting in without so much as an explanation. He was insane.

We walked into class, and Eli took the seat next to mine in the middle of the classroom. Then he turned to face me.

"I know how it must sound but—"

"Stop! Until you can give me a valid reason, I will not stop talking to him. Even then, I'm not guaranteeing anything!" I'd had enough of this nonsense.

I sat down with a huff. A girl behind me noticed my foul mood and tapped me on the shoulder.

Even more irritated than before, I turned around to discover that she seemed friendly. I tried to recover and smiled back to be nice.

"Having a bad first day?" she asked. She had an unusually round face, and her smile revealed dimples, which made her green eyes seem even warmer.

I was sure her bubbly voice matched her personality.

"Yeah, something like that," I answered sarcastically as I shot a glare in Eli's direction.

"I'm Bailey."

She tossed back her brown hair and held out her hand for me to shake. I took it.

"Abby."

She smiled.

The bell rang, and I turned around to face the front of the room. I was glad to have met someone who wasn't a boy. I thought Bailey seemed nice and hoped she would become a good friend. I sure could use one of those right about now. Maybe she could even help me out with Pete and Eli. It sure would help if I knew why Eli was so against Pete.

I turned to see if Eli was engrossed in Mr. Lang's discussion. I felt a little relief to see that he wasn't. I took out a piece of paper and tried to look as though I was paying attention. Our conversation bothered me, and he seemed adamant that Pete was bad, but I had a nagging feeling that I shouldn't ignore him. I wished I could push that sense away, but it stuck in my head.

Eli-
You have to tell me why. What is so wrong with Pete? I am meeting him for lunch after class unless I decide that what you have to say is worthwhile.
-Abby

I looked around the room in hopes that nobody was watching. The coast was clear. I passed the note to Eli, trying my best not to touch his hand. I was still a little spooked from the last time.

I watched him read my note and noticed that he tensed up.

While I waited for him to write back, I listened to Mr. Lang's lecture. He was explaining some of the things we were going to learn during the year. He mentioned protons and neutrons, which I had already studied.

I was startled when something hit my elbow. It was a note from Eli.

Abby-
Cancel your plans with Pete today at lunch and have lunch with me instead. I will try to explain better then. Please?
-Eli

So he was going to try and explain, which was what I had asked him to do. But why did I have to cancel lunch with Pete to hear it? And while I wasn't one to turn someone down, I also wasn't the type to cancel plans. That nagging feeling in the back of my head pushed me to say yes to Eli. *What if I went to lunch with Eli and didn't agree with his reasoning?* I would regret canceling with Pete. Then again, if Eli told me something compelling that changed my mind, I would be grateful. There were a lot of unknowns, but I decided to go to lunch with Eli and tell Pete it was because we had to discuss homework. I hoped he would take it well and wouldn't be too disappointed. I didn't want to lose any chance I had with him.

Eli-

I guess I'll go to lunch with you today, but don't think that this changes anything with Pete yet.
-Abby

When the bell rang, I walked out of class with Eli, trying to think of the best way to let Pete down gently. Bailey followed us out of class.

"Hey Abby, wait for me!" she called.

I turned and waited patiently to see what she wanted.

"Hey, Bailey."

"Hey, want to have lunch with me today?"

Three people asking me to go to lunch with them all in the same day? When did I become so popular? I was flattered.

"Actually, I'm having lunch with Eli today."

"Ooh okay . . . I guess I'll see you later then."

She scrambled away before I got the chance to say anything else. I was glad I didn't have to try to make up a lie about why she couldn't join us, but I felt horrible at the same time. I wanted so badly to have a friend, especially a girl. I promised myself I would go to lunch with her the next day. Maybe I could convince Pete to have lunch with Bailey and me.

I sighed, glancing at Eli. "Well, let's get to lunch."

We walked in silence, mostly because I was too engrossed in my thoughts. I had a lot to consider, and it was only the first half of the day! I felt overwhelmed.

When I saw Pete up ahead waiting for me, my heart beat faster. He looked so excited to see me, and it made me feel twice as nervous. I'd never been good at letting people down. Instead, I was the people pleaser. To upset someone by canceling plans was really hard on me. It made me feel like a flake. I hated it when my friends were flaky, and I held myself to the same standard.

"Hey, Abby!" Pete called.

I cringed, hoping Eli would be appreciative of how hard this was on me. Then again, how could he understand? He didn't even know me.

"Hey Pete, I have some bad news."

Eli stood at my side, looking smug. Probably for Pete's benefit. *What's his problem anyway?* I wished he had just gone inside to wait for me. Instead, he decided to be an audience to my discomfort, making the situation that much harder for everyone.

"What's wrong?"

"I have to cancel our lunch plans today." I frowned.

"Oh," he said. His shoulders drooped downward.

"I'm sorry! I just have to talk to Eli about some stuff for our class."

"All right.How about tomorrow?" He perked up a bit when he asked, seeming hopeful I would agree.

"I have plans with Bailey, but if you are okay with Bailey joining us, that would be fun." I hoped he didn't thinkI was trying to avoid him.

"Okay, see you tomorrow. Have a good lunch."

He walked away, looking a little less defeated.

I sighed.

"Shall we?" Eli motioned toward the cafeteria, extending his elbow out for me to take.

"Yep, let's go," I said, pushing past his arm.

I heard him chuckle, and I rolled my eyes.

My stomach was grumbling as I ordered my lunch, but I patiently waited for Eli to finish ordering while I munched on my French fries.

Eli suggested we sit at a table in the far corner of the cafeteria. I could only guess he was trying to get as far from everyone as he could, but I was fine with that. Nobody would overhear our conversation. I hoped the conversation wouldn't get back to Pete, even though I wasn't sure what was going to be said. I didn't want anyone to think I was talking behind Pete's back.*Even though that's exactly what I was doing.* I didn't want to earn a bad reputation for gossiping.

"Let's hear what you have to say," I demanded after we started eating.

He finished chewing his first bite of spaghetti.

"This isn't about me being jealous. I want you to know that from the start. I don't know how to explain it, other than just saying it bluntly." Eli paused, and a few seconds passed. "I think he killed someone." He stared into my eyes.

Murder? This was what he wanted to tell me?

"I don't believe you. He's in high school! There's no way he could have *murdered* someone!" I shot back, not realizing my voice had risen to a shriek.

I blushed in embarrassment when I realized there were people staring at me. My voice carried in the big room, but I could only hope that the hum of voices had masked what I had said.

He rolled his eyes. "Well if you're over the theatrics, can I finish explaining?"

"I'm sorry, but that's absurd!"

"Can I finish?"

I sighed. "Go on."

"I went to a football game here last year. Pete was on the team. They lost the game, and needless to say, Pete was really upset. One of the guys on the other team gave Pete a hard time, and the coach had to get after Pete about his temper. Pete left alone that night, and nobody saw him until the next day. The guy on the other team disappeared. I don't know if anyone at this school even knows about it. I read in the paper a few days later that he was missing, so you can see what I'm talking about when I say Pete's no good."

"There has to be some other explanation."

"Like what?" he asked.

My mind raced as I tried to think of something. Neither of us said anything for a long time. The longer the silence passed, the harder it became to admit that I didn't have any other ideas.

"I don't know," I whispered. "Maybe the guy just ran away from home. Maybe he wasn't happy with his parents or something."

"Do you honestly believe that?"

"Yes," I said, hoping he couldn't tell I was lying. "It certainly is possible."

"I suppose it's possible, but is it likely?"

"I don't know. It's not like you can judge someone you've never met."

"I just wish you wouldn't put yourself in jeopardy like that."

"I can take care of myself," I said, trying to sound tough. "Why do you care?" Deep down, I was questioning my decision to be friends with Pete. Getting into the wrong crowd right off the bat wouldn't be good.

But what if it wasn't true? That wouldn't be fair to Pete. *There are a lot of explanations, right? There must be.* It would only be fair to give him a chance. But could I be objective? I figured there was only one way to find out.

"You can take care of yourself against a six-foot-four defensive lineman?" he asked, snapping me back to the present.

"Yes," I replied, avoiding eye contact.

"Somehow I'm not convinced."He looked up and down my slender body.

I couldn't hold in my giggle.

"So, you see my point?"

"I guess," I murmured.

I finished the last bite of food while I looked around the room. I felt unsure of what to say next, so I avoided eye contact and willed the bell to ring.

"What are you doing after school?"

"I'll probably just go home."

"You want to hang out or something?" he asked.

What? Did I hear him right?

"You want to hang out with me?"

"Yeah, of course. Why wouldn't I?" He seemed confused.

"I don't know. I thought you just wanted to boss me around about Pete. I didn't realize you were interested in being friends."

"I do want to be friends with you. I mean, if that's okay with you. And to be clear, I'm not trying to boss you around. I'm merely giving you information before you jump in."

He wanted to be my friend. I was surprised, but not as surprised as I was at my excitement about the prospect. Despite his bossy nature, I kind of liked him.

"Sure. Let's hang out. What did you have in mind?"

"I don't know. Would you be opposed to me coming over to your house? Maybe I can help you with your homework."

"Actually, that'd be nice."

I didn't have any homework yet, but it would be nice to have some company. Mom wouldn't be home until later so I would be alone otherwise. After living in Arizona for a week, I'd had enough of being alone.

Lunch ended after we finalized our plans for that afternoon. Eli walked me to class, and we agreed to meet in front of the school at the end of the day so he could drive us to my house.

I couldn't believe he already had his license and a car. I wasn't able to get my license for a few more months, and it was crazy to even think about owning a car. I didn't have any money saved, and until I had a job, my mom wouldn't even talk about getting one. Her theory was if I couldn't afford to pay for the gas, I shouldn't expect to have a car. I couldn't fault her—it was a valid point, but it didn't make it any easier. If I wanted a job, I had to find one I could walk to, which didn't leave very many options.

Eli's news during lunch had confused me. I had no clue what to believe. It was so strange. *Maybe Eli was stretching the truth.*

In reading class, I listened to Mrs. June go over the course syllabus. She outlined the books we were going to read, and one of them was a favorite of mine—*To Kill a Mockingbird.* She announced that there would be a book report on it when we were finished. I knew I could write an A+ report just based off what I remembered about it.

My last class of the day was P.E., and I was grateful to have it last so I didn't ruin my hair and makeup for the rest of the day. It turned out that Bailey was in my P.E. class, too. The teacher said we would start swimming the next day. I enjoyed swimming, but swimming at school didn't sound appealing.

After class, I caught up with Bailey.

"Hey Bailey, wait up!"

"Oh, hey Abby," she replied, sounding a little sad.

"I was wondering if you wanted to have lunch with me tomorrow."

I could tell she was surprised, and I felt bad.

"I'm sorry about today," I said."Eli and I just had some things to take care of."

"That sounds great Abby!"she said, her voice bubbly again.

"Okay. I'll see you tomorrow!" I called over my shoulder as I walked to the spot where I had agreed to meet Eli.

Eli and I walked out to the parking lot together, weaving between cars as we went. He stopped abruptly next to a cherry-red convertible. This was a special car; it didn't take a genius to figure that out.

"What kind of car is this? It's gorgeous!" I gushed as I circled the car, checking it out from all angles.

"It's a 1969 Camaro. You like it?"

"I love it!"

I marveled at the inside—flawless black leather seats with what looked to me like a new dashboard. The gauges seemed updated from their original style; they glowed bright white, and the mileage readout was digital. It had been restored so tastefully. I was more than impressed.

Eli pressed a button, and the convertible top slid down out of view. I had never been in a convertible before, and I loved the feeling. I couldn't even tell how hot it was with the wind blowing in my hair. When we stopped, the Arizona sun beat down on us, making it feel like a sauna. But thankfully, those stops were few.

"This car is amazing, Eli. Where did you get it?" I asked.

"It was my dad's. He and I started to restore it about two years ago, and finished it right before he died."

"I'm sorry. I didn't know." After an awkward moment, I spoke again. "How did he die? If you don't mind me asking."

He was silent for a long time. I gave him space and time to answer when he felt comfortable. It would be the courtesy I'd expect someone to give me if the tables were turned.

"No, I don't mind you asking at all. He died of lung cancer. He smoked. We knew he was dying for a few years beforehand. In a way, it gave me the time I needed to come to grips with the fact that he was going to be gone soon. I think that's helped me grieve faster, but I still miss him a lot."

"When did he die?"

"Six months ago."

A wave of sadness washed over me. He didn't look away from the road the entire time we talked, and his blank expression never changed. Even though my dad was in another state, I couldn't grasp the concept of never being able to see him again. Never being able to talk to him or ask for his advice. I admiredEli's ability to hold it together so well.

"It must be so hard to talk about. Let's talk about something else." I searched for a new topic of conversation. "How long have you lived in Arizona?"

"Since I was about three yearsold. I was born in Colorado."

"So you're used to the heat here. I can't imagine ever getting used to it!"

He laughed. "I don't know that you ever get used to the heat, but you survive it."

"Great!" I said. "Thanks for the hope!" I shoved his shoulder.

He let out a deep, throaty chuckle. I liked it.

I found it easy to be around Eli, which made it hard to imagine upsetting him by being friends with Pete. I was attracted to Pete though, and I thought I might want more than friendship with him somewhere down the road.

After thinking it over, I decided to give Pete a chance. He seemed nice enough.But I wasn't going to mention that to Eli. He would find out soon enough. I was enjoying our time together too much to ruin it.

CHAPTER TWO

Pulling up in front of my house was strange. It didn't quite feel like home yet. Before the move, I had lived in the same house since birth. *Maybe this won't ever feel like home. At least not in the way California did.*

The house itself was a newer model built three years earlier. The yard was impeccably landscaped, with spiky green grass in the center lined with tan gravel. A flowerbed filled with rosebushes ran along the walkway to the front door. The huge roses stared at me in a rainbow of color—crimson, peach, and lavender. I truly loved our new house, especially the inside. It was exactly what I would have chosen if it were up to me.

For just the two of us, the four-bedroom home was larger than we needed, but it gave us a room for an office and a guest room. The guest room was right next to mine. I secretly imagined my dad coming to visit and staying in that room. I knew it might not happen, of course. I didn't know if my parents would tolerate staying under the same roof, especially overnight, but I liked to think about it.

The kitchen was tastefully designed with black granite countertops. A dining room adjoinedthe kitchen and brandished an exquisite chandelier that would hang over our table once we bought one. I most loved the shiny hardwood flooring that gave the house a sense of elegance.

Since we had moved in a week earlier, we had eaten our meals at the breakfast bar in the kitchen. I could care less, but Mom hated eating anywhere but at a proper table.

The living room had a built-in entertainment center with room for a big-screen TV that my mom said we would eventually get, but for now, it held the 37-inch TV we had brought with us.

Eli followed me into the house, checking it out as he went.

"Would you like something to drink?" I asked as I set my backpack down on the kitchen counter.

"Sure, a soda would be great." He sat down at the bar. "This house is pretty awesome."

"Thanks, I like it a lot. I don't have any homework. Do you?"

"Nope." He grinned.

"Want to watch a movie or something?"

"Sure."

Eli picked an older comedy about two brothers who were interested in the same girl and didn't know it. It was actually one of my favorites, but I didn't tell him that.

When the movie was half over, I realized it was time for me to start dinner. I stood up and stretched. I hadn't noticed how stiff I was getting.

"Is something wrong?" Eli looked up at me, his eyebrows raised.

"No, I just have to start dinner. Tonight is my night to cook. I should be done in a few minutes."

"Actually, I probably should be going. My mom will be home soon, and she'll be worried if I'm not there."

He stood up, and I walked him to the door. He lingered outside on the porch.

I didn't make eye contact. "Well, I guess I'll see you tomorrow. Thanks for the ride home. It was nice hanging out."

"Sure, anytime. Um . . . Abby . . ." He hesitated. "Have you thought about what I told you today?"

I wasn't ready for that question. I couldn't look him in the eyebecause I couldn't be truthful with him.

"No, I haven't made a decision yet."

"Allright, I'll see you tomorrow."

I watched him walk down the driveway and speed away in his gorgeous car. I felt horrible lying to him, but I couldn't face his reaction yet. As I walked into the kitchen to make dinner, I contemplated what I would say the next day.

I planned to make one of my favorite dinners—baked chicken with creamy mashed potatoes and gravy and crisp green beans sautéed in olive oil. My mouth was watering just thinking about it. I started making dinner and timed everything to be done right when my mom got home.

I took my backpack to my bedroom and sat by the window to

watch another amazing sunset. It was nothing like the one I had seen the night before. In Arizona, the sunset was never the same—the colors that painted the sky changed each night. That evening, the entire horizon burnedgolden orange, with the brightest ball of light in the center. I loved having a front-row seat in my bedroom.

I sat long enough to think about what I would say to Eli. Since I began making dinner, I had gone through what seemed like hundreds of scenarios.

I vaulted the stairs two at a time when I heard the timer for the potatoes. They were perfectly soft on inspection and ready for mashing. I was just finishing mashing the potatoes when my mom walked in the door.

"Mmm, Abby—dinner smells delicious!"

"Hi Mom!" I called back. "It'll be ready in about ten minutes."

We dished up our plates buffet-style and sat down to eat at the bar. The chicken was better than it smelled, the mashed potatoes were the perfect comfort food after a confusing day, and the green beans were flawlessly crisp and full of flavor.

"So honey, how was your first day at school?"

"It was allright. I met a few new friends. One of them came over after school, and we watched a movie. Well, part of a movie. I had to start dinner in the middle, but he had to leave anyway."

"He?" She looked a little surprised.

"Yep, he seems really nice. He's only a friend, though, so don't get any ideas!"

"You know me all too well."

"Always playing matchmaker," I answered sarcastically as she giggled.

I finished dinner and helped clear the breakfast bar. Since I had cooked, it was Mom's job to do the dishes. I was glad to relinquish that chore to her whenever I could. I would rather do any other household chore over washing one sink full of dishes.

I wandered into the living room to watch some TV. There wasn't anything interesting on, but I didn't care—I wasn't really watching it anyway. I kept zoning out, thinking about the next day at school. More and more, I hoped Pete hadn't done anything serious. It still seemed so far-fetched to even consider. *Murder?* Actually, I felt ridiculous even thinking it. I wondered if Pete and I would become more than friends at some point. My mom would *love* that! She was unusually in love with love, always looking for a happy ending. Ironic, considering she was recently divorced. If I ever showed even a slight interest in someone, she got excited. Not that there had been many. I didn't want her to know about Pete until I was sure he was safe. Hopefully, that would happen sooner rather than later, not only for my sake but for Eli's, too. I knew he would worry about me, and I wondered if he would even talk to me again. He seemed like a great guy, and I didn't want to lose him over a friendship with Pete.

I trudged upstairs to shower before bed. I was tense, to say the least, and the knots in my shoulders felt like they were starting to restrict my movements. The shower helped ease some of my tension.

Afterward, I figured I would write an email to Kelly, my best friend in California. In all the chaos, I'd almost forgotten—I had promised to write her after my first day of school.

Kelly was just like me in almost every way, including looks. It was why we were best friends in the first place. Her brown hair and blue eyes matched mine perfectly. We spent most of our time together at the beach or shopping, but I would miss our sleepovers the most. I promised her that I would write her every chance I got and that we wouldn't grow apart, but deep down we both knew we probably would anyway. It made leaving that much harder for me.

I pulled out my laptop and began typing.

Kelly,
  We made it. Man is it hot! Everything is going okay. I hope your first day went great. How are all of our friends doing? I miss you all, and I can't wait till you can visit me.
  I had the weirdest day. I don't want to go into too much detail because I'm really not sure about a lot of it. Some of it may be rumors. But on the upside, I met a few new friends. The funny thing is two of them are boys—very unlike me!
  Although after tomorrow, it may only be one boy. I'll have to tell you more about that later. Well, I should be getting to bed now. Hope all is going well with you.
        Abby

I climbed into my bed and thought of my dad. I should have called him to check in. I knew he would be wondering how my first day went, but I was just too tired.

I sank into the sheets and got cozy in my down comforter. I fell asleep more quickly than usual and was relieved the next morning when I awoke and couldn't remember a single dream.

I hopped out of bed with more perkiness than usual. I dressed as fast as I could, giving myself ample time to call my dad before I went down to breakfast.

"Hello?" He answered on the second ring. His voice was huskier than usual, as if I had woken him.

"Hi Dad," I said.

"Hey, Abbs!" He was the only person I let call me that. "I'm so glad you called."

"How's everything going?"

"Good! I've been working a lot. The store has been pretty busy."

My dad owned his own sporting goods store, and since hunting season was coming up in a few weeks, everyone was getting ready to go. I imagined him amid a sea of targets, tents, and propane tanks. It was familiar, and I liked it. I always thought when I was old enough I would work in my dad's store. As it turned out, that wasn't my destiny.

"That's good."

"How was your first day of school?" he asked.

I knew my dad genuinely cared about what was going on in my life. I could always count on him.

"It was allright, I guess. It's almost time to leave for school. I probably should be getting downstairs to breakfast. I just wanted to call and say hi, but I'll call again soon."

"Okay, I'm glad you did. I miss you."

"I miss you, too."

"I love you, Abbs. Have a good day."

"I love you too, Dad. Bye!"

I hung up before I heard him say goodbye. I skipped down the stairs, my mood improved after talking to him.

There was a note on the refrigerator in my mom's neat handwriting.

> Abby,
> I had to go to work early this morning. Breakfast is waiting
> in the microwave. Sorry, you'll have to walk to school today.
> Have a good day!
>> Love,
>>> Mom

It wasn't unusual for my mom to have to leave suddenly in the morning. She worked as an editor's assistant at a publishing company. She could have to go in early for a number of reasons—if someone called in sick, if the boss needed an earlier coffee fix, or if she had a bigger workload due to the book production schedule.

Pancakes with strawberries on top and sausage awaited me in the microwave. It was still warm and tasted delicious. I didn't mind eating alone; it was actually nice to enjoy breakfast without having to carry a conversation.

    We didn't live far from my school, but since I had never walked before, I was unsure how long it would take. I walked as quickly as I could, but I didn't get far before I heard a car horn honk behind me. I turned around and was surprised to see Eli rolling down his passenger window.

    "Want a ride?" he asked.

    I was relieved that I wouldn't have to walk to school after all. I had already been late once to my first class, and I certainly didn't want to repeat it.

    "Hey, why are you driving down my street?" I asked as I climbed into his car.

    "Well, good morning to you too."

    "Sorry. I'm just a little surprised, that's all."

    "I usually cut through this neighborhood on my way to school. It's quicker. You're just a bonus today." He smiled.

    The compliment caught me offguard, but it made me smile anyway. I knew he didn't mean anything more than that he was happy to hang out, but I couldn't help it when my ego swelled ever so slightly.

    "Well, thanks for the ride."

    "No problem."

    We fell quiet for a long time. I hoped he wouldn't bring up the issue with Pete. I was pretty sure I knew what I wanted to say. I just didn't know if I would have the guts to actually say it. Nothing ever came out the way I planned in stressful situations. I tried to think of something to talk about that would divert the attention away from Pete, but I came up empty. The silence dragged on, and my hands fidgeted in my lap. I hated it when I couldn't think of anything to say.

    We pulled into the crowded school parking lot, and Eli parked his car in the middle of the lot. He turned the car off and sat there, staring straight ahead. It was like he was trying to summon the courage to ask me a question.

    "Well, off to another day of torture," I said to fill the silence.

    I started to climb out, hoping he would follow. He did.

    "Yep," he said solemnly.

    "Thanks again for the ride. I really appreciate it. Plus, I got to ride in the most awesome car!" I threw the last part in as a distraction.

    That did it—he grinned from eartoear. I smiled back, knowing I had avoided the Pete conversation for the time being. I did feel a little guilty about toying with Eli's emotions for my own personal gain, but I wasn't going to fret about it. The conversation would happen in due time.

    We walked into school together but went our separate ways to class. I felt excited to see Pete, despite everything that Eli had said. When I walked into the classroom, Pete wasn't there yet, and I was disappointed—more disappointed than I cared to admit.

He walked in the door right as the bell rang, so he wasn't technically late. That was good because,otherwise, he would have gone to "Sweep," which was basically detention during class. On the first day,I had been given an exception, but today was different. If we were late from the second day of school on, we would have to go to Sweep. Studentsweren't allowed to do anything there, not even homework, which was a pointless waste of time in my opinion.

Wearing dark blue jeans and a green shirt that made his eyes stand out brilliantly, he looked just as good as he had the day before.

"Hey, Pete!" I said from behind him, trying to be as quiet as possible.

"Hey," he whispered over his shoulder.

I wanted to talk to him more, but class was well underway. I would just have to wait. The time ticked by slowly, and I eagerly counted the minutes—30, 29, 28. I sat there, tapping my foot as I anxiously anticipated the bell.

A white flash shot over Pete's shoulder. A note. My stomach did a flop as my jittery fingers fumbled to open it. Pete had neat, precise handwriting.

> Abby,
>> So, are we on for lunch?
>> Pete

I realized I had never let Bailey in on the fact that Pete would be joining us. Hopefully, Bailey wouldn't mind. I wrote him back almost immediately.

> Pete,
>> Yep! Bailey's in too.
>>> Abby

Without caring who was watching, I slipped it over his shoulder, brushing him with my hand. My stomach leaped at the brief contact. I felt a little more careless when Pete was around. Maybe it was his sense of ease or his careless personality.

He read my note, looked over his shoulder, and flashed his beautiful white smile at me. I could have melted. *What was wrong with me?*

He folded the note and put it away. I was dejected that he wasn't going to write me another, but I knew I should pay attention to Mr. Robbins. It would be easy for me to fall behind in math, so I needed every ounce of focus to keep my mind on track.

Pete walked me to my next class, which was something I could get used to. I strolled alongside him, trying to get as much time with him as I could.

"So. How was your lunch with Eli yesterday?" he asked.

I sensed a little sarcasm in his voice, maybe even a hint of jealousy. Could he be jealous? I felt butterflies in my stomach.

"It was good. We mainly talked about school stuff." I tried to make it sound like nothing.

"Well, that's good."

I assumed he meant it was good we only talked about school stuff. Or maybe I was turning it into what I wanted it to be. It was a good thing he didn't ask me to elaborate on what 'school stuff' meant because I didn't have an answer for him. I really needed to get better at lying, or this web would swallow me whole.

"Sorry I had to cancel. What did you end up doing?"

"I found a few friends, a big group actually. It was nice seeing a lot of the people I hadn't seen over the summer. We all got to catch up."

"That's good." I was relieved that he'd had fun. "I guess it was a good thing I had to cancel then." I looked at him and giggled.

"Ha. At least I get to have lunch with you today—unless you decide to cancel again, that is," he joked, shooting me a sideways glance.

"No! There won't be any canceling today."

"Good." He nudged me with his shoulder playfully.

We were standing in front of my class now. Absentmindedly, I grabbed the straps of my backpack. I fidgeted, twisting and untwisting the straps.

"See you at the same place we met yesterday?" he asked.

"Yep." I smiled.

I turned to leave, and that's when I saw Eli staring at us—except, this time, I was the only one getting the glare. I could almost feel his eyes searing me, and the disgusted look on his face sickened me. The cat was out of the bag, so to speak. I just hoped he would still speak to me.

I didn't notice Pete say goodbye, but I was sure he had.

Eli walked into class without a word. I had to jog to catch up.

"Can I talk to you for a minute in the hall, please? I know you're mad, but I want to explain."

"Why should I?"

"We're friends. At least let me explain."

"Fine!"He dropped his books on his desk with a thud.

Several classmates jumped at the noise and gave Eli dirty looks. He didn't make eye contact with any of them. In fact, it seemed as if he didn't notice them looking at him at all. A blush of embarrassment crept over my cheeks.

We walked into the hall. I tried to be as discreet as possible in such a public hallway. He turned around and looked at me expectantly.

I didn't know where to start without making things worse than they already were. My rehearsed lines went out the window the moment he saw me with Pete. They didn't matter since he already knew; now I just had to convince him it was okay.

"I know that me being friends with Pete is a problem for you. I don't know what or who to believe. I'm new here. I don't know you or Pete very well. I understand your concern but—"

He cut me off.

"My *concern?* You have no idea what you're getting yourself into. No, I don't have proof, but if you aren't willing to believe me, I don't know why I even bothered!"

He stormed off before I could get another word in. It wasn't exactly how I wanted the conversation to go. I decided to write him a note with my phone number and invite him over after school that day. If he wouldn't come over, maybe he would at least call me.

As I walked into class, I noticed that Eli was still sitting in the seat next to mine. I hadn't seen Bailey come in, but she was sitting right behind my seat just as she had the day before. I wasn't really in the mood to talk, but I also didn't want Bailey to think I had something against her. I wanted so badly for us to be friends, so I would have to put my best foot forward.

"Hi Bailey," I said as I sat down.

"Hey Abby!"

The bell rang. The phrase *saved by the bell* rang in my head.

Mrs. Mosebee was busy assigning an essay that would be due in two weeksonthe career of our choice. I wasn't looking forward to writing it. Writing took a lot of time, thought, and organization—not my idea of fun. She left career books from the counseling office at the front of the room so we had something to reference. I picked up the law book and started writing down some crucial facts—the amount of time in school it took to get a degree, information about the bar exam, and the different specialties I could choose from.

After I thought I had what I would need for my essay, I pulled out a new sheet of paper to write a note to Eli.

Eli,

I know that you're mad at me. I really would like to explain.
Whether you agree or not, I feel I owe you that much, but you have
to let me. Will you come over after school today so we can talk? If
you don't want to come over, at least call me 555-9236. I'll be
walking home today, so I might be a little late.
Abby

I got up to bring the law book back to the front of the room, and on the way back to my seat, I slipped the note onto Eli's desk. It was pretty coy, especially for me. I saw him read the note and slip it into his pocket. *Better than throwing it in the trash*, I thought. Progress, one baby step at a time.

I wondered what he would decide to do, but I hoped he would come over. It would take up my thoughts for the better part of the day.

I finished working on the outline for my lawyer essay just as the bell rang. Gathering up my things, I shoved them into my backpack and headed out of class. I had hoped Eli was waiting for me outside the room, but he wasn't. I tried not to let my disappointment get to me, but it didn't seem like a good sign. Bailey, on the other hand, was waiting for me as expected. My mind had been so preoccupied that I had forgotten to ask her if she minded that Pete was going to join us for lunch.

"Hey Bailey, you don't mind that I invited Pete Denali to eat lunch with us, do you? I figured it would be nice to have a group to eat with." We began walking to our third hour.

"I don't mind! The more, the merrier. And it doesn't hurt that he's cute!" She giggled, and I couldn't disagree with her.

Eli didn't move away from me in science, but he refused to even look in my direction. I hated seeing how angry he was, knowing it was entirely my fault. I felt terrible.

After science, Bailey and I met Pete near the cafeteria where he and I had met the day before. He was smiling his bright, beautiful smile. It was enough to make me go weak at the knees.

"Oh my," Bailey whispered in my ear.

I giggled. It was nice to see I wasn't the only one he had that effect on.

The three of us walked into the cafeteria together and bought our lunches. Today they were serving burgers with fries, which was fine by me. I filled my bun with ketchup, mustard, pickles, and tomato before sitting down with the others.

I didn't see Eli anywhere, but I guessed he wouldn't want to see me eating lunch with Pete. I would have happily included him, but he was going to need some convincing.

Lunch went quickly with Pete sitting at my side. A few of Pete's friends joined us, and before I knew it, I was seated in a large group. There were three boys and two girls: Austen, Zach, Mason, Breanne, and Alexis. They all seemed really nice as far as I could tell.

A few different conversations buzzed at our table. I couldn't follow all of them, so I decided to pay attention to the ones Pete was involved in. He was engrossed in a discussion about football with the boys since they were all on the football team together. They were talking about drills or something for practice that day. None of it made sense to me.

From what I gathered about the group, Zach and Breanne were dating, and Mason and Alexis liked each other but didn't have anything concrete yet. They both seemed too shy to do anything about it.

I caught wind of Breanne, Alexis, and Bailey discussing the upcoming homecoming dance that was happening in three weeks. Breanne was going with Zach, while Alexis wanted Mason to ask her. I suspected she would get her wish.

I liked going to dances, though it was pretty rare for me to actually go with a date. I couldn't deny, at least to myself, that I wanted Pete to ask me. Even if he didn't, I planned to go. I didn't care about being a third wheel because dances were always fun regardless of whether I had a date or not.

Once lunch ended, I said goodbye to Bailey, and Pete walked me to my class.

"What did you think of my friends?" he asked.

"They were really nice."

I truly could see myself becoming friends with them. Their endless banter at lunch reminded me of my friends back in California, which just made me miss them even more. I couldn't help but feel like I wanted to be back in my home state.

"Oh yeah? I'm glad. Ihoped you'd like them. I've been friends with them for a long time."

As we arrived at the door of my class, we slowed to a halt.

"Well, I should get to class," he said.

"Yeah, me too. I'll see you tomorrow. Thanks for walking me."

He winked before he turned to stride away. I watched him until I could no longer see him in the crowded hallway.

The rest of the day passed uneventfully, but I hit the nail on the head when I thought I wouldn't like swimming at school. Thankfully, my bathing suit was a one-piece. I would have been mortified in front of the class in a two-piece.

After changing into my clothes after swimming, I checked the mirror to see how I looked. Just as I had thought: terrible. My makeup had smeared under my eyes, making me look like a raccoon, and my hair was matted from the water. I took a few minutes to clean my face and tame my mane before I headed home.

As I began to walk home, I wondered why I had even tried to make myself look presentable—it didn't take long before I was drenched in sweat. But I wasn't even out of the parking lot before a car pulled up behind me and honked. Expecting to see Eli, I turned around with a friendly smile. I was surprised when it was Pete, and immediately, I felt relieved that I had the extra few minutes to make myself look presentable.

He was driving a newer silver Honda with chrome rims. It wasn't as nice as Eli's car—that much was obvious. But it was still decent.

"Hey Abby, I didn't know you were walking home. Let me give you a ride. It's sweltering out here," he called out his window.

"That would be great! Thanks!"

The charcoal gray interior of the car was clean and smelled good. The lights for the gauges above the steering wheel glowed bright neon blue. *It must be a guy thing to want your dashboard to glow different colors.*

I was happy not to be walking home in 105-degree weather, but I was already in Pete's car when it crossed my mind that Eli might be waiting for me when I got home. It was far too late to change my mind. If he was waiting for me, I couldn't imagine him wanting to talk to me after I pulled up with Pete.

Pete was attractive, and I transformed into a frog that couldn't utter a word. Apparently, neither could Pete, so we sat in silence. Thankfully, it wasn't awkward; it was actually comfortable. I would take a comfortable silence over an awkward conversation about the weather any day.

We pulled onto my street, and I looked ahead to see if Eli's car was waiting. It was. I silently cursed myself for having been so stupid. Getting a ride from Pete had been a bad idea when I knew I had invited Eli over. What was I thinking? *Oh yeah. I didn't want to walk in the heat. Oh well. Eli would just have to understand.*

"My house is the one right there with the car in front." I pointed toward Eli's car.

"Whose car is that?" he asked.

I wondered if he was admiring it. I knew I did every time.

"It's Eli's, from school."

Pete stopped in front of the driveway.

"Are you guys friends or something?" he asked.

"Yeah, sort of."

"How come he didn't give you a ride home if he was coming over anyway?" He seemed almost perturbed.

"He told me he was staying after school, but it must not have taken as long as he thought it would.He wouldn't have known where to find me." The lies were coming easier and easier each time. It was becoming a really bad habit.

"Oh," he responded, seemingly unconvinced.

"Well, thanks for the ride."

"You're welcome. Are you walking to school tomorrow?"

"I don't know. It depends on my mom's work schedule."

I opened the door and stepped out.

I trudged over to Eli's car and peered in the window. He looked mad—worse than he had earlier in the day. His hands gripped and relaxed on the steering wheel, his knuckles turning white each time. He wouldn't even look at me.

Finally, he got out and looked at me from over the car.

"This isn't exactly what I expected when I came over. Why did you ask me to come? To show me you don't care about anything I told you?"

"Come inside. I want to talk. I'm sorry you're upset. I didn't plan on getting a ride fromhim. He saw me walking and offered to bring me home."

"Does it really matter? Either way, you rode with him. If you wanted a ride home, I would have preferred you got it from me, even if I'm mad at you."

He took a few steps around the car and headed up toward the house. I was relieved that he was still willing to come inside, but I wasn't pleased with his dad-like approach. I decided to brush it off instead of dwelling on it.

I unlocked the door and stepped into the cool air, making room for Eli to follow behind me. Thank goodness for air conditioning—I had broken a sweat just walking from the car.

"I didn't plan it. You haven't exactly been reachable, anyway. You wouldn't talk to me." I motioned toward the living room."I'll meet you in there."

I set my backpack in the kitchen, grabbed two sodas, and went into the living room. I handed one to Eli and sat down next to him on the couch.

"I realize you're uncomfortable with my friendship with Pete, but I don't see any danger yet. I want to see if I can figure out what happened. But until then, I'd like to be friends with him. I was hoping that you'd be willing to help me."

"Help you?"

"Well, I sort of thought I could get information from Pete, and we could figure it out together."

"I don't want you to get close to him just to figure out what happened to that football player. Just leave it be. The past is the past."

"What about that guy's family? They must be wondering where he went and probably want closure if he's gone for good. I'm hoping that isn't the case, though."

"I'll think about it, but even if I agree, there will be conditions. For example, you shouldn't be alone with him."

He almost seemed convinced. I was fine to agree to not be alone with Pete. Until I knew the truth myself, being alone with him didn't seem all that appealing. Of course, I would never admit that to Eli. I hoped Eli would change his bad attitude toward Pete if he were around him enough. He would get to know him better, and we could all be friends. That was my overall goal—but first, I wanted to know the truth.

CHAPTER THREE

The next day, Mom couldn't bring me to school again, but Eli found me walking just like he had the day before. His cheerful demeanor was back in place, and I could tell he wasn't mad anymore. It was as if his bad attitude had been a dream.

"So, I've been thinking about what you said about Pete yesterday." He paused. "I don't know that this is something we should be getting involved in, but I don't see a way to talk you out of it."

"Nope." I smiled, feeling triumphant.

"Exactly what I thought. I don't want you to do it alone. I really have no other choice but to help you."

He was going along with my plan, and I couldn't have been more pleased.

"You have no idea how happy that makes me! Thanks, Eli."

I saw him smile, although I didn't think he intended me to notice. Just as quickly as it crossed his face, it disappeared again.

"Remember, I said I had my conditions if I agreed."

"Yes, I do," I said, almost dreading his conditions. I had no idea what he might say.

"My first condition, as I told you yesterday, is that I don't want you to be alone with Pete, meaning no more rides home from school, no eating lunch with him if I'm not there, etc. . . ."

"I'm fine with that, though it'll be hard because he's in my first hour and walks me to second hour every day."

He thought for a second. "I guess I'm okay with you walking to second hour with him, but I'll be waiting outside of second hour for you."

"Sounds fair enough, I guess."

I was probably more accommodating to his conditions than I would usually be because he had agreed to do what I wanted. I wasn't about to make it harder on him, at least not on purpose. "What else?"

"I'll drive you to and from school every day."

"Driving me to and from school?" I scrunched my face at him.

"Well, I don't want to chance Pete seeing you walking alone and offering you a ride again."

"I can't complain about that, though it seems like you're going to a lot of trouble."

I had to admit—it sure would be nice to not worry about getting to and from school every day with my mom's hectic and unpredictable schedule. She might even be excited because Eli was a boy, and of course, she would think he was interested.

"I won't risk your safety, and it's sort of my fault that you're in this mess in the first place. I just couldn't let you be around himwithout knowing what he's capable of."

"It's not your fault. I'd be involved with him regardless. You just showed me I shouldn't let my guard down. And it's an *if* he is capable of it. That's what we're trying to find out. Innocent until proven guilty, right?" I said. "Anything else?"

"That's all I came up with for now."

Once we arrived at school, Eli walked me to my first class. I guessed it was just the start of his terms. While it was nice to have the company, I wondered if I would get tired of having someone around all the time. For the time being, I liked it. Eli was pretty awesome. He never seemed to run out of things to talk about. I hadn't realized it, but Ihad gotten pretty lonely before school started. I was used to having someone around a lot when I lived in California. Living with both my parents meant there was usually someone else home anytime I was. Now with my mom's work schedule, I was home alone a lot more than I had ever been.

The first half of the day flew by. We were assigned homework in math, we worked on our essays in English, and in science, we prepared for an experiment with different sources of power. I looked forward to doing projects in science. It beat sitting and listening to a lecture that never seemed to make sense until you could apply it. To top it off, Eli was my lab partner. He made me laugh as we worked.

Lunch was pretty crowded after I added Eli to the mix. Pete seemed surprised he would be joining us for lunch. I couldn't tell if it was a good thing or bad thing yet—but I had a hunch.

"I didn't realize how close you guys were,"Pete whispered to me as we stood in line to buy our lunches.

Despite what Eli had against Pete, lunch went well. I couldn't even feel any tension radiating from him. I had been worried about how Eli would act around Pete, but now I knew that had been silly. What did surprise me was Pete's apprehension about Eli. I couldn't guess why.

"I'll walk you to class, Abby," said Pete as we all stood up to leave.

I looked at Eli to see if he had heard Pete. Of course, he had. He hadn't left my side since we met Pete at the cafeteria door.

"I'll walk with you guys. I'm headed in that direction," Eli chimed in.

I knew that wasn't true. I didn't know what his problem was—it wasn't like it was any different than earlier in the day. Plus, when you're walking through the halls, you aren't really alone. Hundreds of other students would be in the halls. If you asked me, I thought he was going too far out of his way. It was going to get old quickly. I made a mental note to talk to him about it later. We said goodbye to everyone else and walked out of the cafeteria together.

Suddenly,I sensed enough tension to render me speechless. It seemed to have the same effect on Pete and Eli because our group was dead silent amid the chatter of the students around us engrossed in their own conversations.

We stopped in front of my classroom after what seemed like the longest, most awkward walk ever. An extended silence followed as we stood there, and I couldn't make eye contact with either of them, so I tried to appear interested in the people around us. *Gosh, this was painful.*

Finally, Pete broke the standoff. "Well, I was hoping I could get a moment alone with Abby," he huffed, looking at Eli.

I gazed at Eli and wondered what he would do. I could tell he was annoyed.

"Allright, I should get to class anyway. I'll see you after school, Abby.Same spot?"He shot Pete a smug glance.

I couldn't figure out why they were having a pissing contest. *What had gotten into them?*School could get really ugly if this continued.

"Yeah," I said, smiling at him.

He turned and strutted away, but I noticed he didn't actually leave. He lingered, striking up a conversationwith someone I didn't know just out of earshot. I would have to try to make it quick with Pete so Eli wouldn't be late. This was stressful!

I looked back at Pete, who was staring at me. It startled me. He had caught me staring at Eli again, and I hoped he didn't notice the color rising in my cheeks.

"I was sort of wondering if you had any plans this weekend . . ."He trailed off, avoiding eye contact.

"I don't know. Did you have something in mind?"

"Would you like to go to dinner and a movie with me?"

So he was*interested in me.*Butterflies flapped in the pit of my stomach. I was excited and nervous all at once. Then I thought of Eli, and all my excitement vanished. What could I say? If I went, it would violate Eli's trust, but if I didn't, I would be deprived of something I really wanted. *But what would I say?* I didn't want to make him think I wasn't interested.

I hoped I hadn't already taken too long to respond, so I said, "I think that sounds great, but I have to check with my mom first just to make sure it's okay with her. Which day were you thinking?" I breathed a sigh of relief because I knew he wouldn't question that excuse.

"Saturday, if that works. Here's my number," he replied, handing me a folded-up piece of paper. "You can call me to let me know, or you can just tell me tomorrow."

"Okay. I'll talk to you later."

"Bye." He smiled and turned to walk to class.

I looked at Eli after Pete walked away. He smiled before leaving for class.

I had two good friends, a whole group of people to eat lunch with, and a date, and it was only Wednesday!Well, I had a date if I could find a way around this set of rules Eli and I had established for our "mission." I had never had so much happen in one week before, and it wasn't even over yet.

Reading and history class passed slowly. I was bored and struggled to focus. Racking my brain, Itried to find a way around Eli's rule when it hit me—a genius plan that just might work. I could ask Pete if a double date was okay. Then Eli could bring a date and come with us. I would hate to cancel with Pete, especially using the mom excuse. But who would Eli bring? I would have to ask.

I met Eli at our agreed-upon spot. I had failed miserably the first time I tried to talk to him about a tricky subject, and he had to know that something was up since Pete wanted to talk to me alone. I hoped I wouldn't put him on the spot. In the end, I would have to tell him that Pete asked me out, and I wanted to go. It seemed easy mapped out in my head.

"How was your day?" he asked.

"Good, how was yours?"

"Different."He paused as if he were thinking. "I'm not used to being around Pete and all the people we ate lunch with. Since that football game, I have tried to avoid him and that whole crowd as much as I could."

"It wasn't so bad, was it?"

"He's allright," he said reluctantly. "The rest of them are pretty cool though, I have to admit."

"See!" I gloated. After a long pause, I said, "Well, I kind of have a dilemma."

"What's your dilemma? Should I be worried?" His smile faded.

"Depends on how you look at it." I paused. "Pete asked me out." I waited for his reaction.

He didn't answer right away, so I stole a glance at him. I expected him to look a little upset—maybe stressed—but he didn't. He looked like he was contemplating something.

"What are you thinking?" I asked.

"I'm trying to figure out what the dilemma is."

"I want to go," I said, kicking myself for not having any tact. I sounded like a child throwing a tantrum.

"It's against the rules *you* agreed to."

"I know. I was sort of hoping you'd double with us so I could go." I waited for his outburst. It never came. We stopped in front of my house. I turned to look at him, but he was staring straight ahead again. Neither of us made a move to get out.

"And who did you think I'd take on this 'double date'?" He put his fingers up in air quotes.

"I don't know. Isn't there someone you're interested in?"

"Maybe, but who said I was planning on doing anything about it?"

"Nobody, but I was hoping you would," I replied timidly.

Hegave a dark chuckle. He was taking it exactly how I had expected him to. I had hoped it would go better than this, but at least it didn't take me completely off guard. I was asking a lot, and I knew it. I'm not sure I would feel different if I were in his shoes.

"You don't have to, but I just thought maybe you'd do it for me, as a friend," I said, feeling guilty that I had pulled the friend card. After all, he owed me nothing. We hadn't even known each other for a week. I figured he might need some time to decide, so I got out of the car to give him the space he needed.

"You're welcome to come inside and hang out if you want. Thanks for the ride if not."

"I think I'll go home. I have some homework I need to work on."

I guessed that wasn't the only reason he wanted to go home."Okay." I didn't want to put any more pressure on him than I already had. "I'll see you tomorrow."

I hurried up to the house, knowing he wouldn't drive away until I was safely inside.

I turned and waved as he pulled away. I wondered who Eli had a crush on, but I probably wouldn't find out until he was good and ready, if ever.

When I walked through the door, I was surprised to hear Mom in the kitchen.

"Hey, Mom," I said.

"Hey, Abby."

I shuffled into the kitchen, but she wasn't there.

"Where are you?" I called.

"In the dining room. I have a surprise!" She sounded excited.

I walked in to see her placing a three-candle centerpiece on a beautiful cherry dining room table. The table was rectangular and large enough to fit six people. The chairs were entirely made of wood and sported thick white cushions.

"I hope you don't mind that I picked it out without you."

"Are you kidding? It's gorgeous!" I exclaimed.

The table was truly more than I would have expected Mom to buy. It was exquisite and must have cost a fortune.

"I'm glad you like it." She beamed.

"How come you're off work so early?" I asked.

"They didn't need me this afternoon. My boss was off for a last-minute doctor's appointment. I figured I would go buy us a table so we could stop eating at the breakfast bar for every meal. I also thought we could go out for dinner to catch up. What do you think?"

"I'd love that!"

Due to our hectic and unpredictable schedule, it had been a long time since we had gone to a sit-down restaurant. It would be really nice to have some time with my mom.

We chose an Italian restaurant that we had seen the day we moved in. It looked small and authentic. It seemed larger on the inside than it looked from the outside, and the environment was just how I imagined a restaurant in Italy to be. We ordered our usual favorites soon after sitting down.

"How's school going?" she asked.

"Good so far. I have tests on Friday in history and math that I'm sort of dreading." I shrugged.

"Oh." She made a face.

"Yeah . . ." I said, sticking out my tongue. "I've made a few friends, too. More than I thought I would. It's weird. But they all seem nice."

"Really? I'm so glad to hear that, but I hope you don't let it affect your grades."

"I'm sure you do!" I smirked. "How's work?"

"It's allright. I've been busier than I expected, but that's a good thing. I'd rather be busy than bored, except that I don't get to see you as much as I'd like." She frowned. "Unfortunately, I think I'll have to go in early almost every morning from now on, so I won't be able to give you rides to school in the morning."

"Oh, that's fine. My friend Eli offered to pick me up in the mornings and drop me off in the afternoons. I guess it's on his way."

My stomach grumbled as the waitress brought us our salad. It came out in a large bowl, with tomatoes, cucumbers, onions, croutons, and Italian dressing. The salad was tasty, and I ate almost half of it on my own, but I wanted to save room for my Alfredo so I stopped myself from having more.

"I'm glad you have someone to take you to school. I was a little worried about you walking every day."

"You worry too much."

She laughed. "I know, I know. I have to, though."

A few minutes after we finished our salads, the main course came. Romano cheese topped my Alfredo, with garlic bread on the side. It tasted fabulous!

"How's your dinner?" I asked.

"It's great. How's yours?"

"Very good," I replied with a full mouth. I laughed when I looked up and saw Mom giving me a dirty look. People who talked with their mouth full were a huge pet peeve of hers, so instead of finishing the bite in my mouth discreetly, I smiled at her with food laced through my teeth. I couldn't help but laugh when the look on her face shifted from a scowl to a grin that she tried to hide.

"You are lucky I love you!" she giggled.

We ate the rest of our meal silently. We had been so hungry that it didn't take us long to finish eating and pay. The food had been excellent, and as we walked out we both agreed that we would be back. We trudged out to the car, our stomachs feeling as though they might burst.

"Have you talked to your dad since Sunday?" asked my mom.

"Yeah, I talked to him yesterday but not for long. I plan on calling him and having a good conversation this weekend."

"That's good to hear. I'm sure he's worried sick."

"That's one thing you guys always had in common. Both of you worry too much!" I knew I'd said too much. The divorce had been bad and hurt them both. Sometimes I didn't stop to realize it was too soon for me to say things like that.

It was quiet the rest of the way home. I felt bad that I had turned our night sour. Mom wouldn't hold it against me, but that thought didn't make me feel any better.

I checked the voicemail when we got home. There were two messages: one from my dad and one from Eli. I decided my dad could wait until later. I couldn't believe that I had missed Eli's call. Thankfully, he left his number so I could call him back. I ran upstairs to call, but he wasn't home, so I left a message with his mom.

I was concentrating so hard on my homework that I jumped, startled, when my mom called toward my room. "Abby, someone's here to see you."

Who could be here to see me? I ran downstairs as fast as I could and was happy to see Eli talking to my mom.

"I called you, but you weren't home," he said.

My mom stood behind Eli and mouthed,"He's cute," before leaving the room. I tried to hide my giggle.

"I see you've met my mom."

He smiled. "Yep!"

"Come on!Let's go in the living room."

He followed me and sat down on the couch, fiddling with his hands like he didn't know quite what to do with them.

"I came over because I wanted to talk about the doubledate you suggested."

"I hoped that's what you wanted to talk about. What do you think?" I asked, trying to sound lighthearted.

"Well, there's someone I'm interested in, but I can't ask her out."

"Why not?"

"I just can't."His tone grew aggravated.

"Oh," I said.

Why couldn't he ask her? I got the feeling he didn't want me to know anything about it, but I couldn't help but feel even more curious about the identity of this mystery girl. For now, I had to let it go. I didn't want to anger him again by pushing him to tell me something he clearly didn't want to reveal.

"I don't mind going with you, but . . . will you help me get a date?"He looked away shyly, and any hint of aggression dissipated in the blink of an eye.

I hadn't seen that side of him before. He was always so confident and sure of himself—or at least he seemed that way. I usually felt like the awkward one, so it was nice to know I wasn't alone.

"I don't . . . really have much experience with girls."

He's shy? I couldn't believe it! He hadn't seemed to have a hard time approaching me or being around girls for that matter. Not to mention he had a great personality and was a blast to hang out with. How could he be self-conscious?

"Of course I'll help! What do you want me to do?" I asked.

"I don't know. I don't even know where to start,"he said nervously. "Every time I try to ask a girl out, I end up talking to her about something else, and we wind up being just friends. I think a lot of it has to do with not knowing how to bring up that I like them. By the time I've broken the ice, it feels too late.Like it would be awkward to ask."

"I'm not sure what I can teach you, but there's really not much to it. You take a deep breath and ask." I looked at him to make sure he was listening. He was, more so than I had expected. I almost jumped at the sight of his eyes staring at me so intently. "Like when Pete asked me out, he started by asking me what I was doing this weekend. Then he suggested going to dinner and maybe a movie," I said, shrugging. "There's nothing really to it. It just takes a little bit of courage."

He contemplated that for a few minutes.

"I don't know if I have the nerve to do that."

"I think you do.You approached me, didn't you?"

"Well, that was different."

"No, it wasn't. Approaching a girl you like is exactly the same. You just need to stop thinking of it as a daunting task. Maybe you could start with a girl you don't necessarily like so you can see how easy it can be. This weekend's date can be practice."

He seemed to be thinking really hard. "Who would I ask?"

"I don't know." I thought about it for a minute."How about Bailey?"

"Uh, I guess that could work."

"So, you'll double with us?"

"Yeah, as long as I don't chicken out tomorrow," he said faintly.

"It'll be fine.You can do it."

"Whatever you say." He didn't sound convinced. "I should be going. I still have some homework to finish before I go to bed."

I walked him to the door, and we said goodbye. I felt bad for him. He seemed so nervous about asking someone out. I hoped he could musterhis confidence. If only he could see himself as I saw him, he would be set.

After Eli left, I went upstairs to finish my homework. I was so happy that Eli had agreed to go on the date with Pete and me, but I decided I wouldn't call Pete to let him know just yet. I wanted to see how things panned out with Eli and Bailey. I couldn't say I had done anything to make a difference, so it would all be on Eli. But I had faith in him.

I showered and climbed into bed, but I wasn't able to fall asleep right away. I tossed and turned until onein the morning. My mind wouldn't stop racing, darting from thoughts about what Pete and I would look like as a couple to envisioning Eli and Bailey as a couple and then to the extreme—whether Pete was a murderer or not. My mom and dad would pop up every now and again, too. I wondered how they were each doing without each other. Mostly, I worried about my dad.

I awoke early with a start and a racing heart. I wished the nightmare would go away for good—but I also wanted a little insight into why I was even having it. Up until six months earlier, I had only had a few bad dreams in my whole life. Now I felt like I'd had enough nightmares for five lifetimes.

I was surprisingly excited for school that day. Just four days earlier, I had been dreading it. It was amazing how things could change. My expectations were high when I thought of Eli asking Bailey to doubledate with Pete and me. I truly thought Bailey would love to go on a date with Eli. Who knew—maybe they would hit it off. After all, Eli was quite a catch, and as far as Bailey was concerned, Eli would be lucky to have her.

When I got downstairs, my mom had already gone to work. I was just finishing up the remnants of my breakfast when I heard a soft knock at the door. It was Eli, so I grabbed my backpack.

On the way to my first class, I searched every face for Bailey's in hopes that Eli could ask her, but I didn'tfind her. Eli didn't linger outside my classroom door. He seemed jittery and not quite himself. I guessed his nerves were getting the better of him.

"See ya," he said over his shoulder as he walked out of sight.

I waved.

Once Pete walked into class and sat down, he turned around immediately.

"Hey, did you talk to your mom about this weekend?"

Wow, he didn't waste any time. He completely put me on the spot. I was glad I had rehearsed what I would say. "I did, but she didn't give me an answer. She told me she would let me know this morning, but she had to go to work early again. I'll call her later to get her answer, but I don't know if I'll get one today."

"Oh, all right."

He turned back around to face the front of the classroom and didn't speak to me the rest of the period. I wasn't sure if it was because he wanted to pay attention or he was upset with me, but I hoped it wasn't the latter.

We were checking our homework, and mine was fairly good. I had gotten most of the answers correct.

Pete walked me to second period and was definitely more quiet than usual. I couldn't help but wonder if it was because of me or if there was something else eating at him. He certainly didn't seem like his usual self.

"I'll see you at lunch?" he asked.

"Yep! See you there." I walked over to where Eli stood waiting for me. He looked happy.

"Have you seen Bailey yet?" I asked Eli.

"Yep!"He beamed. "I asked, and she said yes!"

"Wow, that's great!" Now I just needed to convince Pete that a doubledate with Eli and Bailey would be fun, which might be harder. He didn't seem so keen on Eli.

"I know, isn't it? Thanks so much for your help! It was as easy as you said it would be! Although, I'm not sure it would have been so easy if she'd said no."

It felt so good knowing that I had helped him. Maybe all he had needed was a confidence boost.

"Glad to hear it. Thank you for being willing to go with us."

"Sure," he said as his face turned from happy to serious. "I'm not thrilled about the idea, but I feel better knowing that I'll be with you."

He was so protective. I had never known a guy that was so protective of me other than my dad. It made me feel safe. I wanted to give him a big bear hug, but I refrained. He might think it was weird.

In third hour, Bailey seemed even more full of energy than usual. I could tell she couldn't wait to tell me the news.

"Eli asked me out!" she squealed in my ear as I walked into the room.

"I heard! That's awesome!" I responded, relishing her excitement.

"I can't believe he asked me out!"

Eli went to talk to Mr. Lang before class, and I could only assume it was to give us the opportunity to discuss it. I was sure he knew how much girls liked to gossip about guys. Chatting about a date with your best friend was half of the fun of going!

"I know, isn't it great? You guys are going on a doubledate with Pete and me!"

"It's even better that you'll be there. I've never been on a date before," she confessed.

I wondered if she truly liked Eli. If they started dating, it would make things easier if Pete wanted to continue to date me. We would always have double-date partners. Now I knew I was getting ahead of myself. We hadn't even had our first date yet—but it couldn't hurt to dream, could it?

I couldn't wait to tell Pete the good news. Ironically, the one thing I did forget was to actually talk to my mom. But she was going to think it was a group outing, and it wasn't completely a lie. I was being extra cautious about her knowing all the details about Pete. The last thing I wanted was for her to get invested in a relationship I wasn't sure about yet.

Bailey, Eli, and I walked to the cafeteria. Pete, looking amazing as usual, stood there waiting for us. His face lit up when he saw us coming. He seemed to be out of the funk he had been in earlier in the day. *Gosh, he seemed moody earlier.*

"I have good news!" I said to Pete as I walked up to him.

"She said yes?" he asked.

"Yep!"

"Great!"

"I had an idea," I whispered as I pulled him aside from Eli and Bailey. He towered over me, and I had to stand on my tiptoes to be as quiet as I could. "What do you think about making it a doubledate?"

"A doubledate? With who?"

"Eli and Bailey."

"I didn't even know they were dating," he said.

"They aren't yet. Eli just asked her out today."

"Oh, I see. Sure, why not," he replied with a shrug.

"Great!" I said, reaching up to give him a big hug. I wasn't sure what came over me—it wasn't like me to be so bold—but I went with it, and it made Pete chuckle.

During lunch, nobody paid much attention to Pete and me, which gave us ample time to chat.

"What time do you want me to pick you up on Saturday?" Pete asked.

"Well, I was going to ask Bailey to come over Saturday,so there's no reason you guys would need to come pick us both up. You and Eli can come over, and we can all drive together. What do you think?"

"Sure, I suppose we can drive together. Carpooling's good for the environment, don't you know?" he said with a laugh.

He seemed so easygoing. That made it even harder to grasp the thought that he might be trouble. He didn't seem like he had an angry bone in his body.

"Great! I'm really looking forward to it," I blurted out. As soon as I said it, I wonderedif I had said too much, so I blushed and refused to make eye contact. I didn't want to sound desperate or too eager. Pete could easily have any girl in the room. I didn't want to scare him off.

He reached over and squeezed my hand. "Me too," he said, shooting me a flirty smile.

Pete and Eli walked me to fourth hour in silence. It was beginning to feel comfortable that way, but I chose to break the stillness.

"Eli, we're all going to meet up at my house before the date and drive together. Does that sound okay?"

"Sure," he said.

Pete stayed quiet. I wrote my number down and gave it to him before we all split up to go to class.

For once, I was able to pay attention in the last few classes of the day. In English, we received our copies of *To Kill a Mockingbird.* And in history, we were given the opportunity to work on our study guide outlines for the test the following day. I had already completed mine, so I used the time to study, which I definitely needed after not paying attention all week. We were still in the swimming section of our P.E. curriculum, and I was looking forward to being done with it.

Once school ended, I was looking forward to going home, especially since I didn't have any homework to focus on.

Eli didn't hang around after he dropped me off. He said he had some homework and studying to do. That was fine with me—I planned on relaxing and wasn't in the mood for entertaining. I made some popcorn and put in a movie, and for the first time that week I felt truly at ease. It was Mom's night to cook dinner, but since I had extra time on my hands, I decided I wouldsurprise her by cooking and having it ready when she got home. That would be a nice treat for her.

Halfway through the movie, the phone rang. It was Pete. I hadn't expected to hear from him.

"Hey Abby.How's it going?"

I cleared my throat. "Hey! Good, you?"

"Pretty good. I was just calling to see if you were free tonight. I thought maybe we could study together for the math quiz."

"I'm sorry, Pete. I was planning on spending time with my mom tonight. Thanks for the offer though."

"I totally get that. Don't be sorry."

"Maybe next time," I said.

"Yeah. I'll see you at school tomorrow."

For the next several minutes, I couldn't stop thinking about Pete. He seemed so genuine and caring—qualities I thought were great in a boyfriend. Maybe I was blinded by his charm because I couldn't see any of the bad things Eli had told me about. Maybe that was why he was so worried about me. I didn't feel blindsided, but I guess that's why it's called that: You don't see what's happening right in front of your face.

It was getting late in the afternoon, and I needed to start dinner if I wanted it ready when Mom got home. I checked the cabinets and decided to make homemade macaroni and cheese with Parmesan-crusted tilapia. Mom loved fish and always talked about how good it was for your heart or something.

Once dinner was in the oven, it needed to cook forthirty minutes, so I went upstairs to put my backpack in my bedroom and check my messages for the first time that week. I smiled when I saw one from Kelly.

Abby,
I was so happy to read your email today. I'll write you back a good long message soon. I hope you don't think I'm ignoring you. Things are so crazy right now with school starting up. I already have two essays to write, a book to start, and two tests tomorrow. Yikes! I'm sure you're just as busy. I'll talk to you soon! Hope things are still going well.
Kelly

It was nice to hear from Kelly. I missed my friends in California. Even so, I was having a lot of fun in Arizona. *I would love Kelly to come visit me and meet my new friends.* I wondered what she would think of them.

I heard my timer going off. Kelly would have to wait. Mom would be home in five minutes, and I had just enough time to get everything out of the oven, dish up the plates, and set the table. Just as I finished, my mom walked through the front door.

I sat down at the table as she walked into the room. Her face lit up.

"What's all this?" she asked, surprised and happy.

"I thought I'd surprise you with dinner. Plus we haven't had a whole lot of time to spend together this week, so I thought I'd give us extra time."

She smiled. "You're right. We haven't. Thanks, honey!This is so sweet. I had a rough day, and this is the best thing to come home to."

I was glad she appreciated it—but she always did. It melted her heartwhen I thought ahead and did something special for her.

"I made your favorite, tilapia."

"Even better! Yum!"

"Oh, before I forget to tell you, I made plans to go out with some friends on Saturday night, and I was thinking about having my friend Bailey over during the day. Is that okay?"

"Of course! Actually, I was hoping you'd make plans. I was invited to go out to dinner with some co-workers, and some of the girls are going shopping beforehand. I wanted to go, and that should give you girls some alone time."

"Thanks,Mom!"

"So, who are you going out with?" she asked.

"Bailey, Pete, and Eli. We eat lunch together every day."

"That sounds fun."

It was the first time I wasn't feeling grumpy toward my mom about the move. I hadn't realized how much I was actually enjoying myself—that in itself was a huge turning point for me. No longer would I give her a hard time about moving, at least for now. She seemed to have enough on her plate as it was, and I was sure I hadn't been helping with all my complaints.

"Well, since you made dinner, I'll do the dishes," she said, standing up with an empty plate in her hand.

"Okay!" I grabbed my plate and glass to bring into the kitchen. "I was thinking we could sit down and watch a movie or TV together."

I flipped through the channels while I waited in the living room for my mom to finish up in the kitchen. When she emerged, we sat down and watched a chick flick we both loved. By the end of the movie, as always, Mom was crying. We watched the credits for a few minutes, lost in our own thoughts.

As I stood up to turn off the movie, I tripped on the leg of the coffee table and tumbled to the ground, banging my shin as I fell. Even though pain shot through my leg, I couldn't help but laugh. *Typical klutzy move*. Even so, Mom immediately jumped up.

"Are you all right?" She grabbed my arm to help me up.

"I'm fine! Just being my usual self, I suppose."

"You're bleeding!" she exclaimed, looking at my head.

"I am?" I reached up and touched my forehead. A smidge of blood clung to my fingers. I must have bumped my head on the coffee table, too.

Mom cleaned my forehead, and I looked in the mirror. It was horrible. The cut itself wasn't deep, but it was swollen and already starting to bruise. I looked like I had been in a car accident.

I headed to bed shortly after we put a butterfly bandage on it but not before I took an aspirin for the headachethat was beginning to build between my temples. I hoped it would be gone in the morning.

I rummaged through my nightstand drawer for my chapstick and instead found a picture of my dad, my mom, and me at the beach. Thinking about the fun we had together brought a smile to my lips, yet it also made me sad. I knew those happy times together were over. I drifted to sleep while looking at the picture, my chapstick all but forgotten.

I awoke Friday morning with a start, though not from a dream this time. My mom was sitting on the bed next to me, watching me sleep. She smiled.

"I brought you breakfast in bed. I thought it would be a nice treat."

"You were worried about me, weren't you?"

"Can ya blame me?"

I took a deep breath to steady my heart. After all, the only thing she had ended up doing was scaring the crap out of me!

I rolled my eyes. "Well, thanks for the breakfast in bed."

"Of course. I'm headed to work. I'm already late, but I wanted to see that you were okay before I left. Your friend Eli is going to drive you to school, right?"

"Yep," I said.

"Good. I didn't want you to have to walk to school after your *trip* last night."

She laughed at her own joke, and I couldn't help but laugh, too. "Yeah, yeah, yeah."

She kissed my forehead and walked out the door.

I sat in bed for awhile, enjoying my fresh oranges and Belgian waffles smothered in strawberry syrup. I got ready at a slower pace than normal—my head was killing me. I debated wearing a hat to cover the obnoxious mark, but it hurt too badly *Did I have to go to school? Because all I felt like doing was climbing back into bed.*

I heard a car horn honk as I trudged down the stairs.

"Morning!" I said as I climbed into Eli's car.

"Good morning. Oh my god—what *happened*!?" Eli practically shouted the last word.

I grimaced. "Oh, this?" I pointed at the cut on my forehead."I tripped last night on the coffee table and hit my head on the way down. It's nothing, really. It looks worse than it is." It was going to get undeniably old telling everyone how much of a klutz I really was.

"It looks terrible. Are you sure you're okay?" He looked concerned.

"Yeah, I'm fine, *really*.Everyone worries too much."

"I knew there was a reason my mind was pushing me to call you last night." He spoke so quietly that I almost didn't catch it at all.

"What?" I asked.

"Oh, nothing. I'll leave you alone about it. Let me know if I can do anything."

"All right, I will. But I think you're doing plenty already."

"Friends do whatever they can for each other, right?" he asked.

I nodded.

"So there's always more I can do."

I couldn't have asked for a better friend. He was a different breed, and that was rare to find—a diamond in the rough,if you will. I smiled to myself, thinking about how lucky I was.

We got to school in record time, though it wasn't necessary. I was in no hurry to get to class for my math quiz. On the other hand, I was happy to see Pete.

Pete was also worried about my head. He grabbed my backpack from my shoulder and helped me into class, as if I was having trouble walking or something. I assured him I was fine, but it didn't seem to make a difference. Then again, it was nice to have him fawning over me.

Bailey was the only one who didn't go off-kilter about the bruise. She seemed surprised, but she didn't freak out. She even admitted she had the klutz gene too.

"I hope it doesn't leave a scar," she said.

I hadn't even considered that it could scar. I looked at it more closely in the mirror during a bathroom break. It did look pretty nasty, but only time would tell. I sighed, thinking of how ugly it would be to have a scar right in the middle of my forehead.

The entire day consisted of tests and reading, but I was lucky enough to get out of swimming. I found a note in my backpack from my mom to my P.E. teacher, excusing me due to my head. I hadn't thought about it, but I guessed it probably wouldn't be a good idea to get it wet. So I ended the day on that good note and didn't even have any homework.

I asked Bailey to come over Saturday so we could get ready together. She was ecstatic and, after a call to my mom and her dad, we made plans for her to spend the night as well. She was set to arrive at my house just before lunch. Since I had no homework for the weekend, all I had to worry about was buying the ingredients for the homemade pizza we were going to make.

Eli dropped me off at home and left as quickly as he had come. I could tell he was anxious about the date. So was I.

Mom said she would be home early, so I hurried to get dinner on the table so we could go to the store. I threw some potatoes in the oven and started marinating a couple steaks. Then I went upstairs to put away my backpack.

I needed to finish unpacking all the boxes I had avoided because I was upset about the move. I wanted my room to look nice when Bailey arrived. Plus, I needed the space for the trundle bedunless Bailey preferred to sleep in the guest room.

I opened the first box, which was full of clothes. I had already unpacked most of my wardrobe, but there were still a few boxes left. That specific box contained my dressier clothes, and it was the precise box I had hoped to find. I needed to pick out a date outfit that was prettier than my normal, everyday clothing. I hung each piece in my closet, and before I knew it, the box was empty.

I checked my watch and saw that it was 5:14 p.m. I needed to get the steaks and corn on the grill.

Mom must have arrived home sometime while I was cooking outside because she came out onto the porch to greet me just as I was taking the steaks off the grill.

"Hey there! Steaks tonight?" she asked.

"Yep."

"Sounds like a delicious Friday night dinner to me."

"I'm glad you think so," I said, grabbing the plate of steaks and corn. I handed it to her. "Can you bring these in while I shut off the grill?"

"Of course. Anything else I can do?"

"If you want, you can take the potatoes out of the oven."

Soon enough, we were sitting at the dining room table to eat.

"So, I was hoping we could go to the store and pick up some groceries for Bailey and me tomorrow."

"Sure. We can go when we're done eating. I'll clean up later."

My mom was so accommodating, especially when it came to my social life. She always wanted to make sure I was surrounded by friends as often as possible. She stressed that friends were important, that I needed people who would stay by my side. Everyone needed a little support now and again.

I finished eating before my mom, so I began clearing the table while she finished up. I was putting the last dish in the sink when she came in, carrying her plate.

"Ready to go?" she asked.

CHAPTER FOUR

Bright light woke me from a deep, peaceful sleep. I knew it had to be late if that much light was streaming through my window. I rolled over to look at the clock: 11:10 a.m. I had just under an hour to shower and get dressed before Bailey arrived.

I jogged downstairs to check if Mom had left yet. There wasn't a note this time, only a piece of paper with an arrow pointing to the handle of the microwave. Inside lay some bacon and toast—a small breakfast that was just the ticket in a time crunch. I gobbled it up and ran upstairs to shower.

I was ready just five minutes before Bailey arrived. We started making the pizza right away, and it didn't take long to get it into the oven.

I had felt like the ultimate girl the night before when I picked out three outfits from my wardrobe. Of course, in typical girl fashion, I wanted Bailey's opinion. She had felt the same way and brought her choices with her. It was exciting to think about the night ahead of us. After about twenty minutes of trying on different outfits, we had both decided. I was going to wear a knee-length black skirt and a red v-neck shirt with a shimmering silver heart in the center. It was one of my favorite shirts. Bailey chose a cool blue dress with sequined flowers. It came midway down her thigh and looked beautiful on her. Eli would be impressed.

I heard the timer for our pizza going off and ran downstairs. Bailey followed right behind me.

"So, what do you want to do with your hair tonight?" I asked while eating my first slice of pizza.

"I don't know! I was hoping you might have an idea. I'm totally lame when it comes to doing my hair, especially thinking of new hairstyles," she admitted. We laughed.

"I know a few hairstyles, and I've seen you in some cute ones, too. We can experiment when we're done eating. Either way, I think we should both go with straight hair. What do you think?"

It was rare that I actually straightened my hair, but this constituted a special occasion, so it deserved the extra time.

Girl talk flowed abundantly, ranging from boys to cars to jobs. I didn't realize how much I missed being able to gab about all my favorite things. Even though I never seemed to run out of things to talk to Eli about, this was different.

"Do you know how to surf and stuff?" Bailey asked.

"Well, of course. You don't live in California and not take full advantage of the beach!" I exclaimed.

"Wow, that's so cool! I've never been to the beach."

I had just finished straightening Bailey's hair when the phone rang. It was my mom checking in. After hanging up, I hurried back into the bathroom.

"Was that your mom?" Bailey asked.

"Yeah, she was just checking to see how we're doing."

"That was nice of her. My dad doesn't think of doing that kind of thing."

"What about your mom?"

"She died when I was four."

"Oh, I'm sorry. I didn't know. How'd she die, if you don't mind me asking?"

"Car accident. Someone ran a red light."

"That must have been so hard."

"I don't really remember anything from back then. I don't even really remember her, just little images here and there. It was harder on my dad, of course. I can see he still misses her. He never dates." Her expression grew somber as she fiddled with the clips and hair ties in her hands.

"I couldn't even imagine."

"What about your parents?"

"Divorced. My dad lives in California, where we just moved from."

"When did that happen?"

"Officially? About a month ago, but they separated six months ago."

"How do you feel about it? I've heard divorce is really hard."

"It's been a rough adjustment, but I'm okay with it as long as my parents are happy. They hadn't been happy for quite a while. I just wish I didn't have to move away from my dad. I'm going to miss him the most."

After my hair was straight, Bailey started trying a hairstyle on me that I remembered seeing her wear on the first day of school. With a clip, she pulled back about an inch of hair from the front of each side. It was simple yet elegant. I had a beautiful black clip with rhinestones that made it even better.

"It's perfect. I think it was exactly what I was looking for. You need to give yourself a little more credit," I said. "Let's get started on your hair."

I wanted to take her side-swept bangs and pull them back to give her some volume. I always thought it was a cute look, but I had never been able to manage it with my own hair. It just wasn't the right texture. But back in California, a friend showed me how to do it on someone else's hair, so I was sure I could pull it off for Bailey. I started working with her hair, and before long, I was finished. It looked fantastic and turned out exactly as I had hoped it would.

"Done! Do you like it?" I asked.

"I love it! I haven't been able to figure out how to do this on my own."

By then we only had an hour and a half before the boys were going to pick us up.

I applied shimmering silver eyeshadow on Bailey to match her dress, along with berry-colored lipstick. After seeing how her makeup turned out, I decided to have her do mine the same way.

My forehead hadn't healed yet, but it was looking a little better. Bailey did most of my makeup, but I dabbed the foundation around the injury so she didn't hurt me.

We were ready with thirty minutes to spare, so we went downstairs to watch TV and wait for the boys.

"I'm so nervous!" Bailey squealed.

I giggled. "Sounds like you're excited too, though."

"Yeah, that's true!"

"I'm right there with ya!"

A knock sounded on the front door. My stomach flopped.

"They're early!"

I answered the door. It was Eli. I had assumed it was him when I heard the knock. He was such a worry-wart and had to be there before Pete, even though he knew Bailey was here.

He looked amazing in a button-up blue, red, and gray plaid shirt with dark denim pants and black shoes. He clutched a bouquet of beautiful flowers.

"Hey, Eli! Those are beautiful! Bailey will love them."

"You really think so?" he whispered.

"Of course she will," I said. He seemed nervous. "Bailey, Eli's here," I called.

As soon as the words left my lips, she glided around the corner, andEli's face lit up.

"You look beautiful," he said shyly.

"Thanks."She blushed.

Everything between Eli and Bailey seemed to be working out well so far. I thought he seemed to really like her, though it might not have occurred to him until he asked her out.

Another knock sounded on the door—Pete was also early. *What was with these eager beavers? Didn't they know that women typically ran late?* It was a good thing we had both been ready. I answered the door.

"Wow, that was quick! You must have been standing there waiting for me," he teased.

I shoved his shoulder and laughed.

"Eli got here just before you did."

"Sure he did."He winked. "You look nice."

He hadn't brought me flowers, and I couldn't help but feel a little jealous of Bailey, even though I knew she had nothing to do with it. Why hadn't Pete been as thoughtful as Eli? I tried not to let it bother me.

"Shall we go?" I asked.

"Sure," Pete, Eli, and Bailey all said in unison.

"Where are we going?" Bailey asked.

Pete jumped to answer the question. I figured it was only fair that he planned the date since he had been the one to suggest it in the first place.

"I know I mentioned going to a movie, but I figured that we wouldn't be able to talk much. So I was thinking we could grab something to eat and go mini-golfing."

"That sounds like fun!" Bailey said.

"What about pizza?" I asked. Even though Bailey and I had eaten it for lunch, I still thought it sounded good. I hoped Bailey thought so.

"That's actually what I was thinking. I know a great place." Pete smiled and winked at me. "Great minds think alike."

He slid his hand around my back, guiding me through the

doorway. He kept his hand resting there as we waited for Bailey and Eli to exit the house so I could lock up. Eli and Bailey were a little more shy toward each other. They didn't touch the whole way to the car.

We left in Pete's Honda since Eli's Camaro was only a coupe. I sat in the front seat with Pete, while Eli and Bailey sat in the back. I glanced back at them after awhile and saw they were holding hands. I felt another twinge of jealousy and couldn't understand why. I brushed it off, figuring it was probably because I wanted Pete to hold my hand. Of course, he couldn't while he was driving.

Pete took us to a small, casual restaurant I hadn't heard of called Rosali's. We ordered two medium pizzas to split between the four of us. I was impressed at how quickly the pizza arrived.

"I've never been here before, but this pizza is so good!" I said after a few bites.

Only one pizza place I had been to even came close, and it was my go-to spot back in California.

"I love eating here. It's one of my favorites," Pete said.

Bailey and Eli were engrossed in their own conversation.

"I enjoy going to hole-in-the-wall placesthat aren't big chains. They usually have the best food," I said.

"I completely agree."

I smiled.Our eyes met. It was one of those moments you only see in movies. The intensity of it made me blush, and I had to look away. Moments later, I glanced up at Pete through my eyelashes, hoping he wouldn't notice. He was looking down at his plate, smiling to himself, and a moment later, I found myself doing the same thing.

As we drove to play mini-golf, everyone was in great spirits. Pete turned up a popular rock song, and we all sang along. Nothing could compare to the freedom we felt at that moment. We were having the time of our lives.

We came to a stop at a red light, and Pete took that moment to lean over and place the gentlest kiss on my cheek. My hand drifted up to touch the spot his lips had just brushed. I looked up at him, and our eyes met. Time seemed to stand still.

Then we heard screeching tires.

A car slammed into us from behind, the impact jarring us forward. Luckily, we were all wearing our seat belts.

Pete turned toward me. "Are you okay?"

"I . . . I think so," I stammered.

"You guys?" He turned to face Eli and Bailey.

Eli spoke for the two of them. "I think we're allright. Just a little shaken up."

"That moron!" Pete screamed. "We could have been hurt. What an idiot. I can't—"

"Bailey, Abby," Eli said. "I think we should get out of the car to see if everyone else is allright and give Pete a moment to collect himself."

"I don't need a moment alone, thank you!" Pete's face reddened as he jumped out of the car. "What in the world were you thinking?"he shouted at the driver of the other car.

Pete was already at the back of the car by the time the rest of us clambered out. I headed toward him, but Eli grabbed my arm and held me back.

"You and Bailey need to stay here. Pete's out of his mind right now, and I don't want you two to get the brunt of it," he whispered.

I didn't disagree with him; it scared me to see Petelike that. I stayed behind with a panicked Bailey. She had borrowed Eli's cell phone to talk to her dad. I didn't even know Eli had a cell phone, or I would have called my mom. *Except, I don't know the number forthe place she's at.*

By the time Eli reached Petewas still yelling at the driver by the time Eli reached him, and his voice was only getting louder. The other driver apologized profusely, trying to calm Pete down. I could see that Eli wasn't sure how to defuse the situation.

"Did you call the police yet?" Eli asked the driver in between Pete's outbursts.

"Yeah, I did." The other driver looked relieved to have someone calm in the conversation. "They should be here soon. Is everyone okay?"

"We're all fine. Are you okay?"

"Glad to hear it. Yeah, I'm fine. I just wish the cars looked better." The driver had stopped talking to Pete and was only paying attention to Eli, but that didn't stop Pete's rant. "I'm so sorry. I looked down for one second, and the next thing I knew you were stopped."

Both cars had sustained significant damage but nothing to prevent them from driving away. Pete's had a humongous dent in the bumper and trunk, and one of the taillights was broken and would have to be replaced. The other car wasn't as bad. Both headlights were intact, but the bumper was dented, and it would need a new grill.

"It's fine," Eli said."Accidents happen. Do you have your insurance information?"

"Fine? Yeah right! You better have insurance!" Pete said.

As the driver went to get his insurance card,I overheard Eli talking to Pete in a hushed tone.

"You need to calm down. You're embarrassing yourself and

scaring the girls.”

“I am not embarrassing myself. You're embarrassing me!” Pete hissed.

I couldn't believe the way he was acting. It was such a turn-off. Eli saidsomething to him that I couldn't hear, but it seemed to just make Pete more upset. He got in Eli's face, and I could see Eli getting mad. Then he must have said something Pete really didn't like because Pete winced and grabbed his ears as he backed away. I could finally see what Eli was referring to when he said I shouldn't be around Pete alone in case something set him off. I had underestimated his anger. I would not want to be on the wrong end of it.

The police arrived before the other driver could come back with his insurance card. Pete's demeanor changed drastically once they arrived, as if he had put on a mask. One of the officers asked Pete for his information and made note of everyone's account of what happened. As expected, they found the other driver at fault and gave him a ticket.

“I think we should call it a night,” I said as the police left, hoping not to upset Pete further.

“I think that's a good idea,” Eli said.

“Fine!” Pete spat.

He flipped a U-turn, sending us all flying into the right side of the car. I sighed, wondering if I should have just listened to Eli in the first place when he warned me to stay away from Pete. I think Eli sensed I was upset because I felt a hand rubbing my right arm reassuringly. It helped to know I wasn't alone—that he was there for me. We were just pulling up to my house when I felt his hand slip away.

“Sorry about your car,” I said once we got to the door. Bailey and Eli went inside to give us time alone, but I figured Eli was watching from a window.

“It's not your fault. I'll see you later,”Pete said, leaving without so much as a hug goodbye.

I lingered on the porch with my arms crossed, waiting for the night to sink in. I felt completely lost. I had been so looking forward to the date, and now I wasn't sure about Pete at all. I had a lot of thinking to do and hoped I wouldn't hear “I told you so” from Eli. Instead, when he stepped out onto the porch, he greeted me with a big hug. It was a huge relief. I could see that he had been worried, but I couldn't understand why he was so worried about me. We had all been in the car.

“Bailey and I were thinking the three of us could watch a movie since our night got cut short. You in?” he asked gingerly.

“Sure,” I said in a faint voice.

“You okay? You look really—”

I cut him off. "I'm fine, really. I just feel a little stupid. Where's Bailey?"

"She went to pick out a movie.And you're not stupid,"he said. He turned my head to face his. "Got it?"

"Okay, I'll be right there. Just give me a minute."

"Allright, but if you aren't in there in five minutes, I'm sending a search party," he said with a wink.

I smiled as he went back into the living room to be with Bailey.

I stood on the porch for a few more minutes and then took a deep breath and headed into the living room. I realized I had an amazingfriend in Eli, and that couldn't have made me feel more at home. There was no question about it—he was my best friend.

The movie seemed to drag on forever. I guessed it was because I couldn't pay attention. All I could think about was Pete. I couldn't believe how he had reacted to a simple accident. I felt terrible, especially since Eli had warned me about his temper and I had dismissed it. I hated to be wrong. I didn't want a relationship with someone who flew off the handle like that all the time. It would be dangerous.

Then again, maybe it had been a fluke. Maybe he didn't always have a temper like that. He had been distracted by Eli and maybe even felt a little competition from him. He could have been overwhelmed and acted irrationally and out of character. I couldn't figure out if I should give him the benefit of the doubt or not. Despite the circumstances, it was unacceptable to act that way. And Eli would be disappointed if I gave him a second chance, so I couldn't talk this through with him. I also wasn't sure how Bailey would feel—she was rightfully upset and would probably tell me to move on. I felt so alone.

I was glad when the movie ended. My emotions were all over the place, and I couldn't wait to go to sleep. Bailey walked Eli outside, and I went upstairs to leave them alone and get ready for bed.

When Bailey strolled into my room, she sported a big grin. I knew she had been excited to go on the date, and I was sad that Petehad ruined it. But she didn't seem upset. In fact, she looked blissful.

"What's that big smile for?" I asked, eyebrows raised.

"He gave me a big hug and a kiss on the cheek! Ahh, isn't he great?"She beamed, plopping down on the bed next to me.

"He is." I meant it. However, I couldn't help but feel remorseful as I said it.

"I hope he asks me out again."

"Yeah, hopefully, next time doesn't get cut short like tonight did," I said.

"Well, technically it didn't get cut short. Our plans just changed.

I'm sorry about your date, though. Here I am, excited about Eli, and you're probably upset. You're not hurt from the accident, are you?"

"No, I'm fine. Just shaken up, I guess. I don't know what to do now. I don't know why Pete acted the way he did."

"He definitely overreacted. Seems like he can't control his temper."

"Yeah."

"I'm beat,"she said.

"Me too."

Bailey went to the bathroom toget ready for bed. I fixed up the bed in my room for her and fell into bed before she returned.

I layawake for a long time. Around 3:30, I finally fell into a troubled sleep, my nightmares even more realistic than normal. I could feel the heat around me and the dust in my lungs. I felt out of breath when I opened my eyes, as if I had actually been running.

CHAPTER FIVE

I woke up after ten a.m. and slinked downstairs in my pajamas and tank top. I found Bailey sitting at the table, eating breakfast with my mom. There was a place set at the table for me next to Bailey, and in the center of the table lay a plate overflowing with pancakes, bacon, and scrambled eggs. A large pitcher of orange juice sat off to the side.

"Good morning, sleepyhead!" Bailey said.

"Morning," I said, still feeling a little groggy.

"Bailey was just telling me that you were in a car accident last night," Mom said sternly.

"Yeah, it wasn't a big deal. Just a fender-bender. I'm fine, and so is everyone else."

"You never called me."

"I didn't have a number to call you at, and you weren't home when we went to bed. I didn't want to leave a note and worry you for nothing. I figured I would tell you when I got up this morning."

"Next time—and hopefully there won't be a next time—I want you to find a way to get ahold of me. I'll get a cell phone today to ensure it won't happen again."

"Okay," I said, slightly annoyed.

Even though Bailey hadn't meant any harm, I was irritated that she had told her before I got up because she was probably worried sick. I told myself that Bailey had no way of knowing how much my mom worried.

"You need to call your dad, too. He'll want to know about it."

I had planned on calling him after Bailey left, but I had been on the fence about whether to tell him about the car accident. Apparently, Mom had made that decision for me. He didn't worry quite as much as she did, so it wouldn't be that big of a deal to tell him. On the other hand, now that I was in another state, it might be worse since he couldn't see that I was fine.

"I planned on it," I said.

Bailey broke her silence. "Wow, Abby! Your mom makes such a good breakfast!"

I doubted she could be any more obvious with her subject change, but I was thankful anyway. She could probably tell I was getting aggravated—it didn't take a rocket scientist to read my expression.

"Yeah, Mom is really big on breakfast," I said. I could see my mom smile at the remark, though she never looked up from her plate.

"Well, I'm done,"Mom said, standing up. She grabbed her plate andempty glass. "You girls enjoy your breakfast."

She walked out, and it was silent for a moment.

"How'd you sleep?" I asked Bailey.

"Good. You must have too because you were out like a light. You're definitely not a light sleeper." She laughed.

I chuckled too. "I can be really hard to wake up sometimes."

Actually, I usually was a light sleeper, even with nightmares. I often woke up at the drop of a hat, as if it was my body's defense against the dream. I couldn't understand how I could have slept so heavily the night before.

We finished the rest of our meal slowly and quietly, lost in thought. Then we cleaned up the breakfast dishes together while chatting and joking to make the time go by faster. Bailey would have to go home after she got ready since she still had homework to do before Monday. I was glad I would get some time to myself.

As soon as Bailey left, the phone rang. It was Pete. Surely he knew I was upset about what had happened on our date. I didn't even know if I felt like talking to him at all.

"Abby, I want to talk to you about what happened yesterday. Can I come over?"

His sincere voice almost convinced me to say yes, but then I remembered I wasn't supposed to be alone with him. Rules aside, as I thought about it a little more I realized I didn't *want* to be alone with him.

"Actually, no. I have some things I need to get done before my mom gets home, and tonight she and I are supposed to spend some time together."

"Oh. Well . . . I just wanted to tell you I'm sorry for the way I acted yesterday. I don't know what came over me. I overreacted. I'm really sorry you had to see that. You shouldn't have."

I didn't really know what to say. Did he mean I shouldn't have had to see it because he didn't want me to see the real him or because it wasn't a normal occurrence?

"It's okay, I guess." I really wasn't over it. His apology didn't make up for it in the slightest, but I didn't know what else to say.

"I hope you'll forgive me. I'd like to have a second chance to take you out."

"I'll have to think about it."

"Okay," he said, sounding defeated. "I guess I can understand that. I'll let you get back to what you were doing."

"Allright, bye."

I felt a little better knowing he was remorseful. I wasn't sure I could ever trust him again. I rubbed my temples, trying to easemy stress headache. I wasn't sure how he could have expected anything else from me.

The front door opened and shut.

"Hey Abby!" my mom said."I have a surprise for you! Where are you?"

"In the living room," I called back. She skipped into the room, holding a phone up in the air. "Oh, you got a new phone. Cool."

"It's for *you*."

She had bought me a cell phone. *Holy cow!*

"Oh my gosh, Mom! Thanks!" I squealed.

I had wanted a cell phone for the longest time and had been hinting at it for ages. Not having to find a phone every time I needed to call to check in would make life so much easier. Plus, almost everyone my age had one, so having the ability to text my friends was exciting. It sure beat passing notes, although that would still probably happen. I was sort of behind when it came to technology.

"You're welcome. I thought about it, and if you're going to be able to call me in case of emergencies, you're going to need a phone."

"Thanks,Mom," I said as I hugged her.

I grabbed the phone and ran upstairs to check it out. It was a pink smartphone—my favorite color. I wasn't that great with directions, and learning the area hadn't really been a priority for me so far, so I was glad I would have a phone that I could use as a GPS when I got a car.

"Be careful about how much you talk on it. We're sharing a plan!" she shouted up the stairs after me.

Before long, I had programmed all my friends' phone numbers into it, including Eli's, Pete's, and Bailey's. I loved it, although I had nothing to compare it to since I had never had a cell phone before. I wanted to call my dad on it, but since my mom had cautioned me about the minutes, I called him on the house phone instead.

He picked up on the first ring and sounded like he was relaxing. All in all, he took the news of the accident okay, but he was still worried about me. I tried to set him at ease by telling him about the cell phone Mom bought me. I made sure to give him the number before we finished talking. He was doing well and was considering a visit already. The thought excited me, even if it wasn't for a few weeks.

When Eli picked me up the next morning, I told him about Pete calling me to apologize. He acted shocked that Pete had a conscience. I shoved his shoulder at his poor attempt at a joke. Whether or not Pete lost his temper often, it wasn't like he was going to blow up every time he got mad. He wouldn't have such a good reputation if that were the case. I knew that just as well as Eli, even if he wouldn't admit it.

"He also said he wanted to take me out again sometime to make it up to me," I said, trying not to look in his direction. I wasn't sure how he would take that—I wasn't even sure how I was taking it.

"And what did you say? Please tell me you told him no."

"I told him I had to think about it."

"What? How could you even consider going out with him again? Think of how awful he was."

"Well, I still want to find out what happened. I'm just not sure it's worth it yet. And I'm not sure I still have your support. I'm not even sure I want to be around him at all. There are a lot of things to think about, and it's all so confusing." I crossed my arms and looked out the window.

"Now, more than ever, I'd think you wouldn't want to be around him, but if you, for some strange reason, decide you still want to date him, I'll stand by you. That's what friends do, right?"

"I'm so glad to hear that. I was so worried you wouldn't."

"Why?" he asked.

"Because of how he acted. I figured you'd be mad at me for even considering it. I'm kind of mad at me for considering it," I admitted. I stared at my feet, unwilling to look up for even a second.

"I will say it's not what I expected, but I'm not mad. I don't think you should be mad at yourself either. I may not agree with you, but you've done nothing wrong."

"I know. You don't know how relieved I am to hear that," I said. "Oh, guess what!"

"What?"

"My mom got me a cell phone!"

"Awesome! Welcome to the world of technology."

"Give me your phone. I'll put my number in." I held out my hand.

He pulled it out of his pocket and tossed it into my lap. I was impressed with his nice phone and punched in my new number to save it. Just as I was about to hand it back to him, I noticed his screen background—a picture of a man and woman. I wondered if it was his parents but didn't dare ask. I tried to hand it back to him before he caught me staring at it.

When I arrived at math class, I saw Pete already there. I had been dreading this class all weekend since our disaster date. I had been trying to prepare myself to talk to him, but nothing helped. My stomach floppedin anticipation, and I tried to make as little noise as possible when I sat down so he wasn't alerted to my presence. I was unsuccessful.

"Hi," he said.

"Hi," I responded coldly.

There were still a few minutes before the bell would ring to signal the start of class. The seconds felt like minutes.

"How are you feeling?"

"I'm fine," I said.

"Same here. I'm glad you're feeling better."

He turned around slowly,like he was waiting for me to say something more. But I had nothing more I wanted to say. I hoped he wouldn't bring up the date until I was ready to talk about it. I wondered if he was still planning on walking me to class. I wasn't sure I really wanted him to, but at the same time, I didn't want to be rude or push him away prematurely.

As I suspected, when class ended, he walked with me to my next class. I was thankful for his silence during the entire walk. When we said goodbye to each other, Eli was watching and waiting as usual.

"Well, that looked strained." He was amused.

"Yeah, well I'm not ready to make anything easy on him."

"Good for you."

All I could do was smile because he was pleased, although I didn't know why it mattered to me.

The next two classes passed quickly. Bailey, Eli, and I had fun talking whenever we got the chance. The troubles of the weekend were forgotten until the bell rang for lunch. None of us had discussed it, but I was sure they preferred not to sit with Pete.

We were laughing at one of Eli's jokes as we strolled up to the cafeteria, Bailey and Eli walking hand-in-hand. Just then, a somber and remorseful Pete confronted us. He played the part quite well, but I didn't believe all of it was real.

"Hi guys, I wanted to apologize for the other night. I'm not sure what came over me, and I hope you can forgive me,"he said.

Eli and Bailey looked at each other, wondering what the other would say. Bailey answered for both of them.

"It's okay this time, but if it happens again, I'm not sure I can look the other way." She smiled at Pete and glanced at Eli for approval.

He nodded and said, "I agree," giving Pete a stern look. He must have been putting on the act for Bailey. There was no way he would have been so forgiving if she weren't there. But there was more—something unspoken seemed to pass between Eli and Pete. But I couldn't put my finger on it. *Exactly what was Eli up to?*

"Agreed," Pete said, smiling without letting on that he sensed something more. Then he turned to face me. "Can I talk to you alone for a minute?"

"I guess," I said, shrugging.

We walked over to the side, and Isaw Eli and Bailey talking to each other out of the corner of my eye. Pete held something out to me. I resisted the urge to put my hand out to take it. Staring up at him, I tried to gauge what he was doing.

"Take it," Pete said, nudging me along. "I wanted to give you something to show you how sorry I am."

Hesitantly, I reached my hand out, and a silver bracelet fell into my palm. It was magnificently crafted with one perfect charm—a heart. *How beautiful!*

"A bracelet?"I was astonished. I had never expected something so extravagant as an apology gift, especially since we had only been on one date and I wasn't sure I would go on another one.

"Yeah, do you like it?" He sounded hopeful.

"It's beautiful."

"Good," he said, smiling proudly. "I hope you'll forgive me. Even if you choose not to give me a second date, I'd still like to be your friend."

I thought for a second, staring at the sparkling bracelet in my hands. At first, no words came to me, but when they finally did, I felt I had no other choice. "I haven't decided yet whether I'll go on another date with you, but . . ." I paused, looked up at him, and smiled. "I will be your friend, if nothing else. But only if you promise not to lose your temper like that in front of me again.Agreed?"

He laughed."Agreed." With that, he swept me off my feet and gave me a big hug, swinging me around in a circle.

It wasn't until that moment that I realized just how strong he was. He squeezed so tight I couldn't breathe.

"Can't . . . breathe . . ." I gasped, panicking.

"Oh, sorry." He carefully dropped me back on the ground.

"I don't think I can accept this," I said solemnly as I held the bracelet out to him. "It's too much and not necessary."

"You have to. I won't take it back. It's yours," he said, turning to walk away.

Ugh! Lost that battle. It was a pretty bracelet, but I couldn't say for certain how often I would wear it, if ever. That would all depend on how things ended up going with Pete in the long run.

Lunch was quieter than usual, at least between Bailey, Eli, Pete, and I. Everyone else didn't seem to run out of conversation, and I was I relieved I didn't have to offer any tidbits to jumpstart the discussion. My eyes never left my lunch. I tried to make it seem like I was thoroughly interested in the food on my plate as I pushed it around between bites. *Eventually the awkwardness was bound to go away, right?*

My prediction about the awkwardness proved right. By the following Monday, everything seemed to return to normal. It had been an intense week trying to get through lunches, but in the end, enduring it paid off. The horrendous date seemed to be forgotten by all but me—and of course Eli, though he didn't show it.

I was still undecided about what I should do. I was physically attracted to Pete, and his outgoing personality drew me toward him. But his temper scared me. I was teetering on the edge of danger, and I had to make up my mind. The homecoming dance was this weekend, and he'd already asked me.

I made plans to go dress shopping at the mall with Bailey, who was going to the dance with Eli. My matchmaking had panned out better than I expected—they had gone on a date together the prior weekend, and Bailey was beaming when she came to class on Monday. She couldn't stop talking about him. It did trouble me that Eli didn't talk about Bailey nearly as often. *But he's not as emotive as she is in general,* I mused. *And even if her feelings are stronger than his, that can change. He just needs to spend more time with her.* I hoped she wasn't about to get her heart broken.

CHAPTER SIX

Eli continued in his role as my "bodyguard," and our friendship continued to flourish. For some reason, he still didn't feel at ease discussing his love life, even though I felt more than comfortable discussing mine with him. *Guys were always different than girls about opening up about their feelings and emotions. Why was that?* It was a lot more interesting to have a deep conversation with a guy who was open. Their inner workings fascinated me.

I sat in my bedroom working on homework. It was only Monday night, but I already had three assignments: math, science, and history. We were havinga quiz on the first two chapters of *To Kill a Mockingbird* soon. I had chosen to read it over again, and by the time I finished the assigned chapters, it was well past eleven. I went straight to bed but tossed and turned despite my exhaustion. Reading was one of my favorite things to do before bed. It made it easier to sleep. Usually. Apparently, tonight was not one of those nights.

Once I finally fell asleep, it didn't last long—I woke up screaming. It was still dark out, so I knew Mom was still home and probably in bed. I hoped I hadn'twoken her up. Moments later, my door opened. Mom peeked her head in and peered at me through sleepy eyes.

"Is everything okay, honey?" she asked in a groggy voice.

"Yeah," I sighed. "Just a bad dream."

It was the first time since my recurring nightmares started that Mom knew about even one of them. I would have liked to keep her in the dark forever. I figured they would eventually go away on their own—or at least I hoped they would.

"Do you want some warm milk?" she asked.

"No that's okay. I'm fine, really. Go back to bed."

"Are you sure?"

"Yes."

"Okay, but let me know if you need anything."

She left quietly, and I hoped she wasn't worried about me. After a while, I fell back asleep and slept peacefully until my alarm went off. I grudgingly climbed out of bed, thankful for the uninterrupted sleep I was able to get after my nightmare. I wasn't sure if my mom would confront me about my dream. Knowing she was downstairs made me get ready much more slowly. When I finally arrived downstairs, I was relieved to find she wasn't at all concerned about it.

"Good morning," she sang.

"Morning," I replied.

To my astonishment, Mom never even mentioned the mishap from the night before. I was so relieved I wouldn't have to lie to her. I had been sure she would ask me if it was the first time, but I guessed she hadjust assumed it was.

I felt exhilarated, and when Eli arrived to pick me up, I could tell he was in high spirits as well. I soared through the first half of the day blissfully happy, and by lunchtime I decided to throw caution to the wind and take Pete up on his offer to accompany me to the dance that Saturday. I couldn't wait to tell him, and I knew Eli couldn't get out of doubling with us because he was already going with Bailey.

As soon as I saw Pete standing by the cafeteria, I ran up ahead and pulled him aside. I couldn't help but blurt out the good news.

"So . . . I've decided I will go with you to the dance on Saturday, if you still want me to," I said in a rush.

He stared at me. He looked like he had to clamp his mouth shut so it wouldn't flop open.

"What? Really? What made you change your mind?" he asked in bewilderment.

"I don't know!" I laughed.

"Well I'm glad you did," he said, putting his arm around me as we walked into the cafeteria to join Eli and Bailey. Eli's eyebrows lifted when he caught sight of Pete's arm around me, but he didn't say a thing.

Our good spirits persisted, and the rest of the day went on without a hitch. I couldn't see how the day could get any better until I got into P.E. The teacher announced that we would be finished with swimming that Friday and moving onto volleyball the following week. Although I wasn't very good at it, I loved volleyball. I was smiling when I walked up to Eli at our usual meeting place.

"So you're going to the homecoming dance with Pete, huh?" he asked in an annoyed tone.

"Yep," I said with a guilty smirk on my face.

"When did you plan on telling me?" he asked.

"Right now?"

He chuckled. "Oh! Well, okay then."

We strolled to his car as we discussed the dance, figuring out how we were going to work around me going with Pete. We decided I could just meet Pete at the dance. Pete and I weren't planning to go to dinner beforehand, so that would make things easy. Eli would drive me—but we wouldn't tell Pete—and Bailey could catch a ride with another friend.

More than ever, I was looking forward to going dress shopping with Bailey the next day. Bailey's dad was going to pick us up from school and drop us off at the mall, and my mom would pick us up on her way home from work. Bailey would eat dinner with us before we took her home.

Everything was so much more complicated since I didn't have my driver's license. I needed to start applying for jobs so I could get a car soon. I mentioned it to Eli and found out he was planning on looking for a job too. Neither of us knew exactly what kind of job we wanted, but we both agreed that we didn't want to work at a fast food restaurant. I liked the idea of working with clothes, and Eli liked the idea of being a cashier. Most of it depended on what we found close by that would hire employees with no prior experience.

Mom got home early. She was making dinner when I arrived, and I went straight to my room after letting her know I was home. I was hard at work on my homework when she came in with the cordless phone in her hand. It was my dad. I had been so busy with everything else that it had been almost a week since I had spoken to him. I felt guilty for not thinking to call him sooner.

"Hey honey," he said cheerfully. "How's it going?"

"HeyDad!It's going well. I'm just working on some homework right now. How are you doing?"

"I'm good, but I've been missing you. It feels like it's been months since I've seen you," he said.

"It almost has been. I've missed you too. I can't wait until you come and visit me. I want you to meet my friends!"

He was coming in two weeks, and I couldn't wait. To my delight, he and my mom talked it over, and he was going to stay in the guest room. It had been my mom's idea. She had been so insistenton getting a fresh start somewhere new that I would never have guessed shewould be so open to letting him invade our new space. Then again, they had been married for more than seventeen years, and that had to mean something to both of them. Of course, they had me to think about, too. My mom knew how much it meant to me to see him, so she wanted to make it as easy as possible—and for that I was grateful. If he had to pay for a hotel every time he came out, the cost would limit how often he would be able to visit. He planned to leave early in the morning before the sun rose to drive to Arizona. It was a seven-hour drive, and he didn't want to get in late.

"I can't wait either. I've already started tying up loose ends here at the store for when I leave. We've been really busy, and it'll probably get even crazier as hunting season gets closer."

"I know what you mean. I remember how busy it gets," I said.

We talked for a while longer, mostly about his visit. We decidedto go to the pizza place that I had gone to with Pete, but I left out the fact that it had been a date. I told him I was going to the homecoming dance that weekend with a friend but only as friends. I didn't feel like it was the right time to tell him or my mom about my feelings for Pete. I wasn't sure our relationship was going anywhere. After we hung up, I finished my homework just in time to eat dinner.

Mom and I discussed Dad's upcoming visit. She admitted that she was nervous about him staying with us, which I had guessed. It was inevitable. I mean, they had been married for a long time, and it ended badly, but there had to be some feelings still left. You don't just stop caring about someone just because you got divorced.

While I was cleaning the kitchen, I thought of Pete. I wondered if, by the time my dad came to visit, I would want him to meet Pete. I was getting ahead of myself, but it was nice to dream. That was something I didn't do often enough. I longed to go back to the normal, nerve-wracking days of "this is my boyfriend" introductions. It always seemed so daunting, thinking maybe my dad wouldn't like the guy I brought home. Now it was way worse because I wasn't sure how I felt about him. Sure he was as slick as butter when you talked to him, but so were con men, right?

That night, I had another nightmare. I wondered if Iwould ever get to the end of the dream instead of waking without answers or relief. It always ended just before I found out who I was running from. Each time I came to know the desert around me better and better, and I memorized new details: the clearing, the dust billowing up from my footsteps, the cactus only inches away from me. I was growing angrier every time I had the dream. It was one thing to have a nightmare—it was another to be haunted by the same nightmare night after night.

The minutescrept by slowly, and I figured it was because I was anticipating my dress-shopping trip that afternoon. It couldn't come soon enough, but my mood hadn't improved much from that morning. I hoped I could forget my troubles and enjoy shopping.

My mom gave me $60 to spend, but I never dreamed my dress would cost that much. Bailey told me at lunch that her dad was going to give her the same amount, so we both had more than enough to find beautiful dresses and maybe shoes to match.

Bailey's dad picked us up right on time, and Bailey was the spitting image of him—in girl form, of course. I could tell that Bailey and her dad had a close relationship. She hadtold me that there was very little she didn't disclose to her dad, but she did admit that she hadn'ttold him about Pete's outburst after the accident for fear of him not allowing her to hang out with him again. I didn't blame her—I'm sure my parents would feel the same way.

I briefly wondered what it would be like only having a dad. I couldn't imagine having to have "the talk" with my dad. I don't think I could have stomached it. I'm not sure my dad would have made it through the conversation either. There were some things that were just easier to discuss with a mom, but Bailey seemed to be doing just fine.

Bailey found her dress first—a short, pink, strapless dress with rhinestones. The bottom was hemmed diagonally from one side to the other, and it hugged all her curves in just the right ways. Eli was going to love it. To top it off, it was only $40. Bailey was ecstatic, as was I when I found mine a half an hour later. My dress was tight as well, though it was slightly longer than Bailey's. It reminded me of the perfect little black dress, and it was in my price range at $50. We decided to wander around the mall for a little while after finding our dresses, and when five p.m. came, we called my mom to come get us. Ten minutes later, we climbed into my mom's car. It was like she had stood by the phone with keys in hand waiting for my call, though I knew that wasn't the case.

"Hey guys, how was shopping?" she asked.

We gushed about our perfect dresses.

"That's wonderful! You guys will have to model them for me tonight," she said.

Once we were home, Bailey and I put on our own fashion show to show off our new dresses to my mom.

"Wow, you two look terrific!" she exclaimed.

The doorbell rang, signaling the arrival of our Chinese food, so we ran upstairs to change our clothes for dinner. We were back in a flash, and Mom was already waiting at the table with plates, napkins, and sodas.

We devoured all of the delicious Chinese food before taking Bailey home. She thanked us both for the ride and dinner before she went inside.

By Friday, our little foursome was bursting with excitement. We were greeted by even more excitement from our other friends, who seemed to be only able to talk about the dance. The ladies had the lowdown on all our friends' dresses, and the guys were discussing who they were bringing and all the detailing they planned to do on their cars the next morning.

When Saturday rolled around, I spent the morning being lazy. I utilized the entire afternoon getting ready as slowly as I wanted. I accentuated my already curly hair with a curling iron until curls cascaded down my shoulders. Then I pinned my hair halfway up with bobby pins and checked it in the mirror before spraying it with hairspray. I was having a fantastic hair day—the kind where it lays exactly how it's supposed to the first time you pull it back.

I did my makeup a little heavier than I normally did, since I was going for an evening look, and put on a pearl necklace my mom loanedme. She said it would make the dress. I couldn't say that I disagreed—it looked stunning in contrast to the dress.

As planned, Eli came to pick me up at precisely 6:30, exactly thirty minutes before the dance started. He looked great in a red button-up, short-sleeved shirt and black jeans. The red shirt brought out his eyes brilliantly. His shoes didn't stand out because they weren't shiny, but they still looked presentable. He didn't comment on how I looked, but I could tell by the way he looked at me that he was impressed. It almost seemed like he was embarrassed by how much he was impressed. My mom wasn't home to see me off, which I was grateful for because I didn't want to explain to her why Eli was driving me. Not to mention that I didn't want to do the half-hour photo shoot.

We went into the dance separately. I walked inside first and found Pete standing close to the door, waiting for me. He looked striking in dark blue jeans and a blue collared shirt. He really did have impeccable taste in clothes. He slid his arm around my waist, and it felt so good to be in his arms.

"Wow, you look gorgeous." His lips lightly brushed my ear as he spoke, and I felt a rush flood through my body.

"Thanks, you look good too." I blushed.

"Thirsty?" he asked.

"Not right now."

We headed to the dance floor for a slow song when Eli walked in holding Bailey's hand. They strode up to us and started dancing. I smiled at them without saying a word. Bailey looked amazing. She had straightened her hair and left it down. It was a good look for her.

After dancing to a few more songs, fast and slow, the four of us were sweating and decided to grab a table and drink some punch to cool off. We chatted for awhile about nothing in particular, and then Pete asked if I would like to take a walk outside to get some fresh air. I agreed, and off we went.

Leaning against the wall outside, I suddenly felt nervous. I thought Pete looked nervous too. He was looking off into the distance, and then he turned and kissed me. His tongue pushed my lips open, and I let them part. The kiss was sweet and lasted only a moment, but when he pulled away, I could see compassion in his eyes. It was a passionate and sensual moment and definitely ranked toward the top of my list of good kisses. My face flushed. I looked at the ground, smiling until I thoughtthe blush had passed.

He took my hand and led me back into the crowded room where we were engulfed by blaring music and strobe lights. I had to blink to readjust my eyes, but before I could rejoin the dance floor, Bailey grabbed my arm and pulled me in the direction of the bathroom. She dragged me all the way inside and shut the door behind us. As soon as we were alone, she began giving me the third degree.

"I saw you guys kissing!" she squealed.

"Shh! Yeah." I tried to sound nonchalant even though my heart was still racing. I looked in the mirror and checked my makeup and lip gloss to make it seem more believable that I didn't find it out of the ordinary.

"Well?" she said expectantly.

"Well what?" I asked, trying to conceal my grin.

"Are you kidding? You kiss him for the first time, and you aren't gushing? I would be floating on a cloud!"

"Well, it was nice." I grinned. "But it wasn't my first kiss."

"Wow, I didn't know you'd kissed a boy before. I haven't,"shesaid, looking at her feet. "But I'm hoping Eli will kiss me. Do you think he will?"

"I'm sure he will at some point. Maybe even tonight," I said.

"You really think so?" she asked, suddenly more enthusiastic. She smiled absently and then touched up her lip gloss while I used the restroom. I washed my hands, and we left the bathroom together.

By the end of the night, we had spent the majority of the time dancing. I even danced with Eli, and Bailey with Pete. Pete and I walked out hand-in-hand when the dance ended, right next to Eli and Bailey. Eli told me earlier in the night that he was going to drop off Bailey and then go straight to my house. If I weren'thomeby the time he got there, he would call me. It was the first time he had approved of fudging the rules about me being alone with Pete, and I could tell he was nervous. He seemed almost as if he were second-guessing his decision as we parted ways. I mouthed,"It's fine."He seemed to relax a little. As Pete held the door open for me, I felt surprisingly at ease sliding into the passenger seat.

"Well, do you want to go straight home or would you like to go to the park and walk around or something?" he asked once he climbed into the driver's seat.

I looked at my watch. It was already eleven, and even though I didn't have a definite curfew, my mom expected me home before 11:30 unless I called to check in. I knew that Eli was expecting me home pretty soon as well. But I couldn't say it wasn't a tempting offer.

"Actually, I'm kind of tired. It's been a long, exciting day. I think I need to go home. I'm sorry," I said, sounding sad. I really wanted to spend more time with him, but that was against my agreement with Eli. I was beginning to get pretty fed up withthat agreement. How was I ever going to get to know Pete better if we were never alone?

"Don't be sorry—I understand."He smiled, resting his hand on my leg.

I smiled back and felt a tingle of excitement in my stomach. Such a small gesture went far with me. *I suppose it did with a lot of girls.*

We pulled up in front of my house. I could tell that my mom was already in bed, but she was probably reading while she waited for me to get home. Pete walked around the car and opened my door for me. *What a gentleman!*Not many guys still had the class to open doors for ladies. He walked me to the front door of the house, and we stood there for a few minutes holding hands and staring into each other's eyes. It wasn't awkward like I would expect it to be. Finally, he leaned in and kissed me again, and our tongues tangled as our bodies melted together. When I finally felt myself coming back to reality, it seemed like it had been an eternity. I saw headlights in the distance before the kiss ended, and when it got close, I caught a glimpse of Eli's car. He gunned it right before he passed the house.

"I should go. Tonight was great. Thanks for the second chance." He leaned in and hugged me before giving me one last kiss. I noticed he didn't drive away until I was safely inside. I closed the door and watched out the window as he drove away, and out of the corner of my eye, I saw another set of taillights flicker on and a car start before it aggressively sped away. I knew it had to be Eli. I hadn't seen him park, and I wasn't quite sure why he seemed upset, but maybe that was just my imagination.

I couldn't help but wonder if it made him mad that I was getting so close to Pete. I hadn't realized until that very moment that I had forgiven Pete.

CHAPTER SEVEN

I was super excited when I woke up the next morning. A great night, followed by a deep, dreamless sleep was a rarity for me. I threw on my fuzzy white bathrobe and matching slippers and headed downstairs. A lazy morning enjoying TV on the couch in my pajamas sounded awesome.

"How was the dance?" Mom asked during breakfast.

"It was good."

"Did all your friends go?" she asked.

"Yeah, but mostly I was with Eli, Bailey, and Pete." Mom still didn't know that Pete was my date.

"You guys seem close. I'm glad you've been able to find good friends so quickly."

"Me too!How was your night?" I changed the subject.

"It was fun. We played Bunco at one of our co-worker's houses and had a few drinks. It's nice we both are able to get out with other people so soon after moving here. I was worried it might be hard to find friends."

"Yeah."

The awkward silence seemed to last longer than usual. Something was up. Mom was radiating tension.

"Umm, Abby . . . I'm not sure how to bring this up, so I'm just going to say it. How would you feel about me dating?"

"Dating? Dating who?" I had been so caught up in the move and the divorce that it hadn't even occurred to me that my mom would be ready to date so soon—or that she would even date at all.

"Someone at work introduced me to one of their friends. He seems really nice," she replied timidly.

"You've already found someone?" My voice went up several octaves.

"Well, he asked me out last night. I told him I had to make sure it was okay with you. I know it's really soon, but I think it's better to be out there moving on with my life rather than sitting around here sulking because my marriage failed. I really would like to do this, but I needyour support."

I didn't know what to say. I didn't want her to date anyone except my dad. In fact, I still secretly hoped that they would come to their senses and get back together. If she started dating someone else and fell in love, there would be no way that could happen. Or maybe it would make my dad want her more. It was something to consider. To be honest, I truly wanted my parents to be happy, and if that meant my mom had to date, I guessed that would be okay. It wasn't like this person would be around forever.

"I guess if that's what you really want to do, I'll support you," I said through gritted teeth.

"Really?"

"Yep. Whatever makes you happy." I smiled, trying to seem upbeat even though I was totally bummed.

"Great! I'm so glad you're being so mature about this. Do you want to meet him before we go out?" she asked cautiously.

"No, I don't need to unless you really want me to. If you really like him, and you guys hit it off, I can meet him then." I hoped she wouldn't want me to. I doubted I could handle it.

"Sounds like a plan to me. I'm really nervous about it.It's been like twenty years since I've dated anyone other than your dad." She stared off into space for a minute before she spoke again. She seemed like a giddy teenager, not unlike how Bailey and I had acted only a week before. I had never seen her that way before. "Well, enough about that. I'll get this cleaned up and then what do you say we go shopping?"

"Sounds good to me!"

There went my plan to be lazy, but it would be nice to get out of the house and distract myselffrom the conversation we had just had. I hopped up to shower and get dressed.

We had shopped for hours before we realized thatwe had skipped lunch, and it was time for dinner. Mom suggested we grab dinner at a Mexican food restaurant.

There was one we had both wanted to try, so we headed straight there. As soon as we walked in, I spotted Pete with his family. I wanted nothing more than to turn around and walk out. I wasn't ready for my mom to meet him—I wasn't even sure how to introduce him. He didn't have a clue that I hadn't yet told my mom we were dating. Maybe we could get through dinner without him seeing us.

The hostess seated us at a table almost directly across from his. *So much for not being noticed.* He spotted us almost immediately and hopped up from his seat.

"Hey Abby!" he said, giving me a big hug and a kiss on the cheek. I held my breath to make sure my mom hadn't seen and was relieved when I saw she was speaking to the waiter. He slid his arm around my waist, and I pushed it off. I whispered in Pete's ear that I didn't want my mom to know we were dating just yet, but I didn't have time to explain why before she finished talking to the waiter.

"Well hello," she said, greeting Pete.

"Hi," he replied, reaching his hand out to shake hers.

"Mom, this is Pete, one of the friends I was telling you about."

"Oh, it's nice to finally meet you. Abby was telling me how great it's been to have such welcoming friends."

He glanced at me slightly confused, but played along. "It's been nice having her here," he said with a smile. "I should get back to my parents. It was nice meeting you, and I'll see you tomorrow, Abby."

He turned around, still looking confused as he walked back to his table.

"Wow, he's cute Abby,"my mom said. "You should go out with him!"

I couldn't help but laugh. The rest of our meal went on without interruption, even when Pete left. He waved to say goodbye,butmy mom didn't notice.

An hour and a half after sitting down, we walked out of the restaurant feeling as if our stomachs would burst. Later that night when we had recovered from the tremendous portions of Mexican food, we made hot fudge sundaes heaping with whipped cream for dessert.

My mom never brought up Pete again. I could only guess how excited she would be to learn that we were, in fact, dating. On the other hand, I knew she would be shocked if she ever learned about the way he had lost his temper. She wouldn't approve. She probably would have me committed for choosing to be so reckless.

Sunday night I dreamed happy dreams about my night at the dance with Pete. That was a dream I wouldn't mind recurring. It had been such an amazing night.

The dream opened with us walking into the dance, though it seemed different, almost like we were alone. We danced, drank punch, and finally kissed. That's when I awoke, of course—during the best part of the dream! My mind was running the dream on repeat—I wanted to feel his lips on mine again.

I dragged myself out the door when Eli honked. He was running late, and instead of making it to school on time we ended up having to go to Sweep. I wasn't upset to be there. I didn't feel like going to math that day even though I was missing out on my opportunity to see Pete. At least I would see him at lunch. I ended up falling asleep and was surprised when I woke up to Eli shaking my shoulder. The bell had rung, and almost everyone had already cleared out of the large cafeteria. *Oops.*

We made it through the next two classes. I was excited to see Pete, but when we got to the cafeteria, he wasn't waiting for us like usual. He didn't show up the entire lunch period, and I wondered where he was. *Maybe he's sick.* The night before he had told me that he would see me at school the next day. I felt a prick of sadness that I wouldn't get to see him.

I didn't get to speak to Pete until the next day, even though I tried to call him. He said he had been sick, though he seemed fine. *And why didn't he call me back?* I thought it was weird. I decided to express my concerns to Eli, but when I did, he didn't seem concerned. I felt like I must have been reading too much into it.

Since the ice had been broken, we felt free to kiss each other every chance we got. I could tell that Eli and Bailey hadn't gotten to that point yet because they sat in silence. We unsuccessfully tried to hide our stolen kisses, since we didn't want to make them uncomfortable, andwe laughed together when they caught us. As Eli, Pete, and I walked to my fourth-hour class, I told them my dad was coming to town the next week. I couldn't contain my excitement any longer. I didn't want to introduce Pete to him as my boyfriend, even though I knew it would be hard to conceal. I wasn't looking forward to explaining my decision to Pete, and I was actually surprised he hadn't yet asked about being introduced to my mom as only a friend. How could I delicately bring it up to him?

I sailed through the rest of the day and felt relieved when I got to P.E. We were playing volleyball. For the first day, we were paired up with partners to practice hitting the ball. Thankfully, Bailey was my partner,so I didn't have to embarrass myself in front of someone I didn't know well. Bailey and I were equally matched in our ability, which meant we both sucked.

When class ended, Bailey informed me that she was coming with Eli and me after school. They had plans to study together after they dropped me off at my house. I couldn't help but feel a little jealous that I couldn't have the same easygoing relationship with Pete that Eli and

Bailey shared. I always needed a "babysitter." I tried my hardest not to let it show that I felt left out. I knew they needed alone time, but I wanted in on it. Instead, I was going home to an empty house to do homework and make dinner. Maybe I had been wrong to give Pete a chance. Would we ever be a normal couple?

My mood deflated further when I listened to the message waiting on the answering machine at home. It was my mom. She wasn't going to be home until late that night, she hopedbynine. I would be alone for dinner as well. I really needed a little companionship, and there was nobody to give it.

Doing my homework took longer than I expected. I was lonely,which made it harder to concentrate. I was still working on it after I ate dinner. I supposed it gave me something to take my mind off things, but I would havepreferred to be done with it altogether.

After two hours of working, I finally was able to focus, and I jumped when my cell phone rang. It was Eli. I sighed, remembering that he was probably still with Bailey. When I answered, I tried to sound cheerful.

"Hello."

"Hey Abby," he said. "What you up to?"

"Homework, you?"

"Talking to you."

"I thought you would still be with Bailey," I said with an edge to my voice. I heard myself say it and felt bad. I wasn't trying to sound sarcastic, but my comment definitely came off that way. Luckily he didn't seem to notice. *Why was I acting jealous?* Eli wasn't mine. I had never even considered him in that way.

"No, she had to go home for dinner like an hour ago. What are you doing tomorrow?" he asked.

"Nothing so far, why?"

"I was thinking we could go look for jobs like we talked about. What do you think?"

Job hunting would be a great distraction for me. Between my rocky relationship with Pete andmy anticipation of my dad's visit, I could use any distraction I could get.

"Okay, we can go right after school. Let's each make a list of the places we want to check out, and we can compare them tomorrow."

"Okay, talk to you tomorrow!"

I hung up the phone, smiling, feeling my mood lift a bit. I was excited about trying to find a job. It would be something fun to share with Eli, and I would also have something great to tell my dad when he came to visit the following week. *That is, if I find one.* With much relief,

I finished my homework and started on the list of places at which I would like to look for a job.

Suddenly, I heard a knock at the front door. I was surprised to have heard it from upstairs, and I wasn't expecting anyone. Mom wouldn't have knocked, so I was curious and scared. After all, I was home alone. That didn't bode well for unexpected visitors. I padded down the stairs and made my way to the front door as quietly as I could. When I peeked through the peephole, I saw Pete. What could I do?

"Hey," I said, peeking around the doorframe as I opened it a crack.

"Hey, sorry to come by without calling first, but I was driving by and wondered if you wanted to do something."

"Sure, come on in.We can hang out here." The words were out of my mouth before I knew what I was saying.

We made our way into the living room. *Eli will never have to know*, I thought. I was breaking the rules, but I didn't care. I needed the company.

"Do you want to watch a movie?" I asked.

"Sure."

I put one in, but I didn't think it mattered much what it was. We cuddled up on the couch together. I thought of my mom coming home to find us like that. For a moment, I worried a little that she might be upset, but my trepidationvanished once the movie started. Before long, Pete leaned over and kissed me. He was such a good kisser, soon our kisses intensified. I was so lost in the moment that I had no idea what time it was anymore. I ran my hands through his hair as he pulled me closer. His fingers stroked my long hair as it flowed down my back. After quite a while, he pulled away slowly, hesitantly, and announced he should be going. I glanced at the clock.It was almost ten p.m. An hour had passed since he arrived, and I was shocked it was so late already. I blushed, thinking of how I had lost track of time.

"What are you doing tomorrow after school?Want to do something?" he asked as we walked to the door with our arms around each other.

"I already have plans, sorry. I'm going with Eli to look for a job."

"Why are you always with Eli?" he asked, his voice gruff and irritated.

I couldn't tell if he was angry or sad. Either way, I didn't like where the conversation was going.

"What?" I asked, confused.

"Every time I want to do something with you, you're already

busy with Eli. Is there something going on between you two that I need to know about?" His voice elevated until he was shouting.

I was blindsided. I could only think of one other time that I had done something with Eli instead of Pete. *Where was he getting this?*

"Eli and I are just friends." I searched for something else to say because I knew that wasn't enough.

"Friends, huh? I don't think I believe that." He grabbed my shoulders.

"Oww! That hurts," I squealed.

I began to tremble. *What had I done?*

"You need to spend more time with me. I don't want you spending time with him anymore. Do you understand me?"

My ears drummed to the beat of my pulse.

"W-w-whatever you say," I faltered.

"Good," he said, shoving me back. I stumbled backward and almost fell on my butt as he strode out of the room and out of my house. He slammed the front door.

I stood there, shaking. We had just shared an intimate time kissing and holding each other. I couldn't believe he had blown up at me like that. And of all things, for it to happen over—Eli? I was flabbergasted. After he left, it took me a long time to move. I plopped down on the couch, defeated. My feelings ran rampant—confusion, fear, shame. How could I have been so stupid to think he would change? I should have been smart and hightailed it as far from Pete as I could the minute I smelled trouble on our fateful first date.

An urgent knock sounded on the door. My heart raced. *Was Pete back?* It had only been five minutes since he had left. At least that's what it felt like. He very well could have been waiting outside. Maybe he was coming back to apologize.

I peered through the peephole. It was Eli. Relief washed over me. I'd never been so happy to see anyone in my entire life.

I couldn't hold myself back. I flung open the door and threw myself into his arms, almost knocking him over. Tears flooded my eyelids. He stood there, holding me for a long time. His strong, safe arms felt like home. Suddenly I felt strange, clinging to him like my life depended on it. I pulled away, feeling guilty.

"I'm sorry. I don't know what came . . ." I stammered, looking at my feet. I couldn't look him in the eye.

"Stop—I know, it's fine. That's why I'm here."

"It's why you're here? But how . . ."

It was like he understood what I felt, but how could he?

"Can I come in?"

I stepped back without saying a word, allowing him ample room to walk in. He looped his arm around my waist and pulled me into the living room to sit down.

"I know you must be wondering why I'm here, but I can't tell you. Trust me. Please just let me be here for you."

I leaned into the curve of his arm to take in the comfort he offered. There was nothing I wanted to do more than borrow his strength. My head threatened to explode, so I drew in his calm.

My pulse slowed until I could no longer hear it in my ears. I didn't try to speak. Nor did Eli.

The next thing I knew, morning light was streaming through the window, and Eli was gone. Mom stood in the doorway.

"Hey sweetie," she said as she walked into the room.

"Hey Mom," I said.

"Sorry I got home so late. Did you enjoy having the house to yourself last night?"

If only she knew I hadn't been alone. She wouldn't have approved of last night, so I played dumb and ran with it.

"It was okay. Quiet, but I didn't mind."

"I have to get to work, but I left breakfast in the kitchen."

Like I don't already know that, I thought. I was in an awful mood. "Okay. See ya later."

She disappeared from the room. I shut off the TV and headed upstairs to get ready. Every muscle in my body ached from sleeping on the couch. I must have been in a graceless position.

I showered and jogged downstairs in record time. A knock sounded at the door when my foot left the last step—perfect timing as usual. We had a good amount of time before we needed to leave. I wondered vaguely if Eli had planned to be here early.

We shared breakfast in silence. It felt awkward to say anything. I couldn't figure out how he knew what had happened, but I wasn't sure I wanted to know. What I did know was that he had been there for me when I needed him most, and I was thankful.

"Are you okay?" Eli asked cautiously after we sat in silence for the first few minutes.

"I'm fine—confused about more things than I can name—but fine." I sounded more confident than I truly was.

I couldn't tell if he believed me or not, but I couldn't dwell on that. I had enough to think about already. He didn't push any further, and I had nothing else to offer.

After a few more minutes, we got in the car. The longer the silence lasted, the more uncomfortable it became.

"I hung out with Pete last night. Alone." It came out in such a rush, I wasn't even sure if he understood or heard me.

"I know."

He didn't seem angry or mad.He was just straightforward and without judgment. How could he know? *Unless . . . unless he was outside my house watching me?*

"What? Were you spying on me?" I was suddenly hurt, and it all made sense. "You don't trust me, do you?"

"Abby . . . it's not that at all!"

We were already parked at school, so I stormed out of the car. I couldn't believe I had trusted him. Here he was pushing me away from Pete, but he was just as bad! Normal people didn't spy on their friends. They just didn't.

"Abby! Wait!" Eli chased after me.

I was in the building before he even crossed the courtyard. I ran the rest of the way to class, not caring what anyone thought of me. Then I saw Pete and came to a dead stop. He had been smiling until I stopped running, and then his face fell. It was almost as if he thought I wouldn't remember or care about the previous night. I walked right past him into class as the bell rang. At least class bought me an hour before I had to deal with him. I wasn't ready yet. I wished I could press a pause button. *Now that would come in handy, in more ways than one.*

My thoughts raced. *Should I tell Pete off? Should I stay with him and ignore yet another outburst? Should I give him one more chance?* I couldn't decide.

Of course, the one class that went slowly on a normal day flew by on the day I needed it to go at a snail's pace. I took a deep breath and stood up as the bell rang. He stood and turned, grabbing my hand and guiding me out of class. He pulled me out into the hall where Eli was waiting. Had he been waiting outside the whole class period? As soon as Pete stopped, I tried to pull my hand out of his without success.

"Hey guys!"Eli said casually, as if nothing was amiss.

I looked up at Pete, who only glared at me.

"Pete, we need to take a break. I need some space. Give me my hand back." I pulled my hand from him a little more aggressively.

He threw my hand at me and glared at Eli before storming off, muttering to himself.

I looked at Eli and started walking away. I knew I couldn't outrun him again. I was tired, physically and mentally.

"Abby, I wasn't spying on you. I know you aren't going to believe me, but I wasn't. What do I have to do to make you see that?" he pleaded with me.

"What am I supposed to believe?You push me away from Pete and swoop in at the first hint of trouble? What would *you* believe?"

"The same thing you do." His head drooped.

"Well, now what?"

"I'd hoped you'd trust me. I've never given you a reason to doubt me. I'm your friend. I'll always be there for you."

"You gave me a reason not to trust you last night!" I said a little louder than I had planned. Some of the other students were staring at us.

"Please, don't make a scene. I don't want this getting around. Let's talk after school. We can go looking for jobs and talk then. Please, Abby."

I really needed to find a job, so I reluctantly agreed. "Fine."

"Thank you.Can we pretend nothing happened with everyone else? I don't want Bailey to worry or think the same thing you're thinking. The last thing I would want to do is hurt her by dragging her into something she doesn't understand."

"Fine," I said.

We walked the rest of the way in silence. I could tell he knew I needed some space to think. I was grateful that he respected it.

At lunch, Pete was nowhere to be found, and I was glad. I really didn't want to sit through lunch trying to play nice with him and Eli. Other people at our table asked where he was, but, of course, I couldn't tell them. In truth, I hadn't a clue and didn't want to know. The rest of the day passed slowly but remained uneventful.

I met Eli at our usual spot after school, and we went on our way. He drove out of the parking lot, but when we got on the road, he pulled into a neighborhood and turned the car off.

"I know you're confused and angry right now, but I hope that you can look past this and continue to be my friend. I don't want things to be weird between us. I really enjoy having you as a friend, more than I ever thought I would. I don't want to lose that. Please don't be mad at me."

I didn't look at him. I took a few minutes to think before answering, even though I already knew what my answer was going to be. I had been thinking about it all day.

"Okay, you were there for me when I needed you, and you're my best friend, so I can't stay mad at you. I really hope you aren't spying on me. If you were, don't do it again."

"Deal!"

I knew there was still something he wasn't telling me, but I couldn't figure out what. It hurt me to think he could keep something from me. I would never dream of keeping anything from him, but I had to assume he had his reasons.

He started the car. "So, where are we going?"

We reviewed each other's lists and realized we had three places in common. And one of those was at the top of both of our lists: Rosali's—the pizza place where we went on our first double date. We went there first. We spent most of our afternoon filling out applications and turning them in. All in all, we went to seven places, and the best part was that we both got an interview atRosali's on the spot. Turns out they were hiring for three new positions. We scheduled our separate interviews backtoback the next afternoon and decided we would go together.

I told my mom that night at dinner, and she was thrilled. She came upstairs to help me pick out an outfit, and we decided on a knee-length black skirt and a royal blue button-up shirt. Mom said it looked professional enough for a waitressing position.

The rest of the night and the next day at school passed in a flash. I couldn't wait for my interview. I had a ton of confidence that this would pan out to be my first job.

CHAPTER EIGHT

My nerves got the better of me on the ride to the interview. A thousand butterflies fluttered in my stomach. Eli admitted he was nervous, too. He didn't look it, though, and I wondered if he said it just to make me feel better.

My interview was before Eli's. The manager, a woman named Claire who had jet-black hair and brown eyes, was nice but seemed stern when it came to business, which I completely understood. It was important to be professional in order to be successful.

We were both done with our interviews within an hour, and we must have had what they were looking for— we were offered positions on the spot, starting as soon as we wanted. While Eli decided to start on the following Monday, I made sure I could wait until after my dad left. Eli was working as a busboy, while I had been hired as a server.

As we left, we talked excitedly about the prospect of working together. We celebrated with ice cream at a self-serve frozen yogurt place near my house. Eli paid for it, and it made me uncomfortable. I didn't have any money with me so I vowed to pay him when I got my first check.

My mom was ecstatic when I told her about my new job. "I knew you could do it," she proclaimed.

When Monday rolled around, I couldn't wait for a report from Eli. He said it went great, which made me more excited about working there. I couldn't wait to start earning tips. I'd never had a job before so I was nervous about the unknown, but I knew it would be so much easier working with a good friend. We could help each other through things we didn't understand, and time would feel like it was going by faster since we were together.

All the previous issues with Eli seemed to evaporate over the weekend, and things were back to normal between us. Pete, on the other hand, hadn't shown up for school.

By the time Tuesday rolled around, I couldn't wait to see my dad. Just a few hours at school and he would be at home waiting for me!

To my surprise and dismay, Pete returned to school, sitting in his seat in front of me when I walked into first hour. My shoulders slumped. Neither of us spoke to each other, and I couldn't wait for a new seating chart so I could sit as far away from him as possible.

I don't know when I decided it—maybe at that very moment, seeing him sitting therelooking smug—but I knew what I had to do. I had to break up with Pete for good. Time apart wasn't enough to make his problems disappear. Just being near him disgusted me.

I planned to do it right after class so I could leave as soon as I said it. That way he couldn't explode in front of other people, and I could put as much distance between us as possible when hundreds of students flooded the hallway. It would be easy to slip into the crowd.

Once again, class seemed like it was cut short that day. Outside, Pete acted as if nothing had happened, which upset me even more.

"About the other night—"

"Forget about it. I forgive you." He grabbed me and squeezed in an attempt at a hug, but I pushed awayfrom him. Then he put his arm around my waist and pulled me forward to walk with him.

Could he be any more arrogant? We were walking together to my next class. I didn't want anyone overhearing.

"No, umm . . .it's over. I'm done with this. I can't handle wondering if you're going to blow your lid at the drop of a hat. I won't be with someone who tells me who I can and cannot hang out with. That's my decision." I was glad Itold him exactly how I felt. I was proud of myself for formulating the words exactly how I wanted. Now I just had to wait for the outburst.

"You'll be sorry!" He grunted through his teeth before stomping off.

It wasn't what I expected, but I was glad that it was his only reaction. I knew that his threat wasn't something to worry about. He would get over it eventually. Hopefully sooner rather than later. He was more of a short fuse than a grudge-holder as far as I could tell. I saw Eli walking toward me with a concerned look on his face. He must have seen everything. At least I wouldn't have to tell him and relive what happened. I would already have to do that with Bailey.

He wrapped his arm around me as we walked, and it was comforting to know I had the support of a close friend.

After school, Eli rushed me home. I knew my dad would be waiting. I couldn't wait to introduce him to Eli. I wanted him to know the one person who had kept me sane at my new school. My rock.

I ran through the door, leaving Eli in the dust. Dad was in the living room, and he stood up when he saw me. He looked a little tired, and I noticed dark circles under his blue eyes. It also appeared that he had recently gotten his arrow-straight, light brown hair cut. He never kept his hair short, so a haircut meant his hair flowed down his head to the base of his neck. As soon as I saw him, I jumped into his arms and gave him the biggest hug I could, which he returned by picking me up in the air. Eli wandered into the room and cleared his throat. Dad put me down, laughing.

"Well, who's this, Abby?" he asked.

I leaned into the crook of my dad's arm and rested my head on his chest. "This is Eli. He's my best friend." I smiled at Eli. I had never confided to him that he was, in fact, my best friend before, and I could see a surprised look sweep across his face. He almost seemed proud to be introduced with that title, but he recovered quickly. "Eli, this is my dad, Sam."

"Nice to meet you, sir," Eli said.

"Good to meet you. Glad to hear someone is taking good care of my baby," he said with his hand outstretched.

"Dad!" I said as I shoved him playfully.

It was so comforting to have him there. I wanted him to see every aspect of my new life in Arizona and to take part in it all. Then when he went home, he could picture everything I talked about, and it might feel more like he was there instead of hundreds of miles away.

"Well, it was nice to meet you, sir, but I should be getting home. You two probably want to catch up. See you, Abby," Eli said, turning to leave.

"Bye, Eli. See you tomorrow!"

I heard the door shut behind him.

"So, Abbs, I was thinking we could go out to dinner tonight, just the two of us. What do you think?"

"Sure! What about Mom?"

"Well, I already discussed it with her, and she'll be working late tonight anyway."

Again? I thought. *What could possibly be keeping her working late so much?* It seemed like that was the story every night. I couldn't imagine it would make my dad too happy that I was home alone at night so often, so I didn't mention it.

"Well, that works out great then! Where should we go?"

"You're the one who lives here. You tell me."

"Right," I said, giggling. "I have an idea. How does pizza sound?"

"Great!"

"I have some homework I need to do before we go. I'll be back down in a little while. Will you be okay? You can come upstairs with me, but I won't be much company."

"I'll be fine, honey. Get your work done. I won't have you getting bad grades just because I came to visit. Besides, the TV and I need to catch up too," he said, plopping down on the couch with the remote in his hand.

His playful banter made me smile. "Okay," I said cheerfully.

I couldn't have been happier to settle back into the routine of having my dad around. I wished we could go back to that completely and not just once in a while during visits. However, I wasn't going to hold my breath and wait for that to happen.

I took my dad to Rosali's. I hadn't told him I had gotten a job there yet, so I was excited to show him where I would be working. Then he could have a mental picture of the place whenever he thought of me working. Plus, Eli was working that night. It turned out that Dad loved the pizza as much as I did. He was so proud that I had my first job. I was almost embarrassed by his flood of compliments.

When we finished eating, we caught a glimpse of Eli. He came to our table to clear our plates before he hurried back to the kitchen. They kept him busy!

At home, Dad and I talked until almost midnight. Again, Mom was home around nine, but she went straight to bed. I could see the awkwardness on both their faces. They didn't quite know how to talk to each other, and it showed.

For the first time since we moved, I fell asleep as soon as my head hit the pillow, and I slept more soundly than I had in a long time. I even had a good dream where I was on the beach with my mom and dad for the day. We built sand castles and played tag, and my parents were as happy as they always used to be. I could only think of one reason for the sudden turnaround: my dad. He was the sudden burst of sunshine in my world, and sadly his visit wouldn't last very long.

I got up early so I could eat breakfast with him before I went to school. It was oddly familiar walking downstairs and hearing my parents talk over the sounds of clanking silverware and glasses. It was comforting to know my whole family was under one roof, at least for the week.

"What are you planning on doing today, Dad?" I asked, chewing my pancakes. I ignored the dirty look coming from my mom.

"Well, I thought about going shopping. I need to buy some new clothes. I haven't found the time to go lately, and then I'll probably come back here and find a game on TV."

"Keep busy while I'm gone. I'd hate for you to be bored."

"A little boredom might be nice," he said with a smile.

I could hear a car honk outside. "I should get going. That's Eli."

I kissed both my parents before I ran out the door.

My day creptby more slowly than I could have imagined, and I knew it was because I couldn't wait to see my dad again. I was disappointed when I got home from school to find him not there. While I didn't want him to sit around all day without me, I really was looking forward to him being there when I got home. It was a double-edged sword. I decided I should go upstairs to do the little homework I had. I hoped he would be home by the time I finished. I threw in my ear buds and listened to music while I worked. In minutes, I was done. I ran downstairs to see if Dad had arrived, but to my disappointment, he was still gone. I wondered what could be keeping him. When the front door opened, I darted over to see who it was. I was shot down again when I heard my mom's voice flooding the entryway and echoing through the house.

"Hello!" she called.

"Hey Mom," I answered with a sigh as I rounded the corner.

"Well, isn't that just the greeting I was looking for," she teased. "What's got you so blue?"

"Dad isn't here. I thought you were him," I admitted.

"Oh, well I guess I'm just chopped liver!"

"Mo-o-m," I whined.

"I know, I know. I was just kidding. I'm sure he'll be back soon. Besides, I want to talk to you about something."

I followed her into the kitchen and sat on a bar stool while she leafed through the mail. I couldn't sit still as I waited for her to broach the subject.

"What do you need to talk to me about?" I asked, suspicious and impatient.

"Remember when I asked you how you felt about me going on a date?"

"Yes . . ."

"And remember how you said you would be fine with that as long as I was happy?"

"Yes . . ." I answered again, not liking where the conversation was headed.

"Well, I have a date tonight!" she said.

I could tell she wanted me to be excited with her, but I couldn't be. *Why this week of all times?*

"Tonight?"

"Yep!"

What in the world was my mom doing going on a date while my dad was here? Staying in our house! I couldn't comprehend what she was trying to accomplish, unless it wereto make my dadjealous. That had to be it.

"This doesn't have anything to do with Dad, does it?" I asked.

"No, what on earth would make you think something like that?"

"Well, you chose to do this while he's still here. Don't you think that's a little . . . awkward?"

"Only if he makes it that way."

"Is the guy picking you up here?" I hoped she would say no.

"Yes, I want you to meet him to tell me if you approve."

This was not what we had discussed. She was supposed to introduce me to him if it was getting more serious, not on the first date! I especially didn't want to meet him with my dad there. I was furious. She was going to rub it in his face.

"Well, what about this guy you're going on a date with? How do you think he's going to feel about Dad staying here?"

"He knows," she said nonchalantly, looking away.

I couldn't believe how selfish she was being. I felt empathy for my dad and what he was about to be put through. He was clueless. I hoped he wouldn't let it put a damper on his visit. If he acted like I thought he would, he'd brush it off and move on.

"Well, whatever makes you happy, but I don't agree with how you're going about it." I stormed out of the room.

I knew I was being disrespectful, but I couldn't help the way I felt or keep it inside. I began to hope Dad wouldn't come home until after this guy came to pick up Mom.

Of course, that wasn't in the cards either. Five minutes later, he walked through the front door. He came to find me, carrying shopping bags and a pizza.

"I hope it isn't too early for you, but I thought we could have pizza again for dinner," he said.

"No it's not too early—it's perfect," I said. As much as I didn't want him to be there when Mom's date showed up, I could use his support. It was going to be hard for me, seeing her leave with another man.

"That's good! I was worried you might not want pizza again. Is your mother going to join us?"

Great! I was going to have to tell him. The middleman. I got mad at Mom all over again. I wasn't supposed to be the one dealing with all of their issues! That was the whole point of the divorce.

"No, umm . . . she has a date." I couldn't even look him in the face.

"Oh," he said, more surprised than shocked.

"I'm sorry,Dad. I don't know what she's thinking going out tonight. He's picking her up here. It's the first time since, well, you know."

"Thanks for the warning, but it's okay, honey. Your mom is free to do as she pleases."

He was acting open-minded, but I knew better. Deep down, I knew he had to be hurting. Then it dawned on me. *—Was Dad dating too?* It was too much. I didn't want to know if Dad felt the need to date. Then again, maybe I did. I certainly wouldn't ask him. Mom dating was enough to handle for now.

We sat down in the living room to eat our pizza. It was only 5:30, but I liked having an early dinner. It left plenty of time to have dessert later, and I had my mind set on a nice hot cookie with vanilla ice cream. I would need the sugar jolt after all that anxiety.

Before long,Mom came downstairs looking stunning in a little black dress, not unlike the one I wore to the homecoming dance. It looked like it was painted on. I wasn't sure I had ever seen her in anything so revealing. Her hair was curly and pinned halfway up. She was playing dirty, and I hoped it wouldn't taint Dad's time at our house. I didn't want him to be reluctant to visit again.

"Well don't you look nice." Dad's tone was kind and polite.

"Well, thank you,"Mom said graciously yet snidely.

"You're welcome," he said without showing that he had noticed her coldness. Dad was always more civil in that sense.

Soon after Mom made her appearance, her date arrived, wearing black dress slacks and a sport coat with a royal blue tie. His shoes were shined and free from scuffs and his jet-black hair loosely slicked back. He drove a BMW. It made me wonder if he had a lot of money. He almost seemed rude toward my dad, which made me want to be hostile toward him. I refused to say more than "hello" to the mystery man and hoped I'd never have to see him again. They left quickly, and I was relieved.

We spent the rest of the evening playing board games and eating dessert, something we used to do often. My favorite game was Scrabble and Dad's was Battleship, so we played both. It was getting late by the time we finished. Each of us won our favorite games.

I was yawning and so was Dad, so we decided to hit the sack even though Mom wasn't home yet. I wondered when she was going to get home, but I didn't especially care after the way she had acted. I didn't know what had come over her, but she was acting very immaturely, and I was embarrassed by it. That was a first.

CHAPTER NINE

The front door startled me awake. I rubbed my sleepy eyes and squinted at the clock. It was three a.m. I tried to orient myself when it hit me like a ton of bricks—my mom was just getting home. I couldn't believe she had the nerve to come in at that hour! What kind of example was she setting?

I dwelled on it for a few minutes, and the next thing I knew, it was morning. Not surprisingly, Mom wasn't out of bed when I went downstairs. Dad had started making breakfast, and his specialty was just about ready: pancakes. I loved them. He made mine with blueberry eyes, a strawberry nose, and a bacon mouth.

We ate in silence for the first time since he arrived. I could feel the tension in the air, but it was nothing compared to when my mom walked in. The room seemed to ice over. A chill shot down my spine. Nobody greeted anyone—she didn't even say good morning to me. It was at that moment that I knew he had heard her come in late.

I couldn't get out of the room fast enough. I didn't know if she felt proud or ashamed, but I was ashamed of her. For the first time ever I felt like the mom. I expected more from her. I would never disrespect her the way that she was disrespecting me with her behavior.

School was uneventful, despite Pete's sour attitude. The past couple days he'd been extremely petty, which went right along with his temper. He didn't just request a new seat assignment from our teacher in math class—he also got some of the other students in our class to move away from me as well. I was alone in a little circle of desks. Pete had been right about one thing, I was sorry—sorry I ever went out with him, sorry I ever came up my stupid plan, and sorry I ever laid eyes on him.

My disgust with him stayed on my mind as I went home after

school, only to be greeted by the same tension I had encountered that morning. I didn't know what to say to either of my parents, so I did the cowardly thing and went upstairs to do homework. I could hear their muffled voices after I left the room. They sounded furious with each other. My mom's antics were affecting my time with my dad, and it wasn't fair. Shortly after I started my homework, my dad came upstairs.

"Hey kiddo, how are you doing?" he asked, like there wasn't a reason he had come up to see me. I knew better.

"I'm fine."

"Your mother and I are in a spat. I guess we were a little crazy to think we could live peacefully under the same roof, even for only a week." He frowned. "I guess it was inevitable that there would be some bumps here and there." He took a deep breath. "I don't agree with your mother coming home in the middle of the night like she did last night, and I'd be willing to bet you heard her." He looked at me pointedly, and I could only nod in response. "It isn't setting a good example for you. Your mother thinks it's only because I'm jealous."

"I don't think it's setting a good example either. She already knows I disagree with the way she was presenting herself. I told her so yesterday before she came home so late. That's precisely why I haven't been speaking to her."

"Oh."He sounded surprised. "You're so grown up." He sat back. "When did that happen?"

"Dad." I blushed.

"What? You are. That was the type of answer I would have expected to come out of an adult's mouth. You have matured so much in such a short time."

"Thanks," I replied.

"I just wanted you to know what we were arguing about so there was no confusion."

Dad always explained their fights to me instead of keeping me in the dark. In the past, he always said he probably shouldn't because it was above my head but that he would want to know in my shoes. Mom, on the other hand, would deny that they were fighting. She always had a problem admitting that they had problems in their marriage. I gathered that this was part of the reason we moved to Arizona after the divorce— Mom couldn't face her social circle after a failed marriage. I can't say I blamed her. It was embarrassing to say you had failed at something so important. I hoped to never have that kind of disappointment.

"Thanks,Dad."

He grabbed me by my shoulder and pulled me into his chest. "Boy have I missed you, kiddo."

"I've missed you too."

Despite the fight between my mom and dad, she pretended nothing was wrong and decided we should all go out to dinner and then play miniature golf. Neither Dad nor I really wanted to spend any time with her, but we went along to avoid throwing fuel on the fire.

We all ended up having a blast. By the end of the night, we were laughing and had forgotten our troubles. Even Mom and Dad were joking with each other. That surprised me the most.

By the time we got home, it was 11:30. After a long night and enough laughter to make my stomach ache, we each fell into our beds and were asleep in minutes. It had been a long time since I had that much fun, and I suspected it was the same for both my parents.

As Friday rolled around, I realized that the week with my dad was coming to a close. At the same time, we still had the weekend together. I had a few ideas of things we could do that I wanted to run by him. I thought sightseeing and exploring new places together would be great since it was something we both enjoyed. Mom was never the outdoorsy type and was usually a spoilsport when it came to the great outdoors. The whole reason I hadn't explored the area was because my mom wasn't into it. The only person who I knew would appreciate it like I did was my dad. There were a few lakes close by that I wanted to check out. I had also heard that Papago Park was pretty. The Grand Canyon was on my list too, but it seemed a little much for only a weekend trip. I couldn't wait to tell my dad, but when I got downstairs, he had already left. I couldn't figure out where he kept disappearing to. My ideas would have to wait.

When Eli picked me up for school, I wondered if he knew anything about the lakes or Papago Park. I wanted to pick his brain about other places to go as well.

"Hey, have you ever been to any of the lakes that are close to us?" I asked.

"Yeah, I've been to most of them—Saguaro, Canyon, and Roosevelt. Why?"

"Well, I was thinking about taking my dad to a lake this weekend for a day trip, but I since haven't been able to go to any of them, I don't know which would be the best one."

"Personally, I like Canyon Lake the best. Since Saguaro is the closest to town, it's the busiest. It's the smallest, too. Roosevelt is nice, but it's a little further than Canyon for about the same scenery."

"Thanks! You wouldn't want to join us, would you?"

"I would, but I'm working tomorrow."

"Oh, that sucks! You think you could get off? It sure would be nice to have someone there who knows the area," I said, surprised I hadn't thought of it sooner.

"I can try. I'll see what I can do."

When I returned home from school, my dad still wasn't around. It baffled me. Thankfully I didn't have any homework, especially since it was my only weekend with my dad. Before I could even get upstairs with my bag, the front door opened, and my dad walked in.

"Hey honey!" he said.

"Hey, where were you?"

"Just out. I needed some time away from your mother."

I understood. He used to disappear a lot right before they decided to get a divorce, so it all made sense now. It was his way of dealing with frustration and anger.

"Oh. So, I have some ideas to run by you for what we can do this weekend."

"Oh yeah?"

"Since I haven't had a chance to go exploring since I've been here, I thought we could do it together. We could go to the lake or Papago Park or both! What do you think?"

"That sounds like fun," he said.

"I invited Eli. I hope you don't mind. I figured he'd be able to show us around since he knows the area."

"Sounds good to me. You two sound like you're close," he said, his brows furrowed.

"He's my best friend," I answered, smiling.

"Are you sure it isn't more?"

"Of course it isn't. We're just friends."

"So is there anyone you're dating?" he asked, trying to sound casual. He was anything but casual.

"I was, but not anymore."

"That bad, huh?"

"Yeah, I don't really want to talk about it," I said, hoping he would leave it at that.

"Okay, okay—point taken," he said. "I think they both sound great! What lakes are around here?"

"Well, I asked Eli for his opinion, and he recommended Canyon Lake. He said it's the best for scenery and isn't very busy. How does that sound?"

I felt my pocket vibrate and heard the chimes of my ringtone. I yanked it out and ran upstairs to my room as I answered.

"Hello?"

"Hey Abby. Guess what?" It was Eli.

"Did you get off work for tomorrow?" I asked.

"Yep! For the whole weekend! Turns out they didn't really need me this weekend anyway."

"That's great! My dad liked the idea of going to the lake and Papago Park. So I was thinking the lake tomorrow and the park on Sunday."

"Sounds like a plan to me."

"What time do you think we should head up to the lake?" I asked.

"It'll take us around two hours to drive there, so maybe around eight. Does that sound about right to you?"

"Yeah, and we can have a picnic. I'll pack us turkey sandwiches, chips, and sodas. Oh, and some water."

"Mmmm, sounds yummy to me! Don't forget your suits—we can go swimming."

"And sun block!" I said, getting excited.

"I'll see you at 7:45 tomorrow morning?"

"Yep, see you then!" I hung up and hurtled down the stairs.

"That was Eli. He's coming." I beamed.

"That's great! We'll have our own tour guide!" he joked. "Let's go make some dinner." He put his arm around me as we strolled into the kitchen.

While we made dinner, I told him about our picnic plans. He seemed excited about the weekend, maybe even as much as I was.

The next morning, Eli arrived at my house right on time. Dad answered the door and called up to tell me Eli was there, but I was still getting ready. I had packed our picnic lunch the night before, which included six turkey sandwiches with cheese—two for each of us—chips, and cookies for dessert. All I needed to do was put the food on ice in the cooler that my dad had picked up from the convenience store up the street.

"We can take my car if you guys want. The convertible top would make the drive more scenic," Eli said.

"That's very nice of you to offer. That would be wonderful," my dad said.

I knew my dad would be elated when he saw Eli's car. Dad was really into classic cars. Really, I mean what guy wasn't?

We walked outside with our arms loaded with towels, the cooler, and sun block, ready to start the day.

"Wow, that is some ride you've got there, Eli."

We loaded the trunk and climbed in. I squeezed into the backseat, which was roomier than it looked.

My dad and Eli had something to bond over right away: the car. The entire first hour of the drive was filled withcar talk. I didn't have a clue about anything they were saying, so I stayed out of it, but even if I had wanted to join the conversation, I doubted I could have gotten a word in edgewise. At one point they were saying something about horses or horsepower or something.They might as well have been speaking another language. I didn't have a clue what horses had to do with cars.

I couldn't get enough of driving with the top down. I felt like a dog trying to see it all, watching out of both sides of the car. The wind whipped through my hair as we sped around curves and wound through the mountains.

We arrived at the lake just after ten and parked near the marina. The air was warm and comforting, and the bright sunshine sparkled off the water. We all wore our swimsuits under our clothes, and we walked down to the beach to enjoy the lake. We swam for an hour and a half until we grew hungry and then ate lunch on the dock, sitting on our towels and allowing the dry air to evaporate the water from our skin. Afterward, we walked down to the marina. Eli and I wandered around the store little did we knowDad was preparing a surprise. We came out to find him standing beside two jet skis.

"Are those for us?" I asked.

"Yep!For the day."He beamed.

"Oh my gosh,Dad! That's awesome!"

"You like?"

"Like? I love!"

"You don't mind sharing with Eli do you?" he asked.

"Of course not!"

I couldn't imagine trying to drive one myself. I had never driven anything in my life, and I figured it was probably better that I start with something that couldn't sink.

"Allright!Let's go!" my dad said.

We put on the life jackets, and before we knew it, we were speeding around the lake. We had the jet skis until five p.m., and we stayedout on the lake with them the whole time. It was the first time I had ever been on one, and Eli confessed it was his first time too. Eli seemed to really let loose and relax, more than I had ever seen him do. We traded off driving, but I preferred to be the passenger. My favorite part was jumping the waves. A few times we both flew off and landed in the water, but then we'd both come up for air, laughing.

Once we returned the jet skis, we finished off the extra sandwiches in the picnic basket before heading home. I think we were all grateful that I had prepared two sandwiches per person—it was a two-hour drive home, and there wasn't anything to eat on the way. The sunshine had left us famished.

I was sad to leave. It had been exhausting yet amazing, and I hadn't wanted the day to end. I fell asleep on the way home and didn't wake up until my dad lifted me out of the car. I couldn't imagine how he had wedged me out of the backseat.

"Thanks, Eli . . ." I struggled not to doze off.

The next thing I knew, it was morning. We were expecting Eli at 12:30 to go hike around Papago Park—although from what Eli told me it wasn't really a hike since stairs went all the way to the top. Either way, Eli had assured me it was a beautiful view.

I rolled myself out of bed, feeling like I had only slept a few hours. I felt greasy from the sun block I had worn the day before, so I hopped in the shower before heading down to breakfast. It was already eleven, but I was sure that my parents would have breakfast waiting for me.

It turned out that my dad was still sleeping as well so my mom didn't even make us breakfast. But when I appeared downstairs, she was ready and waiting to whip up whatever I wanted for lunch. I decided on some of my favorite comfort food—boxed macaroni and cheese. She made two boxes, knowing I'd eat a whole one on my own. I wasn't surprised to see Dad wander in just as the macaroni was dished up.

CHAPTER TEN

Eli had been right. The top of the mountain at Papago Park boasted a beautiful view. One side sloped down toward a vista of the expansive desert hills while the other overlooked Tempe Town Lake, which was yet another place I wanted to roam soon. We wandered around for a couple hours before deciding we were ready to leave.

When we left, I was famished. We decided to go out to dinner at a Mexican eatery near the park that we had seen on our way. I couldn't help but think that I was going to gain weight if this visit was any indication of how my dad and I were going to eat when he came. Then again, I couldn't complain—it was nice not to worry about wasting our time together cooking and doing dishes.

Mexican cuisine is one of my favorite foods, I mused. There are always a lot of choices on the menu. Plus, the atmosphere is usually so inviting. This restaurant, in particular, was festively decorated, and I loved our bright green table and the red lamp hanging overhead.

My favorite dish was a deep-fried bean and cheese burrito served with rice and beans. Since I was starving, the dish sounded extra delicious. Dad ordered a shredded beef enchilada, and Eli chose a steak-filled quesadilla. While we waited forour food, we munched on the chips, salsa, and beans they provided at no charge.

Before the meal came, I headed to the restroom. Once I had done my business and washed my hands, I opened the door and was confronted by none other than Pete. Fear washed over me but was swept away by relief when I reminded myself that my dad and Eli were in the next room.

"Well, well, well—look who we have here," Pete spat, getting in my face.

"Hi Pete, I was just headed back to my table," I said, trying to discourage him from continuing the conversation. I attempted to squeeze past him, but his stocky body blocked my exit.

"Oh, so Eli is your boyfriend now?" he asked.

"No. I told you he's just a friend. Not that it's any of your business," I said as I tried again to slip out of his reach and back into the dining room. Before I could manage it, he pinned me between his arms against the wall. If I looked straight ahead, I would be staring at his chest, and if I looked up, my face would be inches from his. I chose to turn my head to the side.

I wished there was some explanation for his actions. This was Pete. His temper was a bigger part of him than I could have ever guessed. He seemed blinded by fury. *He must have been following us.* What could I do to get away from him without causing a scene? The last thing I wanted was for my dad to get involved; I would then have to explain to him the rest of the story because he wouldn't believe it was the first time.

"Oh, you didn't think I'd let you get away that easily, did you?" he asked, his voice dripping with pure hatred.

"What do you want from me?" I asked. I was at a complete loss.

"I told you that you'd regret your decision."

Eli marched into view and took charge before I realized what was happening. In a matter of seconds, I was out of Pete's arms and behind Eli, who stood in front of me like a shield.

"Just what the hell do you think you're doing?" Eli demanded, trying to contain his anger.

"Just what I promised, that's all. Nothing that concerns you."

"If it concerns Abby, it most certainly concerns me."

"Is that so?"

"It is, and you know it."

"Whatever Eli. You won't always be around—trust me on that." And with that, Pete walked away, chuckling to himself.

Eli turned around. He looked my body up and down. "Are you okay? Did he hurt you?" He seemed almost frantic with worry.

"I'm fine, really. He didn't hurt me. He just scared me. I didn't know what to do. I'm so sorry, Eli. This is all my fault. I never should have gotten you into this."

"It's not your fault. You didn't know what you were getting into, and to tell you the truth, I didn't either. He's way worse than I could have ever guessed. We'll have to just be more careful from now on until he gets over it."

"Allright."

"Let's get back out there before your dad starts to worry."

"Yeah, I'll go out first, and you can come out once I'm back at the table."

"Good idea.See you out there,"he said, stepping into the men's bathroom for effect.

My dad never suspected a thing, and our meal went on as if nothing had happened. I ate my food, replaying the incident in my mind. It dawned on me that Eli had known something was amiss when he came to my rescue, yet my dad remained in the dark. *How had he known?* My head started to spin. It was happening all over again. How had he known both times I was in a confrontation with Pete? It seemed like too much of a coincidence. I needed to ask him about it later, and this time, he wouldn't get off so easily. I wanted something—anything—to explain what was going on.

We got home early enough that the three of us decided to play a card game. Mom was out again, probably with her new boy toy, and an hour and four games later we decided to call it a night. Eli went home with promises to be there early the next morning to take me to school.

I couldn't wait to soak in a long, hot shower. My muscles ached from all of the swimming and hiking over the past few days. I tried not to take too long since IknewDad would be waiting to take a shower as well, but it felt so good. I had so much dust and dirt on me that I felt like a new person when I emerged from the bathroom.

I melted into my bed feeling refreshed and clean and fell asleep without a hitch.

It was gratifying to wake up from a great night's sleep, but at the same time, I knew it would be my last day with my dad before he went home to California. I hadn't had a single nightmare since he'd been there, and I knew it wasn't a coincidence.

I hoped next time I would still be able to come up with ideas to keep us busy and exploring. It would be nice to go on another lake trip together and maybe even camp out. I would be willing to bet that the lake at night was beautiful, with abundant stars in the night sky. *Maybe once it gets a little cooler out.* I couldn't imagine sleeping in a tent in the autumn heat.

At breakfast,I noticed that the atmosphere had cleared between my parents. They were back to being civil with each other, if not exactly on friendly terms. They only engaged in necessary communication, but that was okay with me. It certainly beat the alternative. As far as I was concerned, Dad didn't need to talk to her at all after the way she had treated him.

After what had happened that weekend, I dreaded facing Pete at school. It was guaranteed to be depressing. My only comfort was that there wasn't a time I would be alone with him.

On the way to school, Eli tried to reassure me that I had nothing to worry about. It brought me back to how he seemed to just *know* when I was in trouble. I didn't want to ruin the day by bringing it up, but I hoped an opportune time would present itself. I would wait for it. I wasn't sure how Eli would react—he might be mad or frustrated. But I deserved to know, didn't I? After all, it did concern me.

I arrived just before the bell rang and saw Pete sitting in the classroom. I tried not to look at him, but I could feel his eyes searing me. Finally, I gave into the temptation and glanced at him. He wasn't even paying any attention to me, and for a moment, I wondered if it was all in my head. I felt silly. I was making him out to be this big monster, and at the moment, he didn't seem to be anything but a mouse. My mind drifted to fractions and percentages for the rest of the period.

When the bell rang, Pete left before I could even gather my things. Maybe he had given up on harassing me, but I suspected I wasn't that lucky. Only time would tell. If he *was* planning something, I almost wished he would get it over with. The waiting was killing me, but then again, maybe that was the point. He was trying to make me suffer. *How fitting for him.*

Eli awaited me in the hall. "How did it go?" he asked.

"Fine," I said hesitantly. I knew his "told you so" was coming.

"Even though I told you so, I'm glad I was right this time," he said as he wrapped his arm around my shoulders.

I liked feeling of his arm around me, but I briefly wondered how Bailey would feel about how close we had become. Then I pushed it out of my mind. I mean, that was how we had always been. Nothing had changed. We were just friends, so there was nothing to be ashamed of.

"Me too," I said.

A few months earlier, I would never have guessed I'd be in that position. It hadn't even been two months since the start of school. I had a boy for a best friend. I had gotten in way over my head in a relationship with someone I shouldn't have messed with in the first place—no matter how tempting and gorgeous he was. I was about to start my first job, and my dad had visited. I had never been so busy in my entire life.

It was time for me to move on with my life and hope that Pete did the same. I knew I would always wonder what had happened with Pete and the missing football player, but I knew I needed to let it be.

CHAPTER ELEVEN

By Christmas, Dad had visited two more times. Our visits were always full of adventure. Once, we wandered around the Phoenix Zoo, which was in the same parking lot as Papago Park. I don't know how I missed it the first time. We took extra time walking through the monkey village, looking at all the tiny monkeys around us. On another visit, we spent the day hiking at the beautiful South Mountain. We managed to time it perfectly so we reached the top at sunset. It was warmer at that point of the day, but thankfully in October, Arizona temperatures resemble Californiain the summer. We even rode the city light rail around, just to dinner and back—another new experience to check off the list.

The tension between Pete and me had dissolved and seemed forgotten. Eli had even backed off since Pete seemed to be leaving me alone. In fact, the entire debacle rarely crossed my mind anymore. Still—I chose to ward off the prospect of any boyfriends for a while, which was easier said than done. A few guys expressed interest in dating me.

Around Thanksgiving, Bailey and Eli broke up. Luckily, it was a mutual decision, and there were no hard feelings. I would have hated it if they were at odds with each other. We all continued to be close as if nothing had ever transpired. They had decided that their feelings for one another weren't romantic anymore, and they weren't sure if they ever were. All in all, they dated about three months.

Both Eli and I worked about twenty-five hours a week, and it was going well. Working together was a blast. We had been there for nearly four months and already received raises, making our wages $5.50 per hour plus tips. I saved almost everything I earned, even though I did go to the movies and shopping every now and then. Despite those occasional outings, I had been able to save $1,500 toward my car. It was a number I took a lot of pride in. My goal was to have at least $3,000 before I began looking for a car, but I wasn't sure I'd be able to wait that long. The lack of my own transportation was starting to frustrate me. I craved independence.

As best friends, Eli and I were closer than ever. I didn't feel, as I once did, that Eli was holding back all the time. On the other hand, I knew there were still things he chose not to tell me, like how he had known Pete had shown up. I still had no idea how he had known there was a problem in the restaurant, but since no other incidents had happened, I left it alone. Maybe one day he would tell me.

Mom ended things with her so-called boyfriend shortly after my dad's second visit. As it turned out, it had taken her that long to figure out that she wasn't ready. I think she had wanted to make Dad jealous butwasn't completely over him. Either way, the tension had long since dissipated, and we were back to our normal, close relationship. She ended up apologizing to me the day they broke up, and I vaguely wondered if she had apologized to Dad as well. I'd never ask, though. That was between them. She hadn't been on another date since. Though we both knew it was only a matter of time before it came up again, I hoped it would be for the right reasons and with the right guy. After all, I wanted my mom to be happy, and if it took dating and meeting another Mr. Right in the process, so be it.

Together, Mom and I went to pick out a Christmas tree. We decided to get a five-foot noble fir, which I thought were the prettiest Christmas trees by far. We would have loved to get a nine-footer if we could, but my mom and I wouldn't have been able to set it up by ourselves. Actually, I doubt it would have even fit in our house!

I went with Bailey, Eli, and a few other friends to look at Christmas lights at the Valley's famous Loop of Lights. We drank hot chocolate and apple cider as we walked down the extravagantly lit streets. A few actually had Santa Claus there to see the kids.

Dad wasn't able to make it out for Christmas Day; things were far too busy at the store to take off at such a critical time, and I understood. Instead, he came a few weeks early to celebrate with me. We splurged with a ski trip to Flagstaff, and Mom even let me miss two days of school. We went to the Sno Bowl, a popular ski and snowboarding mountain. I must admit I wasn't very good on skis, but I had fun nonetheless. I managed to not break anything—which was something short of a miracle—and Dad had fun laughing at me. We stayed at a hotel with an indoor Jacuzzi, and stepping into it each night after a full day on the slopes was like heaven.

On the last night of our getaway, we opened our Christmas gifts to each other. Dad gave me $100 toward my savings account for my car. I was excited to add it to my bank account, bringing me that much closer to independence. I bought him a new sweater and khaki pants to match. It was the "usual" gift I liked to buy him because it was the one thing I knew he could always use. He didn't get out to go shopping much, and he never used to like the clothes my mom picked out for him. Dad and I were similar, so he usually liked what I chose.

Since I was working hard and saving money, I was able to buy Christmas presents for Bailey, Eli, Mom, and Dad without a problem. I tried to put a lot of thought and consideration into what I would buy for each person, but it wasn't hard to decide on the perfect gifts for them. Gift giving was one of the best parts of Christmas, and I usually struggled to conceal my excitement.

For Mom, I found a beautiful white watch with rhinestones encircling the face. She had been looking for a new one for a while without any luck. The minute I saw it, I knew it was just what she was looking for. For Bailey, I bought some new bows, headbands, and clips for her hair. Since she was so uncomfortable doing her own hair, I thought they would be helpful. I'd even made a note to make plans with her to try them all out. But Eli's gift was the one gift I couldn't wait to give. It was positively the most personal of all of my gifts to anyone. I was able to find a picture frame with a figurine of his exact car, right down to the color. I knew it was the perfect gift because he kept a photo of him and his dad standing with his car in the top drawer of his nightstand. It didn't have a frame yet. He showed it to me once. It reminded me of the one I kept in my nightstand of my mom, dad, and me at the beach. I thought it was sweet that he kept it so close at hand, and I hoped he would really appreciate the thought I had put into finding his gift.

I gave my friends their gifts the weekend before Christmas. My thoughtful purchases were the best gifts I could have chosen—but my friends seemed to know me just as well. Bailey bought me an outfit complete with accessories that I was sure came from the store she worked at, and Eli gave me a locket. There wasn't a picture inside, but he said one day I would know how to fill it. It puzzled me, but I guess it made sense that one day a Mr. Right would come along, and that would be the picture I would put inside.

The next time I was at Eli's house, I smiled when I noticed the picture sitting on his nightstand in the frame. Even Eli's mom commented on what a thoughtful gift it had been.

On Christmas, Mom and I celebrated, just the two of us. We

made a delicious turkey dinner with all the trimmings, mashed potatoes, corn, rolls, stuffing, and green bean casserole. We had enough food to feed two large families, but we didn't mind. I made sure to call Dad to wish him Merry Christmas. I couldn't be sure, but it almost sounded like he was holding back tears. I hoped not.

Mom handed over my gift first, and I was surprised to find money from her as well! A hundred dollars, just like Dad. I secretly wondered if they'd talked about what to get me. I was so excited that I was getting closer and closer to freedom. I could almost picture myself behind the wheel. Mom loved the watch I gave her, and she put it on right away.

Usually, my mom and I didn't do anything special for New Year's Eve, but that year we invited a few of our friends over for appetizers and drinks—champagne for the adults and sparkling apple cider for the teenagers. Eli and Bailey came, along with Bailey's new boyfriend, Ryan. They had been dating for almost three weeks, and surprisingly, Eli and Ryan got along really well. I had been worried that once Bailey, or even Eli for that matter, started dating other people that there might be tension between them, but I was wrong. We were all enjoying our winter break from school, but Eli and I were working a lot. I hadn't seen much of Bailey either since she had a new boyfriend and was working at the mall.

At midnight, we gathered in the front yard and made as much noise as possible with poppers and noisemakers, shouting "Happy New Year!" and toasting the year to come. Then we talked and laughed about our New Year's resolutions until everyone decided to head home.

After everyone left, I helped Mom clean up. Around two a.m., I finally went to bed. I layawake for a while, thinking about the holidays. I was sad they were over so quickly; it was my favorite time of year.

Between feeling content with my life and constantly busy with work and school, my bad dreams had been kept at bay for some time. I feared that it wouldn't last long, though. It seemed like they would never stop for good.

Unfortunately, school was starting in just four days, and I was unprepared to go back. In the new semester, our schedules were different. Bailey and I only had one class together. Eli and I had three, which made us both happy. It was always nerve-wracking to start classes with a new schedule. It was like the first day of school all over again, wondering if there would be any friends to keep me company in my new classes or if I would be making new ones. Most people didn't mind making new friends, but for me it was hard. Although since I had been at my newschool, it seemed I had been fairly good at it. I didn't understand why.

I had nothing planned for the last four days of vacation besides work. I was really enjoying all the extra hours I was able to work without worrying about any interfering schoolwork. Plus, my paycheck was definitely going to show my extra effort. My savings account was growing, even after all the money I spent on Christmas.

I hopedI would be able to buy a car in the next month. My plan was to get Eli to help me look for one when the time came since he knew so much about them. Before, I would have asked my dad, but since he was all the way in California, I didn't think that would work out well. Maybe if I were lucky,Dad would be in town when I was ready, and they could both help me. Two heads were better than one, right? They had already bonded so well over cars. In fact, my dad looked forward to seeing Eli when he came to visit. He always asked about him when we talked on the phone.

The last four days of my break were just as I thought they would be: uneventful. Besides work, I didn't do anything except relax around the house. I felt at ease. It was just what I needed to prepare to go back and finish out the school year.

The night before school started, Mom and I had a girls' night. I was a little tired of pizza, which I figured was inevitable since I workedat a pizza place, so we ordered Chinese food and had a chick flick marathon. Welooked at every movie we could think of that had romance and comedy all rolled into one and picked out three favorites to watch.

By the middle of the second movie, we were ready for dessert. We each put chocolate chip cookie dough in our own personal dishes and baked them until the dough was done around the edges but remained super soft in the middle. While the cookies baked, we chatted about all sorts of things. We topped the cookies off with vanilla bean ice cream, which melted around the cookie, making it the best cookie dough ice cream ever. *Yum!*

Monday morning came all too soon. Grudgingly, I climbed out of bed, showered, and got ready for breakfast in less than thirty minutes.

Mom was downstairs eating breakfast, and she had mine waiting for me as usual. Eli continued to drive me to school every day, and I was deeply indebted to him for the favor. Today he happened to be a little early, so he came inside, and Mom offered him some breakfast. He had time for a piece of toast.

On the way to school, we talked about what the new semester would bring. I even disclosed that I was considering getting back in the dating pool—"considering" being the key word. Eli didn't seem too pleased with the idea, but he didn't openly say so.

His presence by my side comforted me as we walked into our first class of the day. I was relieved to see Bailey sitting down next to two open seats. *What luck that we would be able to sit next to each other!* But my excitement was dashed a moment later when Pete sauntered into the room with a sneer directed right at me. He took the last empty seat—directly behind me. *Ugh!* I glanced over at Eli, who looked at me sympathetically and shrugged. Things had been quiet for the past few months, so maybe Pete was over everything, and I had nothing to worry about. After all, the seat behind me *was* the only one left in the room.

Throughout the day, I grew more and more suspicious of Pete. It seemed like he was in every one of my classes. Eli was in my first two classes as well, so it didn't bother me as much. But when third hour rolled around, Pete was there again. I tried to ignore the sinking feeling that I wouldn't be rid of him ever, but I couldn't.

I was relieved when the bell rang, snapping me out of my thoughts. I grabbed my things and headed for the door to go to lunch with Eli and Bailey. We were still sitting at the table where Pete and his friends had welcomed us earlier in the year since we had stayed friends with a lot of those people. Pete had graciously moved to another table before the break.

Just as I rounded the door out of the classroom, someone grabbedmy elbow—hard. I whipped my head around to see who was manhandling me, and I wasn't shocked to see Pete. My heart started racing, and my mind went blank.

"What do you think you're doing?"I asked.

"Oh you know, keeping my word," he said with sickening nonchalance. He didn't even seem angry. I think seeing him so calm unnerved me more than hisanger ever had.

"Stop—let me go!" He was dragging me down the hallway, and he didn't even seem to care about all the people who were staring at us. I couldn't imagine what he hoped to gain from this charade. "Where are you taking me?"

I tried to shake him off without success. I had never wanted to be on that end of his strength.

"You'll see."

He dragged me into the men's bathroom. *The men's bathroom?Why in the world would he bring me here?*

"W-what do you want?" I stammered. I looked around the bathroom, hoping there would be someone there to help. It was empty. *Shoot!*

He whipped me around to face him, backing me against the wall. My heart raced. I panicked. We were alone. I looked up at him and sawrage in his eyes. Rage that hadn't beenthere moments before. I had to get away—I had to get out.

"Oh, don't think that knight in shining armor is going to save the day this time. He has no idea where you are right now. I told you that you'd be sorry. I waited. I knew you would think you had nothing to worry about. I always get what I want, you hear me?"

I nodded shakily. He sounded like a spoiled child throwing a tantrum.

"And I want my girlfriend back, without her little 'friend.' Got it?"

"N-no, I won't be your girlfriend. I'll never be with you again. You need help." I tried harder to pull out of his grasp. One hand broke free and slammed into the tiled wall behind me. The pain engulfed my entire hand and seemed to triple when Pete regained control over it.

"I need help? *I* need help? I'm not the one pinned to the bathroom wall!"

The door burst open, and Eli rushed in. Pete was taken by surprise and turned to look at him right as Eli's fist slammed into his nose. Pete stumbled back a couple steps, then regained his composure and charged straight at Eli. He body-slammed Eli into the wall, and I heard the thud from across the room. Eli's breath was knocked out of him. Pete stood up straight to look at him, and I saw a smile spread across his face. Eli didn't waste any time before he gave him a right hook, sending Pete crashing to the floor.

I stood there, too dumbfounded to move. "H-how?"

"Later," he huffed as he pushed me out into the hall.

We practically jogged the whole way to lunch. I was dazed. I ordered my food as though I was in a trance, and I hoped I would be able to carry the dauntingly heavy tray to the table. The tray was no heavier than it was any other day, but it felt like I was carrying a ton of bricks.

I spoke to no one, and Eli kept glancing at me with a worried expression, although he pretended like nothing was amiss. Bailey kept asking me what was wrong, but I just couldn't tell her, so I said nothing. I had never filled her in on the previous confrontations with Pete because I hadn't wanted her to worry. Plus, I had never really thought there was anything to actually worry about before. Now I wasn't sure about anything.

In the blink of an eye, I was leaving sixth hour. It was amazing how fast time passedina daze. It was as if I was a ghost floating in and out of my classes, and it didn't help that Pete was in all six of my classes. Although he didn't show up to the last three, I knew he was on the roster because attendance was called and the teachers marked him absent. I felt drained. Why would he be in every single one of my classes? That took planning, thought, and pure motivation. But for what? What could he possibly gain?

My mind was elsewhere as I stepped out into the crowd, so it took me by surprise when I was grabbed from behind and pushed out the closest door and straight into a car. Pete's car. He locked the doors before I could get out and sped out of the parking lot.

I hyperventilated. I couldn't even fathom what his plans were. *What was I going to do now? How was I supposed to get away?* Eli wasn't around to bail me out.

Pete had used my lack of attention to his advantage. I felt so stupid to have not been on alert. I should have known he might come back to retaliate.

He ran right through the next red light and changed lanes at an alarming rate. Now it was getting truly scary. He could get into a terrible accident at the speed he was going.

"Pete. Please. Calm down," I pleaded, hoping to slow him down.

"Calm down? Calm down? Your little lap dog comes along and kicks me to the ground, you go running away, and you expect me to just calm down? *Ha!*"

As I looked at him, I saw bruising around one of his eyes and what looked like a fat lip. It made me wonder what Eli's ribs were going to look like after the body-slam into the wall. I hadn't even thought about Eli's injuries; I was such an awful friend. All I could think of was myself. He came to my rescue and was probably in a lot of pain from it.

"Where are we going?" I asked, trying to distract him.

"Somewhere your little friend won't find us."

We were on the freeway. I looked around frantically, trying to think of something to do. Somehow I had to signal to someone I was in trouble or . . . or . . . what? I didn't know. Why hadn't I paid better attention when they spoke at school about getting away from predators?

I looked out the window and tried to spot someone I could signal, but then out of the corner of my eye, I saw Eli's car, speeding toward us like a bullet. I had never been happier to see him. He was gaining on us at an alarming rate. I was scared that something might happen to him, and my heart began to race all over again. Pete must have seen him too because he stepped on the gas and started swerving between cars. The speedometer lurchedupward—80, 85, 90—when would it end? I felt nauseated. *Great. I might pass out. What a girl thing to do.* I chastised myself for being so dramatic. I needed to stop flipping out, or I'd never get my head clear enough to devise a plan of escape.

"Please, Pete. Stop. I'll do whatever you want me to."

"It's too late for that now," he said, laughing to himself. "I tried to give you that chance earlier today!"

He exited off the freeway and headed straight for the desert. I glanced at the clock on his dashboard. It was 4:50. *Already?* How had we already been driving for an hour? I wasn't sure exactly where we were. I knew the basic two-mile area around my house and school, but beyond that, I didn't have a clue. For all I knew, we could be in another state.

"Where are we?" I asked, hoping he would reveal a glimmer of his plan.

No such luck.

"You'll see."

He pulled onto a dirt road. Eli was still far behind us, but he made the turn. Pete pulled over when he saw Eli whip around the corner and climbed out of the car in a flash. Whatever he was planning to do, he seemed to want as few spectators as possible. That did nothing to comfort me.

The sun was on the horizon, starting its slow descent into night. I watched, waiting to see what would happen. I was fearful for Eli and myself. Pete walked toward him, his fists clenching and unclenching, as Eli stepped out of his car. I could see their mouths moving, but I couldn't hear what they were saying.

What could I do? I looked to see if Pete had taken the keys; he had. I grabbed my things and took a deep breath to gather my courage before opening the door. I jumped out in one swift move, squaring my shoulders, and shouted at the two angry figures in front of me. "Stop!"

Pete whirled around to look at me, just long enough to distract him from Eli, who took the opportunity to knock him down.

"Run Abby!" Eli yelled.

I turned and ran. I didn't think—just ran. I tripped going up the embankment and scraped my arms on shrubs. My breathing was getting harder and more strained. Behind me, I heard scrambling, but I couldn't tell if it was someone in pursuit or if a fight had broken out. I didn't, couldn't, *wouldn't* turn around to find out. I didn't stop for a second. My side ached. I struggled to breathe. It was almost completely dark now. I couldn't help but think how quickly the daylight had faded into darkness.

Suddenly, I stopped dead in my tracks as a wave of déjà vu overtook me. My dream. This was my dream. Running . . .running terrified from something.Someone. It was my dream. The scenery, the desert, the clearing, all of it—it was exactly as it looked and felt in my nightmare. I was running from Pete. All those nights I woke up so scared, all that time. I pinched myself once, just to be sure that it wasn't a dream, but sure enough, I was wide awake. How could I have been so naive?

I had heard of people whose dreams came to life, but I never thought much of it. I can't say that I would have believed someone who made that kind of claim. Did this make me supernatural or something? I didn't have time to dwell on it.

How could I keep running? I had to help Eli. What had I been thinking, letting him handle Pete alone? I was the one who had gotten him into this whole mess in the first place. I should be the one getting us out of it. It was about time I faced the nightmare head on instead of always running away.

I turned around, ready to march back to the cars, only to find myself staring right up at Pete. His chest was inches from my face. Heat radiated from his body. I took a step back.

"Where did you think you were going?" he asked through gritted teeth.

"Getting away from you," I spat. "How could you do this to me?"

"Oh honey, I'm not doing anything you didn't ask for."

With that, he grabbed me by the arm and marched me out further into the desert. I pulled, trying to break free of his grasp. I couldn't seem to pry his strong hold off me. Where was Eli? He had come to help me, and I had failed him. Guilt hit me hard. If anything happened to him, I didn't know what I'd do. He was my best friend.

"Where's Eli?"

"You can't get him out of your mind, can you? Admit it! He isn't just your friend, is he? That's all I wanted you to do this whole time. Just admit it!"

He threw me down in an area with little shrubbery. A dust cloud billowed up as my weight slid across the ground, choking me. I felt my hands grind across the rocky terrain. My elbow stung from what felt like cuts all over it.

"You have two choices right now, Abby. I can't have you running around telling the whole school what happened today. You can come back with me in my car as my girlfriend and forget Eli exists. Or I can shut you and Eli up so I won't have to look at you anymore."

"B-but . . ."

"B-b-but," he mocked. "No buts Abby! Make your choice. I'm getting impatient with these games."

I thought about Eli. I didn't know where he was or why he wasn't there, but I knew I had to keep him safe—if that was still possible. It was time I took responsibility for my own mistakes.

I stood up, brushing myself off. I inspected my hands to assess the damage. There was only a little blood on them, so the cuts couldn't be too bad, but man, did they sting. The cuts you can barely see always hurt the worst.

I hoped I was a good actress. I had never tried acting before, but now was my chance. I reached up, put my arms around his neck, stood on my tiptoes, and kissed him.

"I would like to be your girlfriend again," I said, trying not to let my disgust show. It took everything I had not to gag.

He reached around and pulled me close, hungry for more. His hands roamed around my back, sliding lower to grope my rear end. I winced in pain when he grabbed me where I had hit the ground. I pulled back as slowly as I could so as to not make him think I was faking the whole thing.

I put my arm around his waist and turned him toward the car. "Let's go."

His feet shuffled forward in time with mine. He was either very gullible, or I was a good actress. I would be willing to bet that it wasn't the latter.

Eli stood next to Pete's car, waiting for him to return. It was as if he had known everything that had just taken place between Pete and me in the desert. I saw him glance at my arm tucked around Pete's waist. He winced.

"It's time to move along, Pete," he said firmly.

"I don't think so, Eli. Abby has chosen me over you, so you move along."

"Abby, I know you don't want to be with him. Please know that I won't let anything happen to you. Tell him the truth," Eli said.

I hesitated. How could he be so sure of himself? I had already gotten us in so much trouble. I couldn't let him always bail me out; I had to be strong and take care of myself. I looked from Eli to Pete, frozen.

Eli walked closer, and I looked into his eyes. In that instant, a sense of calmness and strength overwhelmed me, like I could do anything. I felt on top of the world. My hair fluttered in the breeze. It was just the nudge I needed to be sure of my move, and before I could think better of it, I pulled my hand from Pete's.

"Pete, we will never be together. I never want to see you again. You have put me through a roller coaster of emotions, and I'm not going to sit back and let it continue. Leave." I couldn't believe I was able to stand up to him. I felt energized.

Tension returned to every bulging muscle in Pete's body. Eli didn't move, but out of the corner of my eye, I saw him close his eyes and clench his hands into fists. His knuckles turned white, and Pete dropped to his knees as if he were in pain. Pete's eyes squeezed shut. He held his head between his hands and let out a groan.

"What's happening?" I asked, turning to Eli.

"It's time for you to be on your way, Pete. I don't want to see the likes of you in this city again. Find a new place to live, got it?"

Pete opened his eyes and stood. "This isn't over, Jacobs!" Pete grumbled as he got into his car and sped away.

I was surprised that Pete had used Eli's last name, but I didn't get a chance to wonder why.

Eli's arms wrapped around me. "Are you okay? I was so scared I wouldn't make it in time."

I pulled away and pushed him back. "What? You wouldn't make it in time? How did you even know where we were? I can't just trust you anymore.Too much has happened . . ." I trailed off, still unable to understand or grasp everything. It was too late for him to explain. I needed answers an hour ago. Days ago. Weeks ago. I stood, looking into his eyes, searching for something I couldn't find. He studied his shoes.

"Abby, I don't even know where to begin,"he said, suddenly shy.

"Well, start with how you always know . . . know where I am."

We strolled to the car. I leaned up against his car and crossed my arms protectively around myself. I couldn't get in yet. I didn't want to feel trapped while we were talking. It was bad enough that I was in the middle of nowhere. My only way home was with someone I wasn't sure I trusted.

"Well, I guess I can't hide it from you anymore." He paused and cocked his eyebrow.

I shot him a snide look, daring him to try.

"Okay.Well. I'm from a group called the Protectors. We are assigned a person to protect, and we protect them for as long as they may need, whether for a few days or even their whole lives. We're there for them to make sure they are safe from anyone who may try to harm them maliciously. We get intuitions as to what might happen sometimes.We even intervene to prevent an accident when it isn't someone's time yet."

"What? I don't understand. Are you saying that you're my Protector?" My head spun. *Why was I important enough to protect? Why did I even need protection?*

"Yes."

"That's crazy. Sure, Pete was aggressive and out of line, but why the heck would I need a Protector?"

"I can't tell you. All I know is that I've been assigned to you. For the foreseeable future, I am needed."

"The foreseeable future? What, like I'm still in danger?" I started to feel panicked.

"Not from Pete. And at this point, I don't see anything problematic for quite some time. That could change, but for now, no. There's no danger."

"So you're telling me you're 'assigned' to me, and you didn't just befriend me because you liked me?"

"Abby—it's not like that. You're my friend, and I wouldn't trade that for anything. I didn't choose this. You are my first assignment. I'm not completely sure how to go about it."

"I want to go home. Now," I said, climbing into his car. He was talking about it like I was his homework or something. I couldn't take it. I needed space to think. I needed to be as far away from this place as I could get.

Eventually, Eli made his way around the car and climbed in. "I'm sorry that I couldn't tell you sooner. I never meant to hurt you. That's—"

"Just take me home."

We drove in silence all the way back to my house. I was so angry at Eli, at Pete, and at myself. I had trusted Eli, and now I had nobody to turn to. He was my best friend, my rock, but now I only had Bailey, and I couldn't even begin to talk to her about the situation. Ultimately, I hadn't even trusted her enough to tell her about the issues I had been having with Pete in the first place. It would only hurt her that I hadn't opened up to her sooner. I felt so stupid.

Eli started to get out of his car to walk me to my door, but I stopped him. "Don't. I don't need to be walked to the door. I can take care of myself. Just leave." I trudged to the front door.

"Abby, please don't be angry. I want to be there for you. Please call me. I will give you the space you need, but please don't cast me aside because of this. I'm sorry."

I shut the door and couldn't be sure if he said any more than that.

What was I supposed to make of all the information that he had dumped in my lap? My thoughts raced. What had he done to make Pete stop dead in his tracks, in what looked like physical pain? I had never really given much thought to supernatural beings like angels and witches, but now I wished I had. Maybe I could have prepared myself better. That's what it was, wasn't it? Something supernatural? I couldn't really be sure. I wondered what else there was to the story that I didn't know yet. Did I even want to know? Between his news and the realization that my dream had come true, I wondered if every supernatural myth I had ever heard was rooted in reality.

I went upstairs to clean up my cuts. Upon closer inspection, only two cuts on my hands and one on my elbow needed medicine and bandages. They were minor and would heal in no time. The last thing I needed was for my mom to find out about what had happened. I didn't know what to make of it yet, and I wanted to have the chance to figure it out before she knew any of it. Luckily, I doubted she would even be concerned if she saw them. I was klutzy all the time anyway. She wouldn't think twice if I told her that I fell and scraped them at school.

Regardless, I was feeling surprisingly calm. It was the strangest thing; I had zero anxiety about it. My anger at Eli was still there, but all my fear had left my body. It was as if it had evaporated into thin air. I ran myself a hot, steamy bath to clear my thoughts enough to sleep.

I knew one thing for certain: My life had changed forever that night. It would never be boring or ordinary again.

CHAPTER TWELVE

Days passed before I spoke to anyone besides my mom. I didn't want to let on that there was a problem at school or with Eli, so I pretended that everything was as it should be. It was a good thing my mom wasn't home in the mornings—I was now walking to school every day, despite the fact that Eli followed behind me in his car, hoping I might hop in. I guess it was his way of showing that he wasn't going to give up. I felt isolated, even though I had other friends. I couldn't talk to any of them about the situation—they would think I was crazy. *I* thought I was crazy. My life had turned into a real-life movie set, and I wasn't thrilled about being the main character.

The only person I felt like talking to was Bailey, and I couldn't even do that. Needless to say, she was worried about me. She even knew my problem involved Eli, but it didn't take a genius to figure out that I wasn't speaking to my best friend. Thankfully, she left it alone. Maybe she thought it had to do with something romantic between Eli and me. Given their history, I could imagine that would have been awkward for her to discuss.

After I hadn't spoken to Eli for a week, he started getting desperate. He tried harder than ever, calling and texting me multiple times a day, passing notes in class—but all his efforts wentunrewarded. I had to admit it was getting hard not talking to him. I really needed my best friend back. It didn't help that I still had a lot of unanswered questions that swirled through my mind, overwhelming me. My wall was weakening, and I didn't just want answers; I needed them. But was I ready for those answers? Would he give them to me? I didn't think he was in a position to be particular about what questions he answered if he wanted to be friends. As far as I was concerned, I had the upper hand.

On another level, I couldn't believe he had kept something so big from me. It made me wonder about our entire friendship. Could I believe anything he had ever said? How had I not known something was going on? I should have realized. Even though he had lied to me, and I was miserably upset about it, part of me knew that if he had felt like he *could* have told me, he would have. At least that's what I chose to believe. I decided I would talk to him that day after work.

It was Friday, and I had already finished school for the day. I walked home with the same thoughts clamoring in my head, and it made me anxious for the end of my work shift. I had just enough time to walk home, change, and grab a snack before I needed to walk to work.

When I stepped outside into the warm, sunny day, Eli was waiting in his car again, just as he had done the rest of the week. Suddenly, I made a last-minute decision and didn't give him the cold shoulder. I marched right over to his car, opened the door, and climbed in. I wouldn't let him know, but I was thankful for the ride to work. I was sick of walking.

"Hi, Abby!"He started the engine and pulled away from the curb.

"I have questions."

"I imagine you do," he said, but the smile never left his lips.

"Can we talk after work?" I asked.

"Of course," he said. "I was hoping you'd want to talk today. Well, that's what I've hoped every day this week, but I had a good feeling about today."

I could tell he was ecstatic, and for some reason, it made me happier than I had been all week. I hadn't formulated all of my questions for him yet. There had been so many sweeping through my head that I wished I had written them down as they came to me. I was nervous that I wouldn't like the answers I received. I think that was why it had taken me so long to reach out to him.

We neared the restaurant's parking lot. "Eli, I know you would have told me if you could have, or at least I hope I can believe that."

Maybe I had been too rash in ignoring him all week. I already felt bunches better after speaking to him. Sometimes feelings got in the middle of things, making you lose sight of what really mattered.

He looked at me with a smile that could light a dark room. "Thanks. You have no idea how relieved I am to hear that."

Work was . . .well, work. We were steadily busy throughout the night, so my mind was kept occupied with pizza, salads, and drink orders instead of the buzz of questions I had been stressing over for the past week. The steady stream of customers helped the five-hour shift go by quickly, and when nine p.m. rolled around, we were both more than ready to leave.

Eli and I walked out of work together, each clutching our own personal pizza and soda. Mine was pepperoni as usual, but Eli liked to change it up so his was bacon and mushroom.

"Do you want to go to the park to eat?" Eli asked.

"Sure."

The park was deserted but well lit for those who ventured there at night, like us. We sat at the closest ramada to the parking lot, next to the playground. On the other side lay a pond surrounded by lush green grass, and all around usstood large pine trees. In the distance, I saw a basketball court awash in light.

After we were settled, Eli spoke. "I know that this is all new to you, and you probably don't really understand much, but I want you to know I'll answer any questions I can. There are some things I can't say. I wish that weren't the case; I wish I could tell you everything from start to finish. But I've been sworn into service, and there are things they don't allow us to divulge. Actually, it is frowned upon to speak of any of it unless absolutely necessary, which in this case it was."

"Okay . . ." I said. "Why me?"

"I don't know," he said. "We don't know right away what the danger is. It's a surprise to us most of the time. Sometimes there are ways we know in advance. You came to me in a dream, just like my dad said you would. I saw you, but I couldn't see anything else."

"Your dad? What does your dad know about all this?"

"Everything.He is a Protector too."

"Is? I thought he died."

"No." His eyes pleaded with me for patience. "I'm sorry I lied to you about him. I had to. He had to move to where his new assignment was. I don't even know where he is and or when I'll see him again, if ever."

The first series of corrections to his lies was tumbling out, and I already felt confused. I was happy to hear his dad wasn't dead, but why did he tell me that in the first place?

"What about the dream?"

"It was just a dream. I was walking along, and there you were. You looked up at me at the same moment I saw you.You smiled. Then I woke up."

That brought my thoughts back to my nightmare and Pete. I hadn't had a nightmare since that night. It was like it had been a warning. I didn't want to think about it, as it brought up so many questions about myself. Was I different too? I couldn't be.

"How do you become a *Protector*?" I pushed thoughts of my

nightmare away.

"I guess you're just born into it. Sometimes one or both of your parents are Protectors as well. Sometimes they aren't and it just happens upon you. In my case, my dad is a Protector, so therefore so am I."

"Oh. Is your mom?" I asked.

He shook his head sadly.

"Okay," I said. I had so many questions. I wasn't sure if I should ask them all at once. I didn't want to overwhelm him or myself, but my mind already felt like it was on overdrive. All of it was so foreign to me. I felt bad for Eli. He was the one who had to live like that, permanently obligated to protect people.

"How long have you known I was your *assignment*?" I asked, sounding disgusted by the word. In truth, I was disgusted with the whole situation. Eli thinking I was some kind of damsel in distress irritated me to no end.

"For about six months," he said. "Six months before you moved here, that is."

Six months. I didn't even know we were moving here six months before we moved. *How?* My chest tightened. I felt dizzy.

"I think I'm going to be sick," I said, trying to breathe through it while I put my head down.

Eli closed his eyes. I felt a breeze on my face, and my nausea faded as quickly as it had come on. The tightness in my chest released, and I felt calm, relaxed, and levelheaded.

I looked up at Eli. "Did you do that?" I asked, wide-eyed.

"Yes."

What?

After giving me a moment, he gently explained. "I can calm you. We are connected."

"Connected?" I asked in bemusement.

"Yeah—that's the easiest way to describe it. I can feel what you're feeling; if you're scared, I can sense it. If you're happy, I know that too. If you're angry, it comes through to me red hot. When needed, I can help you, make you feel at peace. I can change how you feel. I can help you feel better."

"That's how you knew," I whispered. Realization clicked into place, like the last piece of the puzzle.

"Yes,"hesaid. "I'd never spy on you," he added, looking deeply into my eyes.

I believed him. Did that make me crazy?

"But how did you know where we were?" I asked.

"Well, that's where it gets a little more complicated. Our connection runs pretty deep—so deep, in fact, that if your feelings are strong enough, sometimes I get a flash of what you're seeing. It's as if I'm seeing through your eyes. Does that make sense?" he asked.

"So if I'm really upset, you can see glimpses of what is making me feel that way?"

"Yeah, I guess so. When Pete took you, the first glimpse I saw was the inside of a car. I didn't recognize that it was Pete's car at first. I only saw the vague outline of a dashboard. In the second glimpse, I saw an overpass sign. I knew right then where you were, and based on how I felt, I knew I was right. By then I'd come to realize you must be with Pete. He was the only one who had presented a problem, so it was only logical."

I didn't say anything for a while. It seemed too far-fetched, especially to me. Boring girl, mundane life—but then all of a sudden it wasn't boring in any sense of the word. I would have killed for a little boring right then.

Eli let me think before he spoke again. "It takes some getting used to, I know. I'm sorry. The last thing I want to do is make life complicated for you."

"I think we passed complicated a long time ago!" I chuckled.

"Yeah, I guess we did."

So we were connected, and he could feel and change my feelings. It was surreal to know you weren't the same as everyone else. *But wait. What did he do to Pete?* He had seemed to cause Pete physical pain without moving a muscle. I thought I had imagined that part, but if he had the ability to calm me, there must be more to it than that.

"In the desert, what did you do to Pete?"

"Oh that," he said.

"Yeah, what was that?"

"Well, it's a gift from the elders. I'm able to incapacitate others who are trying to harm you or me, but only if they are also otherworldly. It is truly the most useful tool I could have asked for. It gives us a chance to get away without hurting them permanently," he said like he was talking about the weather.

"So these gifts. Do all the Protectors have the same ones?" I asked.

"Nope, every Protector is different, though we all have defenses against otherworldly beings. It makes us harder to fight, especially if you don't know our inner strengths. Our attacks can still include the element of surprise. You'd be amazed at what some of the others can do!"

"Oh." I looked at my hands. Just when I felt like I understood even a portion of what Eli was telling me, I was hit with a jillion more things that my mind struggled to wrap itself around. "What do you mean by otherworldly? Is that what you are? Like from somewhere else?"

He laughed. "No, that's just my word for them. They are just like me, though I know there are other beings out there that are unlike me and unlike you. But the ones I'm referring to are other Protectors who have gone rogue. They choose to no longer accept assignments and intentionally do harm by not protecting their current assignments. There are a lot more than you would think. We can choose to stop protecting the right way if we go to the elders and ask, and they may release us from command—but we lose all of our power and gifts. I guess some people just don't want to lose the power." He spoke so quickly and nonchalantly that I think he forgot I was unaccustomed to his world. When he realized it, he shot me an embarrassed look.

"I'm not sure how much more I can process tonight," I said, rubbing my temples.

"Let me take you home. We can talk more tomorrow after you've had a chance to sleep on it. I want you to know your willingness to talk to me, to give me another chance, means everything to me. I know it doesn't mean things will be the same as before, but I hope we can get past this and be close again." He smiled at me shyly.

Minutes later, I was home. Mom was already in bed, so I went straight to my room. With each question answered, it seemed like there were five new puzzles to solve. I felt like I was never going to get anywhere amid the confusion.

I turned on the radio quietly and sat down at my laptop to check my email. I thought maybe I could take my mind off everything by reading an email from Kelly, but when I opened my email, there were no new messages. I hadn't heard from her in over two weeks. I had dreadedthe moment I would have to admit we were drifting apart.It was inevitable. Now it was apparent that it was beginning to happen. I vowed to try harder to keep in touch with her, starting with an email right then.

I let the music carry me, hoping it would lift my mood.

Kelly,
Hey you! How are you? I'm doing . . . well, I guess, as good as can be expected. Things are kind of crazy right now. I haven't heard from you in a couple weeks. Do I need to come back there and kick your butt? Ha-ha! Seriously, you better write me back ASAP! I want updates, missy. Any new guys hanging around? I'm definitely still warding off any ideas of getting involved with anyone. I'm way too busy to add that to the mix! Mom has been almost a ghost lately. Between work and her social life, I think she is just as busy as me! How is school? Surprisingly, I seem to be holding my own when it comes to my grades. Even in history! I am passing with a B! Won't my mom and dad be pleased!?! Ha-ha. Eli is still the one person I feel like I can

talk to. I thought it would be easier for me to talk to Bailey, but for some reason, she just isn't there like I think Eli can be for me. It's been really nice having someone who gets me like you do! I miss you. I should get to bed.It's almost midnight!

Love ,

Abby

I re-read the whole email before I hit send. I was pleased that I sounded upbeat and happy. It had distracted me as I had hoped but not for nearly as long as I would have liked. The music might have contributed.

I jumped as my computer chimed. It was a message from Eli. He was online too.

Eli: How are you?

I typed a message back. It felt good to be able to talk to himwhen he couldn't see my face with every answer. It gave me time to think, to collect myself.

Abby: I'm doing okay.
Eli: I'm glad. I saw you were online, and I thought I'd see how you were doing. I hate the idea of leaving you to think everything through. It's a lot to think about.
Abby: Thanks. Can't you feel how I am?
Eli: Yeah, I can, but I don't get to talk to what I feel, and I don't know what you're thinking that way. I feel a lot of anxiety coming from you.
Abby: I guess so.
Abby: This is so weird. You knowing how I feel. I guess you've known how I felt ever since you met me, huh?
Eli: Well . . .

It took a moment for him to type up his next response.

Eli: Actually, it's been since you were in my dream, the one thattold me about you. I didn't know what the sensations were at first, but I realized it as soon as I met you.

My body went limp. For six months before he even knew me,he had been feeling my emotions. Everything I felt those last few months with the divorce, the move, and leaving my friends.That was a lot of negativity. He must have felt horrible the whole time. Poor Eli.

Abby: All that time . . . I'm sorry.
Eli: It's not your fault. To tell you the truth, I'm glad that things are the way they are.☺ I couldn't have asked for a better person to be connected

to.

The smiley face was exactly how I imagined he looked at that moment. Only I couldn't figure out why he would want to feel anything I felt. I definitely had my moments of moodiness. I was embarrassed to feel anything now. Realization hit me like a ton of bricks. That was whyI had felt so calm all week instead of stressed and worried. It was Eli. He had been helping me through the whole week, and I hadn't even known. I got teary-eyed. His life revolved around me. It had to stop.

> **Abby: Your life is centered around me. I can't let you give up your life because of me. It isn't fair.**
> **Eli: This is far bigger than you and me, and frankly I don't have a choice. You're stuck with me, like it or not.**
> **Eli: Stop trying to find a way out of this. I was raised knowing this day would come. I don't know anything else. Trust me, I'm not missing anything.**
> **Abby: Fine. We're stuck like glue. Now what?**
> **Eli: Ha-ha, well now we go back to normal and move on.**
> **Abby: Just like that?**
> **Eli: Yep.**
> **Abby: I would love that.**
> **Eli: Have plans tomorrow?**
> **Abby: I have to work at 4, but other than that nothing.**
> **Eli: Go to bed. I'll see you in the morning. ☺**
> *Eli has signed off.*

I sat there for a few more minutes before closing my computer to get ready for bed. He was such a great friend. Now I felt like I could trust him with anything. He was so understanding of everything I brought to him. He accepted me for who I was, no questions asked. He made me feel at ease in ways I never thought possible. Well, of course he did—he could change my feelings. We were going to have to talk about that one. I didn't want him to change them unless I wanted him to. But did I ever want that? Yes, I was sure at some point I would. I didn't know how I was supposed to know if he wereeasing them. I needed to ask him that. For now, I decided to be content with where we were. It was better than where we were a few days ago.

That night, I had an amazing dream. My dad was in town, and we were going to the Grand Canyon. Driving up was beautiful, and mountains full of pine trees surrounded us. We saw deer and elk standing tall, grazing in the meadows. Their antlers seemed to reach the trees. The sky was a vibrant blue without a cloud to be seen. I woke up when my dad and I were standing beside the Grand Canyon, admiring its beauty. The Grand Canyon was something my dad and I were planning on seeing together that summer. After my dream, I longed for it to come quicker.

I rolled over to glance at the clock, which said it was only eight a.m. Normally, I would have preferred to sleep in, but I felt unusually refreshed. I wasn't used to that. Plus, I was excited to eat breakfast with my mom. She'd been gone so much lately, and I had been working so often that I really wanted to catch up, especially now that things were better between Eli and me. I felt better than I had in weeks, and I was ready to enjoy the weekend.

Mom was just getting up and hadn't started breakfast yet. I helped by starting the bacon, which sizzled as it hit the pan. Mom finished making coffee and mixed up blueberry pancakes—my favorite. We maneuvered through the kitchen, finishing the breakfast of eggs, bacon, blueberry pancakes, coffee, and orange juice.

Just as we were about to sit down to eat, the doorbell rang.

"I'll get it," I said, heading out of the room.

I briefly wondered if it was Eli standing on the other side of the door, but if I was honest with myself, I already knew it was.

"Hey, Abby!"Eli greeted me as I opened the door.

"Hey, we're just sitting down to breakfast. Want some?" I asked.

"Sure, thanks," he said, walking into the dining room.

"Mom, it's Eli. You don't mind if he joins us for breakfast, do you?"

"Not at all. How are you Eli?" she asked him.

Before I even left the room to get Eli a plate, he and my mom were engrossed in a conversation about plans for the day. When I returned, Eli had already worked out with my mom that he and I were going to the lake for a few hours.

I was grateful; it felt like everything was back to normal again. I hated when things were strained and awkward. Eli had made himself at home to ensure there would be no lingering tension. He always knew just the right things to do to make me feel better, and I knew he wasn't altering my moods this time. He was just being himself.

"You guys can pack a picnic," my mom suggested, snapping me out of my thoughts. "There's enough food in the kitchen for a banquet."

"Okay, thanks,Mom.Guess we should go get started."

We were already finished eating, but I had no idea where the time or my breakfast had gone. I must have been too engrossed in my thoughts. I wondered what conversation I had missed in my daydreaming, but I pushed it aside, figuring it wasn't anything to worry about.

We packed ham sandwiches, pretzels, and red licorice with cans of soda and water bottles. After such a long, lonely week, it was nice to have something to look forward to. I didn't know that many people went to the lake in January, but Eli assured me that even though we wouldn't swim, we would still have fun.

He decided to take me to Saguaro Lake instead of any of the others because it was so close. It only took about forty-five minutes to get there, and the scenery on the drive consisted of rocky desert full of cacti and shrubs instead of the pretty pine forest I had seen in my dream the night before. We didn't see any wildlife other than a few birds here and there, but I wasn't sure what species were in the area anyway. Maybe I was simply looking in the wrong places.

"There isn't much color in the desert," I said.

"You should see it in the spring. Everything blooms, and there are flowers in so many colors. It's gorgeous."

I had heard once that when the desert bloomed it was supposed to be very pretty, but I had never experienced it myself. Our conversation revolved around the scenery and school the whole drive out. Surprisingly, it never veered toward the one topic I still wanted more of. I knew it was only a matter of time before questions began pouring out of me.

The lake wasn't as deserted as I would have guessed, but as I stepped out from the car, the cold air assaulted my face. I was glad Eli made me bring an extra jacket. I shivered while I waited for him to open the trunk where my jacket was stowed.

"So what's the plan?" I asked.

"How do you feel about hiking?" he asked with a sly smile.

I hadn't been hiking in quite some time, but I was always up for an adventure. "Sounds good to me."

We hiked around the lake to one trail that wound up into the desert. It led us to an overlook where we could see a good portion of the lake. It was breathtaking, and we decided to eat our picnic lunch there. Eli had been kind enough to carry the backpack on our hike, so we spread out our blanket and sat down.

"So, can I ask you some more questions?" I asked him after we were situated with our lunches.

"You can ask me whatever you want," he said after chewing his first bite.

"What's going to happen when I'm not your 'assignment' anymore? Like, if you get a new one?" I was too embarrassed to look him in the eye. The truth was, I didn't want to lose him. If he wasn't able to see his dad, what did that mean for our friendship? That was the biggest thing that plagued my mind.

"I don't know. It's something every Protector worries about." He lifted my chin to look into his eyes. "But I can tell you nothing is going to change for a while, so please don't think about it."

It wasn't the answer I had hoped for, and I changed the subject for fear that I might cry. "It's so peaceful out here. I love it."

"I come out here to think sometimes. It helps clear your head, getting away from it all," he said.

"I used to have a place like that in California, but I haven't had a chance to find one here yet."

He grinned. "Well, we'll just have to do something about that, won't we?"

"How am I supposed to know if you're adjusting my moods?" I interjected.

"Well, if you really pay attention, you can tell, but I've only altered your moods a few times. Those have been when you were with me. Does it bother you?" he asked, sincere concern in his voice.

"A little, I think. It makes me feel weird not knowing if what I'm feeling has been generated by you or if it's what I'm truly feeling." I didn't know if I was coming across in the way I hoped.

"I think I know what you mean. How about this—if I think you need a boost, I'll ask?"

It meant so much to me that he was so caring, but then again he didn't really have a choice in the matter. "That would make me feel a lot better."

"I want you to know that there may come a time when I'm unable to ask beforehand. It may have to do with your safety. When it comes to your safety, I will always act first and ask questions later," he said.

He said it in a blunt manner, which wasn't the way he typically talked to me. I knew it was because he was passionate about that particular subject. It was his job to be. It was so astonishing to think that someone was tied to me just for my protection. I still didn't like the fact that he felt I couldn't protect myself, even though my track record so far wasn't too pretty. However, I had been keeping myself safe for years, and suddenly I neededa bodyguard. It took some getting used to. I was certainly not comfortable yet, and I absolutely wasn't willing to let someone else get hurt on my account. I let it go and concluded with a simple, "Okay."

We finished eating and decided to head down to the shoreline. It was a sandy beach to relax on, and I imagined that during the summer it was packed with people smeared with sunscreen and tow-headed kids building sandcastles and splashing in the water. I sat down in the sand and leaned back on my hands with my legs out in front of me to bask in the sun. I looked out at the water and could only see a couple boats in the distance. I tried to imagine all of the boats and jet skis on the water in the summer.

"Penny for your thoughts?" he asked playfully as he plopped down in the sand next to me.

"I was just imagining what the lake might look like during the summer."

"I'll take you here this summer." He gazed out at the water.

"It's a date!" I said. As soon as the words tumbled out of my mouth, my eyes darted to Eli's. He looked up just as quickly. I don't think that moment could have gotten any more uncomfortable. There I sat, staring at him with a deer-in-the-headlights expression. *Nice, Abby.* "I-I didn't mean it like that," I said shyly, looking back down at the sand so I didn't have to look into his alluring blue eyes.

"I know," he said.

It was the first moment that had ever felt awkward between us, at least in the romantic sense. I wondered if he had thought of me that way. Probably not, with all the drama I brought upon him. I doubted he would ever think of me romantically. I couldn't even understand why he wanted to be friends with me. I had changed everything about his life—but he seemed to want me around. Just as well—we were really good friends, and I would never want to jeopardize that for a fling.

I tried to think of something to say to change the subject, but nothing came to me. The silence was as loud as bongo drums in my ears. I kept my eyes off Eli for as long as I could and glanced at my watch.Two p.m. I had to be at work in two hours. I looked at the sky, watching a bluebird pass over. I wondered what Eli was thinking, so I snuck a peek at him only to find him staring right back at me. I almost jumped.

"How are you, Abby? I know the past week must have been hard for you to take in."

I was beginning to feel better about everything, even though some mysteries would still take time to uncover. With Eli at my side, I knew I shouldn't have to worry about it. He would know the right moment to reveal everything to me.

"Really, I'm doing a lot better than I thought I would be. Once I got past the lying—which I'm still a little upset about by the way—I realized you wouldn't intentionally hide things from me if you had a choice. I wasn't beingfair when I wouldn't speak to you. I'm sorry."

He lifted my chin. "Don't be sorry. These issues are not things most people have to face. You're doing just fine. Okay?"

I nodded.

He released my chin and stood up. "Well, it's getting late, and we should head back so we can get you to work on time."

He stuck out his hand and helped me to my feet before we walked to his car. His arm brushed mine as we walked, and it sent a shiver through my body each time. What was happening? My own body was betraying me. I couldn't stop thinking about him. He was so amazing. I had always known that. What changed?

At the car, I shrugged out of my jacket and handed it to Eli to put back in the trunk for the ride home. He grabbed two water bottles out of the backpack as I took one last look around the lake. I sighed and climbed in, wishing I didn't have to be back for work. The trip to the lake had been exactly what I needed. I couldn't wait to come back and hoped to make it a regular occurrence.

We rode home with the top down, enjoying the sights without anything blocking our view. Convertibles were definitely my kind of car. I would love to have one for myself, but I didn't know if I would have enough money for one. Maybe when I got older.

"What kind of car do you want to buy?" he asked, almost as if he knew what I had been thinking.

"I was just thinking about that! It would be nice to have a convertible." I grinned at him. "But I don't think that will be quite in my price range."

"You never know!" he said.

He was kind enough to bring me home, wait for me to change, and drive me to work. He was off today, but that didn't stop him from coming in and enjoying some pizza while I worked and waited on him.

"Hey Abby, you want me to come back and drive you home?" he asked as he headed out the door.

"Nah, that's okay, I'll just walk. Thanks!"

"Okay, call me if you need anythingat all."

I could tell he was trying to push the point. "I will. Promise."

It was 6:45, and I was going to be off work at 9:30, but for some reason, time moved as slowly as a snail. There weren't many customers to help it speed by. I was given the job of deep cleaning the booths and chairs around the restaurant, and I finished the last red booth in the dining area just before it was time to leave. Since there were still no customers, my boss told me to go home ten minutes early. I walked home at a quick pace, passing other pedestrians, and made it in record time.

My mom was sitting in the living room, eating popcorn, and reading a book.

"Hi Mom," I said as I plopped down on the couch next to her, digging my whole hand into the popcorn.

"Hey honey, how was work?" she asked through a mouthful of popcorn.

"It was long. I had to deep clean the booths because we were slow. I'm beat. I'm going to go to bed. See ya tomorrow," I called over my shoulder as I walked out of the room.

"Allright, sleep tight," she responded.

After a full day of hanging out at the lake and working, I was relieved that the day was over. I had enjoyed myself, but I was glad to be home and go to bed. I took a long, steamy shower, and my muscles relaxed as the hot water cascaded down from my shoulders to the tile floor. My worries melted away.

I curled up in bed, content with the world around me, hopeful for what the next day would bring.

CHAPTER THIRTEEN

Sunday morning came bright and sunny through my window. The smell of maple and fresh oranges made its way into my bedroom. My phone said it was almost 9:15 in the morning, and a text from Eli already awaited me.

I hope you don't have plans! We aren't working today!

I smiled at the text. I didn't have any plans, other than studying for the two tests I had the following week.

I texted him back. *No plans, have to study tonight. What did you have in mind?*

I chose to be lazy and went downstairs to eat breakfast in my pajamas. I padded down the stairs in my fuzzy red pajama pants, black spaghetti strap tank top, and cheetah slippers.

Mom was sitting at the kitchen counter reading the newspaper and sipping her coffee. She had a piping hot bowl of maple oatmeal in front of her.

"Morning," I said.

"Morning," she mumbled.

There was already a bowl of oatmeal cooling on the counter for me, as well as a tall glass of fresh-squeezed orange juice. Mom was not in a talkative mood and seemed interested in her Sunday newspaper, so breakfast was quiet. I ate and headed back upstairs to change for the day.

I checked my phone as soon as I got upstairs and saw a message waiting. I expected it to be from Eli, but it was from Bailey.

Hey, do you have plans this weekend? Want to have a sleepover? I'm off Friday!

The prospect of girl time sounded amazing. I responded immediately.

Absolutely, I'm off too!

I didn't even bother checking with my mom. Normally she wouldn't have a problem with it anyway, but lately,she had seemed pretty uninterested in things that were happening in my life. It was different for her to be so distracted, but I figured she was trying to give me a little freedom. I had been so busy that I hadn't even had a chance to miss her. Thinking about it gave me pangs of sadness. Our once-close relationship seemed to be dissolving before my eyes. I knew it was something that would eventually happen as I ventured out into my own life, but I hadn't realized it would be so soon. Maybe she had been busying herself so I wouldn't feel bad. Either way, I was glad she seemed to understand exactly what I needed, even before I did. I was enjoying my freedom more than ever.

My phone buzzed from across the room. It was Eli.

Downstairs.

He was here? Yikes, I wasn't even dressed yet. I threw on the first outfit I had contemplated and hustled downstairs just as the doorbell rang.

"Hey, Abby! I brought over some movies. How about a movie day?" Eli asked.

"Sure," I said, ushering him into the living room.

He handed me the stack of movies, and all of them were ones I liked. I put in a comedy first. We lounged together on the couch. It was satisfying to put my feet up without a care in my mind until I noticed Eli was being unusually quiet.

"Is something wrong?" I asked.

"No nothing," he answered, but he wouldn't look at me.

"Seriously, what's wrong?"

"I might have to go away for a few days."

"For what?" I squeaked.

"Pete is . . . is causing some problems."He paused. "I didn't want to tell you before because you were already so overwhelmed. I didn't tell you everything about Pete. The truth is Pete and my family goway back. He used to be a Protector. He's one of the rebels I was talking about. They're always causing problems for those of us who have chosen to uphold our end of the deal. Like, for example, when he realized that messing with you would mess with me."He stopped and looked at me.

I couldn't be sure what my face portrayed, but I had a really bad feeling that I wasn't going to like where the conversation was leading. "Go on," I said.

"The original story I told you about Pete was a lie. I'm sorry. For a person to be shunned,they have to blatantly ignore their assignment, allowing them to be hurt or possibly killed."

"And in Pete's case?" I asked, regretting the words the minute they left my mouth. Why did I want to know? Well, the truth was, I didn't want to. I needed to.

"He let his assignment be killed," he said.

"Oh my gosh!" I felt like I was going to be sick. *I kissed that disgusting person.*

"I'm sorry—you shouldn't be part of any of this. I made up the other story about the fight and the disappearance. I hoped that maybe you'd stay away if you thought he was bad news. Then, after the last confrontation, I hoped he would leave town and move on with his life, but it turns out he only went away to return with help."

"Help? Help with what?" I asked.

"I'm not exactly sure what he's planning, but I know he's devising something to get even. He's angry."

"So where do you have to go?"

"I have to go talk to the elders. I need help. I can't protect you and go up against Pete and whomever he has gotten to help him."

"Eli, I'm fine!" My protests came out louder than I had anticipated. I hoped my mom wasn't paying attention. I was frustrated that I was feeling like the damsel in distress all over again. It made me feel so uncomfortable and helpless.

"I've been taking care of myself for longer than I've known you!" I didn't mean to appear so angry toward him, but I couldn't help it.

"Abby, calm down. I'm sorry this is a problem at all. I'm handling it. I won't let anything happen to you. You know that, don't you?"

"Yes, but that's not what I want. I don't want you risking your life for me."

"I'm not risking my life."

"Of course you are. Every time you come to my rescue," I said.

He hesitated. "I didn't tell you this earlier. I'm not sure how you'll handle it. But I can't die." He waited, letting it sink in. "Do you understand?" he asked finally.

He couldn't die? What does that even mean? Everyone dies; that was life. I should have been asking so many more questions. Maybe if I had, there wouldn't continue to be surprises.

"You can't die? What does that make you? Like immortal?" I asked.

"Yes."

It was a good thing I was already sitting down because I might have gone weak in the knees. My best friend would live for thousands of years. He would watch me grow old and die, just like everyone else he became close to. Forever. It wasn't the way things were supposed to work.

"I'm sure you're going through a list of all the things you think you know about immortals, but I bet there are a few things that aren't really true when it comes to Protectors. Our lives are extended because we serve to protect. It is a gift given to help us serve without failing. If we choose to stop serving, our lives still continue to be extended, but we can no longer consider ourselves immortal. We live longer, but we can die just like anyone else. Depending on your history, the elders will determine how much of the gift you will continue to receive or if you will be stripped of it immediately, but ultimately, you will no longer be immortal."

"What about aging?" I wondered out loud.

"I ageat a much slower rate. My childhood progressed normally. Aging doesn't slow until the first assignment. I think the elders typically wait until a person is eighteen years old before giving the first assignment. So from now on, I probably won't seem like I'm aging."He shrugged. "Aging is so subtle as it is, but when you're like me, a person might not look like they've aged more than a year in your whole lifetime." His lips tightened.

"Oh," I said with an apprehensive tone.

"Abby, please tell me what you're thinking," he said.

"My best friend is going to watch me get old and die. I don't really know what to think at this point!" I felt exasperated and tired.

"It's not fair is it?" he said softly.

"No, it's not."

He leaned over and wrapped his arm around me. It felt good to be under his arm. There was nowhere else in the world I would rather be. I didn't know if that close of a relationship was even allowed by his elders, but in that moment, it didn't matter.

When my senses came to me, I pulled away. I couldn't let myself get wrapped up in him. Ever since our awkward moment at the lake, I had been thinking about Eli in a whole new way. Just having those thoughts swirl around in my brain was a risk to our friendship. I had to get past it, and quick. I wasn't willing to jeopardize what we had. Heck, I didn't even know if he felt the same way about me. In fact, I doubted it. He was only as close as he was to me because he had to be.

He looked at me with an almost pained expression.

"I'm fine," I said. "It's just kind of surreal."

"I know." He sat back against the couch with his shoulders slumped.

"Hey, let's go out for lunch," I suggested.

It wasn't until then that we noticed the movie had ended, and the credits were streaming across the screen.

"Yikes! We missed the last half of the movie!" he said, laughing. "Where do you want to go?"

I laughed along with him.

"Know any good places? I haven't been to many new ones."

"I know a good burger place. How do burgers sound?" he asked.

It had been a while since I had eaten a good burger. "Sure, that actually sounds really good."

After checking with my mom to make sure it was okay, we took off.

The restaurant was less than ten minutes away, set back from the road. If I passed it driving, I probably would have never seen it. At first glance, it wasn't much to look at, but on the inside, it was cute and full of 1950s theme decorations. Red-cushioned booths lined the walls, and the tables in the middle had cushioned seats. There was a bar you could sit at just like in the 50s. People around us were deep in conversation, sipping chocolate shakes and devouring huge bites of giant cheeseburgers.

We sat in a corner booth that wasn't close to any other people and browsed through the short menu. I decided to have a single cheeseburger with an order of cheese fries and a chocolate shake. As I waited, I browsed the menu further. There were definitely other dishes I wanted to come back and try.

When the waitress came over, she seemed extra interested in pleasing Eli. She had long, straight blonde hair and captivating blue eyes. You could tell she was active by her super thin, toned body. Any guy would think she was a catch. She pretty much ignored that I was even there except when she took my order. I tried to push away my irritation. She was practically hanging all over him. Eli ordered a double cheeseburger with onion rings and a soda. After the waitress took our orders, she flirtatiously bounced away, casting a look back at Eli. *Honestly, could she make it any more obvious?*

"Well, she was sure interested in you, wasn't she?" I teased once she flounced out of earshot.

"What? I didn't even notice," he said, looking after her with a surprised expression.

Typical guy! Completely clueless unless you smacked them on the forehead with a note saying, 'I like you.' I didn't understand how oblivious guys could be. I thought her interest in him had been obvious to everyone in the restaurant.

Time to change the subject. I thought about our conversation at my house. I couldn't believe I had gone a fullten minutes without thinking about the big mess I called my life.

"So can I ask you another question?" I asked cautiously.

"I'm an open book. Just ask! Besides, I'm guessing you have more than one question," he said.

"Okay." I blushed. *What was wrong with me? Why was I blushing?*"How long do you plan on doing this?"

"Doing what exactly?" he asked, confused.

"You know," I answered. "Being a Protector. You said you could choose when to stop. I was just wondering if you ever thought about it, you know? Stopping." The word *Protector* still felt foreign in my mouth.

"Oh, I don't know. I guess it just depends on how things go. I haven't given it much thought. It's still all pretty new to me, too."

It seemed so simple coming from his mouth, but it couldn't be that simple, could it?

"What do you think Pete is going to do?" I asked, knowing I had already asked him that question. But my mind was struggling to grasp everything that was so not *normal.*

Eli looked at me, his deep blue eyes staring right into mine. His gaze alone spoke to my soul. I felt my insides stirring.

"You are so anxious! I can feel it. I'm getting really good at telling what all these emotions are. You don't have to be anxious. I have everything under control."

"Then why do you have to go away?" I whined.

"I'm not sure that I have to yet. I told you I might have to." He reached out and brushed my hand. "I'm waiting to hear back from the elders about what they want me to do."

Our food was coming, so I twiddled my fingers under the table, trying to keep my anxiety at bay. The waitress set all our food down in front of us and waited to see if we needed anything—and by we, I mean Eli. I didn't know why it bothered me, but my mind drifted back to my confusion about Eli. He was so beautiful, in a manly way, of course. I wondered what it would be like to hold hands with him, but I chastised myself. He was my friend! Nothing more!

I looked up from my food to see Eli staring at me.

"Hello! Earth to Abby!" he said.

"What? Sorry, I was daydreaming." I was so embarrassed to be caught daydreaming about him. I wondered what it felt like to have my feelings mixing with his constantly. I couldn't even keep my own straight. I wondered how I had just come across to him, and that embarrassed me even more.

"Do you want salt or ketchup for your fries or burger?" He held out the ketchup bottle with a grin on his face.

He was amused by my embarrassment. *Ugh!*

"No, thanks," I said.

"Must have been a good daydream! Your mood shifted considerably," he said with a smirk.

"Oh, hush!" I said, blushing and giggling at the same time.

We ate our food in silence for the first few minutes. I didn't realize how hungry I was until then. The food melted in my mouth. The shake was rich and chocolaty, just the way I liked it. Eli seemed to be enjoying his food just as much as I was, but mine was disappearing faster.

"Look, Abby, I know this has been a roller coaster for the last couple weeks when it comes to Pete and all of this new information that is just so . . ."

"Unbelievable?"

"Yes, in a nutshell. Unfortunately, I foresee rougher roads coming."

"Rougher?" I asked.

"Yes. I think Pete is going to try to create more problems." He was so calm it struck me as funny.

How could that be? I was already struggling through everything else. How could this possibly get rougher? Though as I knew all too well, just about anything could get worse. "I thought you said you didn't see anything bad for a while?" I asked. "Also, you foresee? What do you mean by that? Like a hunch or a feeling?"

"No, it's more than that. Remember when I told you that I 'saw' you in a dream, and that's what told me you were going to be my first assignment?"

"Yeah."

"Well, I have the ability to see things that may take place in the future. I don't always know what's true and what's fake, but I can usually feel if it's actually going to happen for real. Sometimes I even get the dreams more than once. I've had dreams with Pete in them three times now, but unfortunately they've all been different. It's almost like he hasn't fully decided what his plan will be."

Back to the prophetic dreams again. If Eli got these dreams so often, maybe my nightmare had been tied to him. I really needed to do some research on it. He had already seen a hint of what Pete was planning, and he was asking for help. It must not be good.

"Okay, so what do I do?" I asked, hoping there was at least some small thing I could help with.

"Just like that? You're taking all this so well. I definitely wasn't as strong as you when I heard all the details. My dad slowly told me over the course of a whole year, and here you are learning it all in a couple weeks! I'm amazed. You amaze me, Abby."

There it was again, another awkward moment. They were becoming increasingly frequent. Maybe that meant we were getting too close. I would have to work harder to maintain our distance.

"And to answer your question, nothing. There is nothing you can do. We have to wait," he said.

I finished my food at the same time as Eli.

He stood without wasting any time. "I'm going to go pay. I'll be right back."

"Okay," I called after him.

While he was gone, I took the opportunity to pull enough cash out of my wallet to pay for my portion of the meal, plus tip. Suddenly, I heard a buzzing. I checked my phone, but it wasn't ringing. I looked over at Eli's side and noticed his phone was sliding around the table with the screen lit. I couldn't help myself. I snatched the phone and saw it was a text message. There was no name on the screen. It only showed it was from a blocked phone number. The message was even more quizzical.

You have approval, and I have answers. Call me ASAP.

Who could it be from? I glanced over to see Eli striding toward me. Luckily, he was looking down at his wallet. I shoved his phone back to his side of the table and pretended I saw and heard nothing. It landed in an awkward position, but I hoped he wouldn't notice. What would he think if he knew I had looked at his phone and invaded his privacy? I felt guilty. It wasn't like he hadn't been brutally honest with me. I had no reason to be suspicious or untrusting. Maybe I was looking for validation from someone other than him. I couldn't explain it, but I felt compelled to know more.

I had forgotten about the money in my hand until Eli asked what it was for. I thrust it forward. "Here, it's for my food."

He pushed it back to me. "No, it's my treat. You've been a rock through all this, and I appreciate it. You could be making things really difficult for me right now. Thank you."

I didn't know what to say, but I wasn't going to fight him on paying the bill. That never worked anyway. Instead, I planned to pay next time. Although that was what I had told myself the last time he paid, and look how well that worked out.

He swiped his phone off the table before we left, and I didn't notice him looking at it until we got back in his car. He didn't mention anything about the message. He didn't even act any differently. Here I was on pins and needles, wondering about the conversation. Yet, he sat there as calm as could be.

It was two in the afternoon already, but Eli was ready to watch our second movie despite the message. I could only wonder why he wasn't ready to jump in the car and call this mystery person. Of course, it wasn't a mystery to him, I was sure. Maybe it wasn't even about what we were talking about, so I decided to let it go.

We watched a love story next, even though I think we both struggled to fully focus on the movie.

We never got to the third movie. When the second movie ended, Eli said he had to go study and do homework. I knew better.

After he left, I went into the kitchen to find my mom making dinner.

"Hey honey, how was your movie day and lunch?" she asked.

"Good. We went to King's Burgers. I've never been there before. Have you heard of it?" I asked, trying to make conversation. She deserved at least that much, even though my mind was elsewhere.

"Actually, I have. I went there for lunch with some co-workers who raved about it. I really liked it. What did you think?"

I nodded in agreement. "What's for dinner?" I asked.

"Chicken fried steak with mashed potatoes, gravy, and corn. I'm cheating though."She winked at me. "I'm using frozen, pre-cooked breaded steaks."

"Sounds good to me! Cheating or not!" I tried to sound enthusiastic, but I think it was a bit overdone. "I have some studying to do. Call me down when it's ready?"

"Of course, honey. Study hard!"

I sauntered through the house and realized it had been over a week since I talked to my dad. Even though I didn't want to hold a conversation with anyone, I decided I had better call him to check in.

He picked up on the second ring. "Hey, Abby! I've missed you so much!"

It made my heart hurt; I'd missed him too. I had to hold back tears. "I've missed you too,Dad. Sorry I haven't called."

"Oh sweetie, it goes both ways. I'm sorry too. I've been so busy with inventory at the store—sort of an early spring cleaning. Got to gear up for spring break and summer campers!"

"Of course." I was happy that he had something to look forward to.

"How are ya doing, kiddo?" he asked.

"Doing really good," I lied.

"That's great! We really need to catch up."

"We definitely do."

"Unfortunately, right now isn't really a good time. I have to go, but I'm so glad you called!"

"No worries, I have studying to do."

"I love you, sweetie! It's great to hear your voice. I'll talk to you soon. Bye." He hung up before I could even say goodbye.

"I love you too. Bye Dad," I said to thin air.

I was glad I called him after all. I felt like I could concentrate better on my homework. It was like I mentally checked one more thing off the to-do list that I hadn't realized I had been keeping.

All of my studying took less than an hour. I was surprisingly focused, and when I was done, I felt ready for what the week would bring—test-wise, anyway. Anything else I wasn't so sure about.

I sat in my room contemplating what I had learned about Eli. I wasn't frightened, as I thought I would or should be. I was excited. Excited that boring California life had ended. Excited that I finally had someone in my life who wasn't going anywhere. Excited about things I didn't even know, things I couldn't explain. Of course, there was fear too, but the excitement was far more overpowering than the fear.

"Dinner's ready," my mom called up the stairs.

Dinner was delicious, as always. Afterward, we relaxed together in front of the TV until bedtime.

I fell into a dreamless sleep that night, sleeping peacefully until morning. I woke with a start, realizing I had overslept. The doorbell was ringing repeatedly with such urgency that I darted out of bed in my pajamas and ran to the front door. I knew it could only be one person. I swung it open, and Eli barged in.

"We're late you know," he said.

"Sorry! I just woke up when I heard the doorbell. I'll be right down!" I sprinted back up the stairs.

He was in the kitchen snacking on my breakfast when I came back down, and I grabbed a couple pieces of the bacon before we headed out the door. We knew we would be headed to Sweep when we arrived, but Eli didn't seem to care. I, on the other hand, was worried about missing our test in first hour.

Eli passed me a note while we sat in Sweep. I wasn't sure how he managed to write it without anyone seeing, but when I looked up the teacher wasn't paying attention.

> I don't have to go away! Help is coming. Hopefully, we can outsmart Pete before he tries anything.
> -Eli

That was great news. I felt victorious even though it was premature. The rest of the day was mind-numbingly boring. The only part out of the ordinary was the new student, Ren, who Eli invited to sit with us at lunch. He and Eli seemed to be fast friends already. I felt a twinge of jealousy. Was Eli upset that his best friend was a girl? Maybe Ren would become his best friend, too. Then I would have to share him. I wasn't sure I liked the idea of sharing him with anyone.

Ren was light-skinned, and his hair was so blonde it was white. He was probably six feet tall and two hundred pounds to match. As much as I wanted to dislike him, I couldn't. He had an outgoing personality and was fun and interesting to boot. He brought something new to our lunch table dynamic.

Eli made plans with Ren after school, so I decided to call Bailey once I got home. I asked if she could come over, but unfortunately, she couldn't.

I did my homework and went downstairs to decide what to make for dinner. I found a note that my mom wouldn't be home until later than normal that night, so I was on my own. I decided to make myself macaroni and cheese since I was already hungry, and I ate in front of the TV.

It had been a long time since I had eaten macaroni and cheese at home, and it tasted really good. It was one of my favorite comfort foods that I used to eat a lot when I was little, and it made me feel good now. I ran upstairs when I finished eating, grabbed my laptop, and brought it back downstairs. I checked my email first.

No new emails. I was thoroughly surprised. What was going on with Kelly? She didn't normally take so long respond.

As busy as I had been, I hadn't had a chance to be lonely before. I sat in silence, watching TV with my knees pulled up to my chin. I never used to get lonely in California. It made me feel homesick.

My phone rang, startling me.

I picked up without looking to see who it was. "Hello?"

"Are you okay?"

I knew in an instantthat it was Eli. "What? I'm fine, why?"

"Your mood shifted, it feels . . ."He paused, measuring the words in his mind. "Sad."

This mood thing was really wreaking havoc on my private thoughts. I couldn't have any emotions that weren't cast out to Eli, like a beacon in a lighthouse summoning him to the shoreline.

"I'm fine. I was just feeling a little lonely, that's all," I said.

"Oh, isn't your mom there?" he asked.

It was 6:30 in the evening, and she normally would have been home by now, so it was only natural for him to ask.

"No, she's going to be late tonight. It's not a big deal. Like I said,

I'm fine."

"You should have called me! I'll be there in five minutes," he said.

"No, Eli. I don't want you to change your plans just for me." I struggled to get the last few words out clearly. I tried to hold back the waterworks. Nobody had ever cared so much about me. In that moment, I couldn't take it.

"Don't cry," he said softly.

"I'm not," I sniffled. "I'm fine!"Tears glided slowly down my face. I couldn't stop them as hard as I tried.

A knock sounded at the door. I hesitated, embarrassed to answer the door looking like I did. I opened it slowly, and in an instant,Eli had his strong, safe arms around me. My tears flowed freely.

"Can I help?" he asked. "Please, I hate seeing you like this. I can't bear it."

I knew exactly what he meant. "Yes," I whispered.

I was engulfed in a light breeze, and my sadness faded. Contentment washed over me like the cool waves of the ocean, filling my soul with love.

He held me until I pulled away. I couldn't look him in the eye so I stared at the floor as I walked into the living room.

"I'm sorry," I said. I felt so silly. Even though he was helping me feel better, I felt guilty and ashamed. I should have been able to control my feelings as well as Eli could, but I'd obviously failed at that. I knew everything was taking more of a toll on me than I had originally thought. Otherwise, being alone wouldn't have bothered me so badly. I had no idea how to make everything better. It was uncharted territory.

He brushed the side of my face with his hand. "You don't have any reason to be sorry."

His touch sent shivers throughout my body, spiraling down from his fingertips. I pulled away and walked across the room, wrapping my arms around myself as I looked out the window.

"Want anything to drink?" I asked, hoping to cover the fact that I couldn't handle his touch. It overwhelmed me with feelings I couldn't face. Feelings I didn't quite understand.

"No thanks," he said quietly.

He must already know how uneasy I felt. It was starting to sink in that he was in tune with my every emotion. It felt like every one of my private thoughts were written across my forehead like a jumbotron at a basketball game, and he was scrolling through them all one by one.

In a flash, I was in the kitchen, gripping the counter, hunched over and taking deep breaths. It was getting harder and harder to keep my distance from Eli. He was such an amazing presence in my life. It was like quicksand, and I was stuck. I took a minute to collect myself before I returned to the living room empty-handed.

"I thought you were hanging out with Ren tonight," I said.

"I did. He already went home."

"You guys seem to have really hit it off," I said almost sarcastically.

"Abby, I thought you realized."He searched my eyes for recognition. "He's not just a student. He's our back-up. He and I go way back. His dad is friends with mine, so I grew up around him, but he's actually quite a bit older than I am."

That sure explained why he was so chummy with him. I felt stupid being jealous.After all, he was there to help us, and he was an old friend. Ren came into Eli's life far earlier than I. I decided I would make more of an effort to be friendly with Ren.

"Oh." I couldn't admit how I had originally felt about him, but maybe Eli already knew. I felt so stupid. I wasn't sure how much of my emotions he felt. It was so alien to think that way. Truthfully, I did like Ren. He seemed like a good person and probably an awesome asset to our us. "How old is he?" I asked.

"Do you really want to know?" he asked carefully.

"Of course I do. Think I can't handle it? I think I've proved worthy," I boasted with a big, cheesy grin.

He laughed. "Yes, yes you have. He is sixty-five."

Sixty-five? Man, he wasn't kidding about not seeming to age. Ren looked younger than I did, but he was a whole forty-nine years older than me, and he definitely acted like the other kids at school.

"Really?" I asked.

"Yep."

"How does he seem so young? I don't mean his looks but his personality?" I asked.

"Well, I guess even though we gain knowledge from the years we're on earth, we still act the age we look. Makes it easier for the Protectors who are really old to blend in. Imagine trying to fit into a younger generation when you're like 150!"

I hadn't really thought of it like that. Whoever had come up with the Protectors' lifestyle really had thought of everything—except the hurt of leaving loved ones behind. It was a concept I didn't let myself think about often. It made me sad that someday Eli would have to leave me. It hurt even more to think that not only would he leave but he would go on to share a similar relationship with someone else. How could he? But I knew the answer to that too—he wouldn't have a choice.

CHAPTER FOURTEEN

The next day, I paid a lot more attention to Ren. I made every effort to make him as close a friend to me as Bailey and Eli. The only problem was Bailey was absent. I wondered if she was sick and decided to call her at lunch to see if she was okay.

As it turned out, Ren was in my first hour, as well as my fourth. I was glad to know he would be in two of my classes. Until then, I had yet to make new friends in my fourth hour, and now I wouldn't have to.

When I was leaving my third hour, Bailey's boyfriend Ryan approached me.

"Hey Abby," he said awkwardly.

He had been to my house and sat with us every day at lunch, but at that moment, I realized we hadn't spoken much beyond the niceties. I felt bad that I hadn't taken more interest in getting to know him, not just because he was a friend but because he was Bailey's boyfriend.

"Hey Ryan, what's up?" I responded cheerfully.

"Have you talked to Bailey today?" he asked.

"No, I haven't. Why?" I asked with concern.

"She didn't answer her phone last night. She didn't call me back, and now she's not at school today. I'm just worried about her."

"I'm sure she's okay, but I'll give her a call at lunch to check in."

He walked with me the rest of the way to lunch.

I whispered to Eli what Ryan had told me as we walked in, and I watched him look at Ryan and then at Ren. I wandered out of the lunchroom to find a quiet spot to call Bailey.

Her phone number was already on my speed dial, so I pressed her number and hit call. It rang for a long time before the answering machine picked up.

Feeling defeated, I went back into the cafeteria, and the look on my face spoke volumes. She still hadn't answered.

"I'll go over to her house afterschool to check on her. I'm sure she's fine," I said.

We were all worried about her. She didn't usually disappear like this. For the first time that day, I genuinely hoped she was sick. Fearful things like car accidents and hospitals raced through my mind.

Our lunch hourwas quieter without her happy, energetic presence. She wasn't talking animatedly about the clothes, shoes, and jewelry she was working with. It was clear that she was the glue that kept our unique group together. She was the one who kept our conversation carefree and happy.

After school, Eli, Ren, and I drove to Bailey's house. Nobody answered. It was strange, but then again, maybe she was sleeping.

When I got back in the car, Eli and Ren stopped talking and stared at me with looks that told me they didn't want to tell me something.

"What?" I asked.

Eli held up my phone. The screen displayed a text message. It was from Pete. *Pete?*

Looking for Bailey? Won't find her there.

My heart sank. I should have listened to that nagging feeling that something wasn't right.

"He has her, doesn't he?" I asked, already knowing the answer.

"I'd say so," Eli answered. His shoulders slumped.

"Why?" I asked.

"To get to us, to get to you,"hesaid.

Ren said, "Why don't you take me home, and you guys can talk. I'll come to Abby's house after I grab a few things."

After dropping Ren off, we got to my house in ten minutes flat.

I couldn't contain my frustration. "Shouldn't we be hurrying? He has Bailey. Who knows what he's going to do! Or what he's already done!" I blurted out. I wasn't frustrated with Eli, but for some reason, that was exactly how it sounded.

Eli grabbed my hands to guide me over to the couch. His touch sent shivers through my body, starting at his fingertips. Color flushed my face.

"Abby, Pete wants to get to you. He knows Bailey is your best friend and that you'd do anything to get her back. She needs you to keep calm. There's only one way to get her back that Ren and I can think of. We're going to have to use you as bait. Do you know what that means?" he asked.

"I have to go by myself, right?" I said in a monotone.

"Yes," he responded. "Can you call him?"

I picked up my phone without answering and pressed Pete's name. He picked up on the third ring.

"Well, if it isn't Eli's girlfriend. Does your boyfriend know you're calling me?" he asked snidely.

Eli's ear was pressed to the back of the phone so he could hear everything. He shook his head, signaling me to say no.

"No," I said quickly.

"At least you have some brains in that pretty little head. I assume you are calling about Bailey?"

He was enjoying his little tirade. I vowed to not let him see how he was affecting me, to hide the emotions I knew were screaming out loud and clear to Eli. It unnerved me that he had the upper hand.

"Yeah," I said. "Where is she?"

He laughed. "With my friends and me, of course."

This was all a game to him, and it made me sick. I could hear others talking in hushed voices in the background. I wondered how many "friends" he had helping him.

"What do you want?"

"Why, you, of course."

"Me for Bailey?" I asked.

"Yep, it's that simple," he answered. "*But*, you need to come alone. I don't want to see Eli's face poking around where it doesn't belong!"

I wondered what Eli thought of all this. I hoped he approved of how I was handling it.

"Fine, when? Where?"

"Papago Park. It seems to be a favorite place of your beau, so let's say meet there in one hour."

"I'll be there," I said. I had never been more sure of anything.

I hung up as soon as the words were out of my mouth. I didn't want to listen to Pete's ramblings any more than I had to. Man, what had I seen in him? He disgusted me. The thought that I had ever kissed that frog made my stomach churn. It was embarrassing that everyone knew of our short romance. I guess that's why they say high school kids are flippant about dating.

"What's the plan?" I asked, turning to Eli.

"You meet him," he said.

"That's not what I meant."

There was a knock at the door.

"I know. I was waiting for Ren," he said as he went to answer the door.

Eli and Ren started formulating the plan, only asking for my input occasionally, though I'm not sure how much it really mattered in the scheme of things. It was hard to keep up so I didn't even try, but when they had finalized every detail, they explained everything to me.

Ren was going to drive me to meet Pete. Eli would follow and meet us there incognito. He would find a place to watch at a safe distance so as not to be discovered. Pete didn't know Ren, so he wouldn't grow suspicious if he came with me as my driver to pick up Bailey. The fact that Bailey wouldn't know Ren was so close to Eli worked in our favor, as she wouldn't give us away. We would trade positions. Ren would leave with Bailey, and I would go with Pete. At that point, Eli would follow Pete in his car to see where he took me. By that time, we were hoping to have Bailey home and Ren on his way to us for back-up. From there on out, it would have to play out as it came. There was no planning for how Pete would react, but we at least hoped to have the element of surprise. The plan was to infiltrate the whole team rather than just Pete to avoid future problems. That would give us an idea of how many and who we were up against.

It was the first time I was scared for myself. What would Pete do once I was alone with him? Plans rarely work as they are supposed to. I knew that better than most. There were always a few bumps along the way. I hoped this would be one time things went smoothly. My nerves got the best of me, and I worried about all the things that could go wrong.

"Don't be scared. I'll be right there with you. I won't let anything happen to you." He held my left hand and rubbed the top with his thumb. "I don't like making you do this anymore than you do, but Ren and I agree this is the only way to guarantee we get Bailey back safely."

Even though it was crazy to have someone in tune with how Ifelt all the time, it comforted me. It made me feel like I wasn't alone even when I really was. I held onto that. I would always have Eli there with me. I squeezed his hand.

I took a deep breath. "Ready?"

"If you are, we are," Eli said, looking at Ren.

I had never seen Ren's car before, but it was as amazing as Eli's. He said it was a 1969 Pontiac Le Mans. It was bright blue with a white pinstripe down the side. I loved it even more because it was a hard-top convertible. The interior was done in cream with black accents. Everything was fully restored to a new glory that it probably never had to begin with.

Ren was such a gentleman. He walked around the car and opened my door for me. One thing was certain—just because he acted my age didn't mean he had lost the gentlemanly ways of an older man. It was a good thing in my book. I only wished there were more gentlemen out there who were my age.

We had a twenty-minute drive to Papago Park. We hoped to get there before Pete so we could decide on the meeting point. Of course, we wanted somewhere in the open so Eli could watch.

I kept my hands folded in my lap to prevent myself from fumbling around with them. It was a nervous habit I was trying to break.

"So how long have you known Eli?" Ren asked when we got on the freeway.

"We met on the first day of school."

"Of this year?" he asked, seeming surprised.

"Yep," I answered.

"Wow, I don't think I've ever seen a bond as strong as yours form so quickly!" he said.

"What do you mean?"

"You and Eli, the closeness you share. It's special. I guess that makes sense, though," he said.

"It makes sense? How so?"

His cryptic words confused me. Why would it make sense that our bond was special or any different from the next? Really? Comparing our bond with others really struck a chord with me. What were the others like? Were they going through what we were? Were these situations always so complicated? I had to imagine they weren't. It seemed anything to do with me had a way of making itself more complicated.

"He hasn't told you?"

I shrugged, not sure what he was referring to.

"Oh, well I shouldn't say anything. I'm sorry.It's just not my place."

Was Eli keeping something else from me? Or was I just missing something? He told me himself he wouldn't keep things from me unless he had to. So I must not have understood something crucial. It was just like me to misunderstand things here and there.

"How long have you known Eli?" I asked.

"I've known him since he was born. His dad and I go way back."

"Wow, you must know a lot about him," I said.

"You could say that. I've sort of been a mentor to him through his Protector journey, at least before you came along. There was a lot he needed to learn before you arrived. After his dad left, I was here for a while. His dad would be so proud if he saw him now."

I was certainly proud to have him in my life.

"He is pretty awesome," I said.

"From what I hear, so are you," he said, a tinge of jealousy in his tone.

I blushed. Maybe I was imagining the jealousy. I couldn't imagine what he had to be jealous of. He hardly knew me. Before I could say anything else, we pulled left into the parking lot. I could see Eli making a right turn behind us. I didn't see Pete's car yet, so it appeared we had beat him. We parked close to the picnic area and sat in the car while we waited. Ren said it was better that way because if Pete decided to try anything underhanded we could make a quick getaway.

From the start, I knew there was a chance Bailey wouldn't be with Pete when he came to meet us. I almost expected him to pull such a trick now that I knew who he really was. I figured all three of us suspected it was a possibility, but we hadn't discussed how to proceed in that event. Eli and Ren probably didn't want me to worry more than I already was, but I had my own plans. I knew in my heartthat I couldn't just desert Bailey. I would go with Pete either way. I had to get to the bottom of it, and the only way to do that was to go with him. But I kept that to myself so I didn't give Eli the chance to tell me otherwise.

It was no surprise to me when Pete pulled up next to our car alone. Pete and I stepped out of our separate cars at the same time, less than two feet from each other. Our cars were parked much closer together than I thought, and it made me extremely uncomfortable. But I couldn't let Pete see it.

My heart thumped. I took a moment to collect myself and gain courage before I said a word to Pete.

"Who's that?" Pete spat, pointing at Ren, who stood inconspicuously on his side of the car.

"A friend. How did you expect me to get here? I don't have a car.Plus, Bailey was going to need a ride home, but apparently, you've forgotten your end of the deal."

"Well, I couldn't lose my leverage when your boyfriend tries to interfere. So you'll just have to come along to get her." He pointed at Ren. "He will have to go on his way without you and Bailey. I'll be sure Bailey gets home."

Ren broke his silence. "Abby will not be going with you unless Bailey is here to stay in her place."

"Is that so?"Pete paused. "Well, I think it's up to Abby. If she does decide to come with me, what are you going to do about it?"

That was my cue to speak up before things got ugly. "If I go with you now, what happens to Bailey?" I asked.

"I call my friend, and he brings her home. Just like that," he said, smiling at me.

"Abby, you can't . . ." Ren pleaded.

I noticed him take a step toward the front of the car, so I took my chance before it was no longer available. I barreled around Pete's car and swung open the door.

"Abby! No!" Ren shouted.

I didn't look in his direction, but I knew Ren was almost all the way around his car before I made it to the inside of Pete's. When I jumped into the car, he turned back to get in his own to chase us down.

Pete was right on cue, and our doors slammed at the same time. His engine roared to life. The tires squealed as they spun, trying to get traction on the asphalt. I saw Eli in my rearview mirror, his arms waving wildly as he ran toward us. At that moment, I felt awful. What had I done? He would never forgive me. I hadn't thought about how it would affect Eli, except that he wouldn't let me do it. I hadn't considered why. All I could think of was how to get Bailey back. My mind only had one track. I didn't want to hurt Eli, but I saw at that moment that I had.

Ren was right on our bumper as we sped out of the parking lot. Pete didn't wait for the stoplight to turn green.

"Where are we going?" I asked.

"A friend's house," he said. "Of course, not until we lose your friend and Prince Charming behind us. You sure do come with a lot of baggage."He chuckled.

He started weaving through the city, whipping down streets at the drop of a hat. He created a difficult but not impossible path to follow until he glided around a corner into a dark parking garage. It was so dark I could hardly see anything else around us. When Ren caught up, I saw him continue driving in the direction he must have thought we had gone. A few cars back, Eli followed Ren.

Pete laughed out loud—he was so proud of himself. It made my stomach roll in disgust.

"Good. Now that we lost the dummies, we can get where we need to go,"he said as he put the car in reverse and drove out of the parking garage.

Now I knew Eli would have no idea where I was. Or would he? He did find me last time. Somehow I had sent him mental pictures of where I was. I didn't know what he would see or even if he would see any of it, but I decided to give it a try. I looked at every possible thing I could as we continued driving, hoping something might be a giveaway. The drive didn't take more than ten minutes, but I felt confident that if Eli saw anything I saw, he would be able to find me. He seemed to know the area like the back of his hand.

We pulled into a neighborhood, and I realized I had one last shot. I willed him to see what I saw with everything I had. I mentally pushed the images out to him as if I could talk to his mind. An estate sign surrounded with wrought iron décor at the entrance of the subdivision, a street sign that said Casper, a bright red house with a broken mailbox and white shutters, a playground structure in someone's back yard with a rainbow canopy, and lastly, as we were getting out of the car, the house number: 5435.

Pete pushed me through the doorway of the house as I dawdled outside, trying unsuccessfully to get one last mental picture of something that might stand out. The house was dark. All the curtains were drawn. He guided me into what I assumed was the living room. It had an impressive entertainment bundle boasting what had to be a seventy-inch TV in the center. There was an action movie on that I didn't recognize. The blood and gore alone were enough for me to not want to watch it.

Two burly guys I had never seen before stood when we walked into the room. One was tall, with brown hair and brown eyes, and the other was shorter but still quite a bit taller than me, with brown hair and green eyes. Both looked about the same age as Pete, but in that new world, who knew what that meant.

"So this is the troublemaker," the taller of the two said.

I wasn't a troublemaker. Pete was the troublemaker. I wasn't going to give him the satisfaction of a remark in return so I shot him a dirty look and crossed my arms in protest.

"This is her," Pete responded as he crossed the room and opened a door that I hadn't noticed until then. "Come on," he said to someone inside. Pete stepped back, exposing a trail of light coming from within the adjoining room. It created a nightlight effect in the dimroom we were standing in. Slowly, Bailey emerged. I was at her side in an instant, hugging her and telling her it was going to be okay.

I held her at arm's length to get a good look at her. She looked healthy, which wasn't surprising since I had just seen her the day before. I cringed when I saw a bruise on her wrist and a scrape on her arm, but other than that she looked fine.

"I'm okay, Abby," she said, sounding different than normal. It was Bailey's voice, but it was stronger and bolder. It made her seem more sure of herself than ever. It surprised me, but it was a good surprise. I didn't question it because I knew she was telling me the truth. She was a fighter.

"Ryan's worried sick," I said.

"Yeah, I'm sure he is."

"Okay, okay, enough of all this reunion talk. Time to get down to business," Pete said.

"What do you want Pete?" I felt like the question was on repeat. It seemed like I was always asking him that. I rounded myself to face him, but I didn't let go of Bailey. Instead, I pushed her behind me as if I were making myself into a human shield.

"Well, I have a bit of an issue with your boyfriend. An issue that I have yet to . . .let's just say, fix. And you two are going to help me. It was really so nice of you to make it so easy to get my hands on you, Abby. I really thought it would be harder."

His triumphant smile made me want to punch him in the face.

"Why am I here?" I asked. "Why is Bailey here? She has nothing to do with any of this."

"Well, my brave one, Bailey was bait to get you here, and you are bait for Eli."

"I get that much, but what do you intend to do with us?" I asked. "You'll never win against Eli."

"You want to bet?"

His whole demeanor changed. His eyes blazed as if a flame was ignited within him. He didn't appear to like losing,but I had to win. The alternative would mean something terrible for Eli. I couldn't be sure what Pete had planned for him, but based on Pete's track record, it wasn't something I cared to find out.

"In case you haven't noticed, I have a little help here. Eli doesn't stand a chance against the three of us," Pete sneered. "Oh, and just to be clear, I let Bailey in on Eli's little 'secret,' which I'm sure you were informed of after our last debacle."

Bailey looked up from the floor at the mention of her name. I could see the hurt in her eyes. Pete must have shared everything with her. I was a horrible friend. The guilt I already felt about not confiding in her resurfaced and threatened to choke me. I wanted to go to her and explain everything and tell her I was sorry, but I knew I couldn't right then. It wasn't the right time. I mouthed, "I'm sorry" to her and moved on for the moment. She shrugged.

"What's next?" I asked Pete.

"Give me your phone so I can call Eli and set up a little meeting."

I hesitated. Eli must be waiting for this. Even though I hadn't followed his plan, I felt bad about it, so I decided that from there on out, I would cooperate. I took my phone out of my pocket and pressed the speed dial for Eli. He picked up before the first ring ceased.

"Abby! Are you okay?"He sounded frantic.

"I'm fine.Don't worry about us," I threw in the *us* to make Bailey feel included and also to let Eli know she was okay and with me.

As soon as the words left my lips, Pete snatched the phone. Strong hands grabbed me from behind to hold me back. I screamed as I struggled to free myself. I fought so hard that he threw me to the ground. My shin throbbed where it struck the coffee table on my way down, and my arm began bleeding. I realized fighting wasn't going to change anything. Pete and his goons had other plans for Bailey and me. The taller guy in the room grabbed Bailey, and they pushedus both into the small room Bailey had come from when we arrived. The door slammed closed and locked from the outside. Trapped.

<h1 style="text-align:center">CHAPTER FIFTEEN</h1>

I could no longer hear what Pete was saying to Eli. I tried to calm myself since I knew my fear would only distract Eli. But the truth was, we were in danger, and it scared me. Trapped in the little room did nothing to make me feel better. Pete no longer seemed to care about what happened to Bailey or me. He had gotten what he needed from us. I looked down at my arm. My blood dripped onto the tile floor.

I found Kleenex on the nightstand and used some to stop the bleeding. Upon closer inspection, the cut wasn't too bad.It wouldn't need stitches, but there sure was a lot of blood. I held the tissue firmly on it until it the bleeding stopped.

The room we were in was a small bedroom with two beds. It only had one exit—the one we had come through. I was surprised to find it was decorated very tastefully. A small TV sat in the corner, and a mini-fridge stood along the wall. I found it was stocked with a variety of food and drinks. The only thing we lacked was a bathroom.

I turned to Bailey, who had taken up residence on one of the beds. She seemed so disheartened, so unlike Bailey.

"I'm sorry that you got dragged into this," I said. "I never would have guessed he would involve you."

"I know. I just wish you had told me everything. I thought we were friends."

"We are, but I couldn't tell you about Eli. It wasn't my place, and I don't really know all the rules about it yet. I wanted to tell you so bad. I didn't have anyone to go to except Eli. I was so lonely."

"That's why things were strained between you guys last week," she said as realization hit her.

"Yeah," I answered. "What did Pete tell you?"

Bailey went on to explain what she knew about Eli's special gift. She left out a few details. Specifically about his bond with me and that Ren was here and was also a Protector. But Pete probably didn't know those things either. I filled her in on the details she didn't know. We needed to be on the same page. I hadn't trusted her before. *Look where that had gotten us.* I wasn't going to make the same mistake again.

"We went by your house looking for you," I said. "Nobody was there."

"Yeah, my dad is out of town on business until Saturday. Nobody probably even missed me," she said, her face fell.

"We did," I said.

"Oh I know, besides my friends.And of course Ryan. I miss him," she said. "What do we do now?"

"I don't know. Wait, I guess."

I sat down on the other bed and looked around, quietly thinking everything through. There was one person I hadn't considered. My mom. *What would she think if I didn't come home tonight?* She would call the police right away. I wondered if Eli had thought of that. In a sense, Bailey was lucky that her dad was out of town all week so he wouldn't suspect anything. She wouldn't have to try to make up some kind of lie to cover up where she had been.

Panic welled up in my throat. It threatened to choke me. I looked around the room. There wasn't a clock in sight, and I tried to think back to when we had met Pete at the park at five p.m. I figured it was probably around 5:45. I hoped she was working late.

Time ticked by slowly, and minutes seemed like hours.

I wished I knew what was happening outside of the room. I couldn't sit still. I paced the small room. I paced so much that I began counting my steps. It took ten strides to cross the room. I counted each time. Then I became frustrated with myself for counting them.

"Abby?" Bailey whispered.

I swiveled on my heel to face her. "Yeah?"

"How long have you known about Eli?"

"Only a week and a half, I promise," I said, closing the distance between us. I sat next to her on the bed.

I was glad she was willing to talk to me. She didn't seem mad, just sad, but I couldn't tell if that was because of our surroundings or because I hadn't opened up to her.

"I'm so sorry, Bailey."

"It's okay. I'm not mad at you. I sort of understand. It's really just a lot to take in. I always wondered why it felt like Eli was more concerned about you when we were dating. It all makes sense now."

"Oh, Bailey, it's not like that." I felt guilty saying that because—for me—it sort of was like that.*But it wasn't back then.*I didn't know if I would be able to stop a romance from developing. I didn't know if I even wanted to prevent it. I felt so vulnerable and wanted nothing more than to be swept up in his arms. He made me feel at home.

"It's okay if it is," she said slowly. "It's like you were already written in the stars anyway. You were his before you even knew him.Before I even knew him."

"I guess so," I said, hoping she meant it.

She took a deep breath and let it out in a rush. "So, how are we going to get out of here?" she asked, radiating more confidence than I had ever witnessed from her. It inspired me.

"Any ideas?" I asked.

We talked through various scenarios for a while until we decided on a plan. We didn't know if it would work, but we didn't have many options.

"Ready?" I asked.

"Yep," she said.

I went to the door and started banging. "I have to pee!" I shouted."Let me out!"

I didn't stop yelling until the taller of the two goons opened the door. He looked angry, so I turned on my charm, hoping to pacify him.

"Hey there, handsome.Mind taking me to the bathroom?" I looped my arm in his and tried to push my way out of the room. He didn't budge. It was like trying to move a brick wall. He hesitated and lookedaround, like he was waiting for something. I'd guess Pete. He came up empty and backed out of the doorway with me still clinging to his arm. He led me through the living room and headed toward a hallway. I was relieved when he left the door to our prison unlocked with Bailey still inside. So far, our plan was working magically.

Halfway down the hallway, our plan started to go south. The shorter thug wandered into view. I had already had enough of that guy. He was obviously unconcerned about hurting Bailey or me. He must have had no conscience.

"Randy, what are you doing? Pete said not to let them out for anything!" he almost shouted.

Randy. I wondered if Eli would know either of them.If I could just get the shorter one's name, I could ask him.

"She has to go to the bathroom. I'm taking her."

"Did Pete tell you to?"

"No, but I'm not cleaning up her pee if she can't wait. Are you?" Randy threw back.

With that,the shorter guard stepped out of the way and let us through, but he headed right for the living room. I had to distract him,or our plan would fail.

"You guys wouldn't happen to have any . . ." I paused and looked each guy in the eye for effect. "Tampons, would you?"

They were dumbfounded for a moment and stuttered a few times trying to figure out how to respond. Speaking of girl matters never failed to make guys uncomfortable. It turned them into bumbling fools, just the effect we wished for.

"Come on, gentleman. You can't expect to keep women hostages unless you have the proper supplies."Despite the dangerous game I was playing, it was proving very hard to keep a straight face.

"We're sorry," they said in unison, as if they were little boys being scolded by their mother.

"I'll go right now to get some," said the shorter guy. I still didn't know his name.

"That's better," I said. "Oh, and I need the slim ones! Thanks!" I strutted back in the direction we had been headed. Getting rid of them was easier than I hadexpected.Pete hadn't chosen them for their brains. Randy followed at my heels, and the other was already out the front door. I hoped he had left the front door unlocked in his haste. I hadbeen surprised when Bailey told me that there was a deadbolt on the other side of the doorto prevent us from escaping. The house was locked up tight.

I took my time in the bathroom. I washed my hands and checked my face, cleaned the cut on my arm, and looked for first aid supplies in the medicine cabinet but found nothing. I laughed to myself that they had fallen for the tampon bit. I didn't actually need one, of course. But it was genius. Bailey had been doubtful; she would be so impressed.

I heard a door close. That was my cue to move out.

"Blaine, is that you?" Randy said.

He was headed back down the hallway toward the front door. I bolted after him.

"I'm finished, Randy," I bellowed, snapping him away from his concern for a moment.

The plan was never for me to get away—it was for Bailey. Of course, she didn't know that. She would be expecting me in the next five minutes on the next street. If I didn't come, she was to leave without me to get Eli. I knew she would probably be pretty upset with me that I never planned to escape with her, but it was a chance I would have to take. There wasn't much chance of us both getting away, and if one of us had to be a hostage, you could bet your butt it was going to be me. My mess, my problem.

I hoped she would be able to get to Eli quickly. I missed him like crazy. He had been such a constant in my life, and now that he was gone, it was hard to think of anything but him. Then I felt him. He was close. I don't know how I knew, but I knew. It was a feeling I was as sure of as if I were to know I was happy. I had never noticed this feeling before. Was it the special bond Ren had referred to? I never imagined I would feel any differently because of it.

My heart quickened at the thought of seeing Eli. A burst of air surrounded me, and my heart slowed. Excitement and happiness filled me down to my toes. Eli was calming me. Maybe that was his way of showing me he was there. I silently thanked him for the boost. I almost couldn't contain my glee.

As soon as we reached the front door, it burst open.A moment later, Randy was on the floor, bound with zip ties so he couldn't move his arms. Eli moved like a freight train, pummeling him. Ren stepped into view, grinning from ear to ear. It almost seemed like he was chuckling.

"I got him," he said as he stepped over Randy to help Eli stand up.

Eli seemed to fly to my side, this time surprising me. He cupped my face with his hands and kissed me hard, and I found myself kissing him back. His kiss was tender, deep, and needy. My stomach flipped with excitement. I didn't realize how badly I wanted it—how much I needed it. My arms flew around his neck and pulled him closer. I felt like my knees would give out. His kiss felt amazing. There was nothing in the world like it. He pulled away slowly, and it was over all too soon. It took me a minute to regain my wits. I had to grab his arm to steady myself. I felt his eyes roaming over my whole body, and it made me self-conscious even though I knew he was just making sure I was okay. His eyes locked on the cut on my arm just as I remembered it was there. Without luck, I tried to hide it.

"Are you okay?" he asked, gingerly brushing his fingertips across the fresh wound.

I winced.

"Who did this?"His jaw tightened, and his eyebrows furrowed.

"I'm okay, really. I'm just so happy to see you," I said, hugging him.

He pulled away. "Who?"

He wasn't going to give up.He was angry. I didn't think I had ever seen anyone as angry as he was atthat moment.

"Blaine, the other guy helping Pete," I whispered, looking at

Randy,who was now standing next to Ren, watching us talk.

I hadn't noticed until that moment, but Bailey was also standing near Ren, her expression blank. I felt for her. She had been thrown into a big mess. Then to watch her ex-boyfriend kiss her best friend—it had to hurt. Eli strode past them, out the door, and into the driveway. He returned a moment later, shoving Blaine. He pushed him through the doorway and into the living room. Ren shut the door and brought Randy in, with Bailey trailing behind.

"What were you thinking when you hurt her? Huh?" Eli growled.

I cringed. This was a completely different side of him I had never known existed. Intense was a mild way of describing it.

After throwing Blaine to the ground, Eli kicked him a couple times. "Where were they keeping you?"he asked me.

I pointed to the open door, afraid to speak. Eli pulled Blaine to his feet and pushed him through the door. Eli stopped dead in his tracks as he stepped into the room.

"Abby," Eli called.

I walked into the room, and my gaze followed Eli's to all of my blood that had dripped onto the floor. The dried blood went from the doorway to the other side of the room and ended next to the bed I had been sitting on. It looked really, really bad—much worse than it had actually been. I knew I wouldn't be able to convince Eli of that. I silently berated myself for not cleaning it up.

"Is this your blood?" he asked sternly.

I didn't want to answer. I knew how angry he already was, and I didn't want to throw fuel on the fire.

"Abby," he probed.

"Yes," I answered, looking down.

Before I could say more, Eli gave Blaine a right hook, hard enough to cause blood to surge from his nose. Blaine landed with a thud on the ground. He was out cold.

Eli wrapped me in his arms and pulled me from the room. Ren finished up by putting Randy in the room with Blaine and closing the door quietly. There was no need for a lock since they were both bound. Ren still said nothing.

"I was so worried about you," Eli said."Are you okay?" He spoke softly, his forehead pressed to mine.

"I'm fine, I swear," I said.

My feelings betrayed me again, and tears slid down my face. All of the emotions hit me at once—happiness, sadness, fear, alarm, love, contentment. He held me tighter, like we were the only ones in the room. I breathed him in. He smelled like the most amazing cologne. It soothed me.

"Can I help?" he murmured.

"Please," I spoke barely above a whisper.

Once again, I was engulfed in a breeze that stirred my hair. I breathed it in and exhaled, feeling immensely better. Remembering we were in fact not alone, I turned to face Ren and Bailey, who were quietly watching us. Ren smirked. I blushed, and for the first time since we had been there, Bailey just smiled.

"That really is amazing," Ren said.

I assumed Ren was referring to Eli calming me. Eli just shrugged it off, but I could tell he was elated at the compliment. In that one glance, I could see how much he looked up to Ren. I was immensely grateful that Eli not only had someone looking out for him but someone for him to look up to. A good role model who cared deeply for him.

Ren cleared his throat. "Bailey, why don't we explore the house and see what we can find," he said, putting his arm out for her to take. I giggled athow obviously they were giving us some alone time, but I was grateful.

Before they were even out of sight, Eli bent to kiss me again. Our lips intertwined. I closed my eyes and took it all in, enjoying every second with him. I had waited for it ever since that awkward moment at the lake. It had been the first time I had ever thought of him as anything more than my best friend.

He pulled away just as slowly as he had before. He rested his forehead on mine, his breathing heavy and uneven to match mine. His enticing blue eyes peered down at me, and my cheeks reddened.

"As much as I've tried to fight these feelings, I can't fight them anymore, and I don't want to. I'm in love with you Abby. With everything about you."

I wished I hadn't tried so hard to push it away for all that time. I couldn't wait a moment longer. "I love you, too."

Eli pulled back from me with a surprised look on his face. It was like his eyes were peering straight into my soul. He hugged me tighter. "You do?" he whispered.

"Yes." I smiled.

"I didn't think you felt the same way."

The ecstasy of our love filled us as we shared our third breathtaking kiss. Nothing felt more right, more perfect, more us. That word made me giddy: us. Our future was uncertain, that much I knew, but I wouldn't let that taint the moment. No other moment in my life had felt that good, that natural.

"I was so angry with you for going out with him. I was so angry with Pete for taking you. I felt so utterly helpless until I got your visions. So clear. You led me right to you," he said.

"You saw them?" I asked quietly."That's how you found us?"

"Yeah, it was awesome. Almost like you were taking pictures with a camera and sending them to me."

"I was in a way, I suppose. I tried to look at everything and push the images out to you. I didn't know if it would work, but I tried my hardest because you said that's how you found me last time," I explained.

He looked into my eyes in awe. "You're amazing. Do you know that?"

I blushed. Nothing could top that intimate moment between us.

He took my hand and led me in the direction Ren and Bailey had gone. The rest of the house wasunimpressive. It had four bedrooms, two of which were empty aside from a sleeping bag in each. I assumed that was where Pete's goons had been sleeping. It surprised me. Our prison had been decorated so tastefully. Maybe that had been for our benefit. Maybe he had moved the things from the two empty bedrooms. I would never be sure, but it didn't really matter.

"Now what?" I asked as we gathered in one of the empty bedrooms. I wasn't directing my question at anyone specific, but Eli responded.

"We wait. Eventually, Pete is going to come back."

"What time is it?" I asked, remembering that my mom was probably worried.

"It's 8:30. I already took care of your mom if that's what you're worried about."

He looked at me with his gorgeous blue eyes. He had taken care of everything. I couldn't believe how he looked out for me. And to top it all off, he was in love with me. My heart leaped.

"How?" I asked.

"You left your purse in Ren's car. I used your keys and left a note for her. She thinks you're working until 11:30 tonight. I hope that's okay," he said shyly.

I hugged him once more. "Thank you. When did you guys find us?" I asked, looking at Ren as well.

Ren spoke up. "We were watching the house for about an hour when we saw Blaine emerge. We were moving in to snatch him when Bailey came out too. It kind of surprised us." I saw Bailey smile. "She explained what was going on, and once we were up to speed, we moved in."

Eli added that he had parked around the corner so his car wouldn't raise any suspicion. I would have never thought of that. It was only a matter of time until Pete returned.

We decided it would be best to hang out in the living room while we waited. It turned out that the TV was set up with the best cable around, and whoever lived there owned a collection of DVDs that would put a store to shame. Eli flipped through channels to see what kind of shows were on. We never really settled on one for more than a few minutes. Despite the situation, we were enjoying ourselves. I couldn't help but feel like a crime-fighting team on a stakeout.

When the lock clicked on the front door, all four of us jumped. Bailey and I backed away toward the door where our captives were being held. We didn't want to be caught up in anything. Eli and Ren took a few steps forward, but they kept out of view so that when Pete stepped into the living room they could take him by surprise.

Pete stumbled into view carrying four bags of take-out. He looked down in the bags, rummaging for something. Eli ambushed him before he even knew what hit him. It amazed me how fast Eli could take out an enemy twice his size. I guessed it was due to his training. Maybe that was one of the things Ren had helped him learn.

Pete was groaning on the floor, holding his side.

"How?" Pete grumbled.

"We're smarter than you," Eli spat. "You really need to learn to leave well enough alone! The elders aren't happy. I'd hate to be you right about now. You are to meet with them tomorrow. Maybe they'll let the thugs in that room go without consequences, but you won't be so lucky, they have assured me."

"You've got to be kidding. Do you really think I'm that stupid?".

Eli smirked. "In case you haven't noticed, you don't really have a choice. Look around. You aren't in charge."

As Eli talked, Pete struggled unsuccessfully to get free.

In the scuffle, the bags of food had wound up strewn around the floor. I stepped forward to collect them. I took out five burgers and orders of French fries and handed three of them to Ren. Bailey, Ren, and I hand-fed all three delinquents without unbinding their hands. We might have been giving them a taste of their own medicine, but we weren't cruel enough to starve them. After all, they had left enough food to feed Bailey and mein the mini-fridge.

Eli went through Pete's pockets and found my cell phone among his things. I was glad to have it back. I didn't know when I had gotten so attached to it.

It was decided that Ren would stand guard that night. The two helpers would be locked in the room, and Ren would watch Pete in the living room.

Eli drove Bailey and me home. We dropped Bailey off first. I felt bad that she was going home to an empty house, but she insisted it was fine and that she wouldn't have it any other way. Before I left her, I made sure she would call me if she needed anything, even if it was just to talk.

After we dropped her off, Eli didn't take me straight home. It was only ten p.m., and my mom wasn't expecting me to be home from work until after 11:30. He didn't tell me where he was going, but I was pleased when we turned into the parking lot at the park where we had eaten our late-night dinner. It seemed like ages ago, but really it had only been a few days. I liked that park. It seemed like it might become "our" place, but maybe that was just me being overzealous.

We walked hand-in-hand around the park for a little while before sitting down at a picnic table to talk. It was comfortable being with him, even more so now that we were truthful about our feelings. The weight of hiding and fighting them had been lifted off my shoulders.

"What are you thinking right now?"

"I should have been honest with you sooner, but the truth is, I was trying to push my feelings aside."

Eli smiled. "So does this make you my girlfriend?"

"Absolutely!" I laughed. "That is, if you want me to be."

He kissed me lightly on the lips. "What does that tell you?"

I giggled.

It felt really good to be carefree. There had been so much going on that we hadn't had a chance to truly relax since Eli told me about his secret identity. I had high hopes that the whole ordeal with Pete would blow over quickly.

He leaned down and kissed me, snapping me out of my thoughts. His kiss was slow and deliberate. I let his kiss take me away, like I was floating on air. For that moment in time, I didn't have a care in the world.

We didn't think about tomorrow. We didn't think about anything except the moment. Selfish? Maybe, but I think we earned it.

CHAPTER SIXTEEN

Eli and Ren weren't at school the next day, but Bailey and I knew they were off handling the riffraff. I couldn't wait to see Eli again. A spark had been ignited inside me, and I couldn't get enough of him.

I also couldn't wait to hear what the elders said at their meeting. I knew Eli was nervous about it, and his nerves made me uneasy. After all, the elders' decision determined our future. If they were too lenient on Pete, then we might have more problems, but if they really threw the book at him, wewould be set.

Bailey seemed to be adjusting well to all the news she had received. While it was a lot to take in, it seemed like she was handling some of it better than I was. She even seemed to be back to her old self again. Ryan was beside himself when he saw her. He picked her up in a giant bear hug. I was happy for them. They walked to their next class holding hands, and it made me sad that Eli wasn't there. I don't know what Bailey told Ryan about where she had been, but I figured it was better that way. I was tired of lying to people.

After a pop quiz in third hour, I was more than ready for lunch. I walked alone, a first for me that school year. Until then, I always seemed to be surrounded by people all the time at school.*Come to think about it, even when I wasn't in school.* It felt good that being alone was a rare thing for me. It meant I had a web of friends to count on. The only problem was that being alone was harder on me than it used to be.

The lunch line was quiet without anyone to talk to, and it seemed to take longer than normal to make my way to the front. It had to be my imagination. I picked a salad for lunch and made my way through the crowds of students to the table where we usually sat.

I looked up from my tray as I made my way through the tables, and there he was. Eli stood with his arms crossed, leaning against the table and smiling right at me. He looked breathtaking. I closed the gap in two strides and almost dropped my salad when I flung my arms around him. He laughed.

Ren was still missing. It worried me, and I wondered where he was. *Maybe he had gone back where he came from?* A part of me hoped he hadn't. I would have really liked having him around permanently. He was a breath of fresh air that we needed.

"You didn't miss me or anything, did you?" he asked as he nuzzled my neck.

Our friends were surprised. They hadn't heard that we were together. It had happened so quickly even for us, but we didn't explain the details. There was more to it than anyone needed to know, so we simply said it happened the night before and left it at that. I couldn't believe that the explanation sufficed for everyone at the table. Maybe they had been expecting it. Bailey just grinned at me—knowing the whole truth gave us a little secret from the rest of the world.

"How did this morning go?" I asked Eli in a hushed voice.

"It went fine but not quite as we expected it to," he said.

"Why?" I asked.

"I can't go into detail now, but I'll tell you after school, okay?"

I agreed. I knew it wasn't smart to discuss at the lunch table. I also just wanted to enjoy the afternoon without worrying about anything except school. Having Bailey back made me realize once again how much she took charge of our group's conversation. That day, things felt more normal than I had thought they would, even though she had fabricated a story about where she was the day before. We also talked about how she was looking forward to our sleepover this weekend. In all of the craziness, I had forgotten about it, though I would never tell her that. It gave me something to look forward to.

I loved walking through the halls, holding Eli's hand. Nothing had ever felt more right. His touch still sent shivers through me, and I wondered if it always would. It was as if his hand sent an electrical current coursing through my body.

Afterschool, Bailey, Eli, and I met at Eli's car. We decided it was best to get together after school to talk about the events from that morning that Bailey and I had missed. Eli hadn't mentioned anything about Ren yet, and I didn't have an opportunity to bring him up until we got into his car.

"Where's Ren?" I finally asked.

"He's back at that house. You know, Pete's house."He paused as if he were waiting for a reaction. I gave him nothing. "That's where we're headed. I'll explain everything when we get there."

I didn't want to go back there. Things must have not gone the way we had hoped. I wondered what Bailey was thinking. I was sure it was the last place she wanted to go.

Walking through the door gave me a sense of déjà vu that made me dizzy. I grabbed Eli's arm for support.

"You okay?" he asked.

"I'm fine, just got a little dizzy."

I wasn't going to explain why, and for once, it seemed like he didn't have a clue. He helped me inside, and we sat down in the newly familiar living room.

"The elders would like to talk about their options before they make their final decision, so they have asked Ren and me to keep watch over Pete until then."

"What about his friends?" Bailey asked.

"His friends were lucky. They were told to leave town and not to talk to Pete or any of us again," he responded. "But I doubt that will be the case. Pete and those two go way back."

It was not the news I had hoped to hear. I couldn't wait to be rid of Pete for good, but obviously, we were going to be burdened by him for a while. But how long?

It was as if I had spoken my question aloud.

"It's only for a week, maybe two. Things will be back to normal very soon. I promise."

He was so sincere it was hard to not feel better just looking into his eyes. He was right. After all, two weeks wasn't so long, and it would be even better if it were only one. I could do it. I had to do it. It was time I was strong for Eli. I knew he wanted the situation to be over just as much as I did, maybe even more.

"Okay," I said. "How do you plan to do it?"

"Ren and I will trade out. He will take a twelve-hour shift, and I'll take the next."

"But you'll miss school." I sounded whiny. *Oops.*

"We will be switching out at eleven each morning and night. I'll only miss the morning of school, and I think I can stand to miss a few days." He laughed as he said it.

Why was he laughing at me? Probably because I sounded downright childish. The truth was, I didn't like not having him at school. Again, my thoughts were on myself. I had to change that. We were a couple now, and I had to start thinking of *us*. I doubted Eli would find selfishness a turn-on.

He put his hand on my knee and went on. "When they reach

theirdecision, we'll bring him to them in Colorado."

Here I thought missing school was the worst part. Now he would be going away, with Pete in tow? I didn't like it. Not one bit.

"I want to go." The words were out of my mouth before my brain had even caught up.

"I want you to go too," Eli said. "But you can't. What would we tell your mom?"

He had a point. It wasn't fair. I hadn't thought about work either. There was no way we both would be able to get off at the same time for more than a day or two.

"How long will you be gone?"

"Probably two or three days."

I knew that those few days would feel like a lot longer than they really were, and I already dreaded it.

"It's okay, Abby. You and I will have lots of girl time!" Bailey piped up, smiling at me and winking at Eli.

I was thankful for such a good friend. I squeezed her hand.

"Did they give you any idea what they had in mind for Pete?" I asked.

"No, they didn't, but I got the feeling it had something to do with his immortality."

"Where is Pete now?" Bailey asked.

This time Ren answered. "He's getting the same treatment you received." He smiled and pointed to the door off the living room.

That made Bailey smile. I couldn't blame her. It served him right. I really had done nothing to deserve the harsh treatment from Pete, and Bailey shouldn't have been involved at all. I still had no idea how Pete had dragged her into it, and I never asked. I wasn't sure that Bailey really wanted to talk about it. Personally, I would rather leave it in the past and move on.

"After this is over, we all need to go out and let off some steam. All this stress is really hard," I said with more force than necessary.

"Agreed," Bailey, Eli, and Ren said in unison.

Eli rubbed my shoulders. I felt the stress melt away and relaxed in seconds. For once, he didn't have to use his gift to help me. His hands did wonders for my aching back. How did he always know how to make me feel better? I wondered if I would ever make him feel the same comfort. I didn't know how I could. I didn't have any gifts to help me.

We didn't have much time to waste hanging around. Eli and I had to go to work at five, and Bailey's shift started at six.

After we had taken Bailey home, Eli and I had some much needed alone time. It seemed like the chaos was never going to end, and it was so nice for the two of us to be together and have a one-on-one conversation.

"After this is all over, you owe me a really great date!" I teased.

"You got it!" he said, laughing.

"Eli?"

"Yeah?"

"When did you know you had feelings for me? As more than as friends, I mean." My curiosity was getting the better of me.

"You really want to know?"

"Of course," I answered.

"From the moment you walked into the classroom on the first day of school," he admitted, avoiding eye contact.

"What?"

"I've loved you from the moment I saw you," he uttered, looking almost ashamed.

"Wow."

"Remember when you asked me if there was anyone I had a thing for?"

I nodded.

"It was you. It was always you."

Nobody besides my parents had ever cared for me as much as he did. I kissed him hard. I didn't know what I had done to deserve such passionate affection.

"I have to say, it was really hard going on double dates with you and Pete. And then trying to pretend like I had feelings for Bailey. I tried—I really did—to like her as more, but when it's not there, you can't force it," he said.

"I'm so sorry!" I said, trying to imagine what he must have felt. It must have been awful to bein that position.

Working with Eli that night was . . .interesting to say the least. Management didn't look kindly on employees dating each othersince some people have a hard time separating work and play. Eli was absolutely not one of them. Secretly, I laughed at just how "professional" he was behaving. We hadn't even acted that distantly polite before we succumbed to our feelings, and I wasn't the only one to notice. One of the other waitresses mentioned it to me.

"Did something happen between you guys?" she asked.

I laughed, feeling like I had to tell someone. "Keep a secret?"

She nodded.

"We're dating," I whispered. "Apparently, he's taking the rules very seriously," I added, making a stern face.

She giggled right along with me. "Wow!"

The rest of the night, I couldn't even walk by Eli without laughing out loud. He actually started to look at me strangely because of it, which made me laugh even harder.

We got off work at the same time and went to "our" park to eat; it was the third time that week we had gone there, which had to be some kind of record.

Eli spread a blanket out on the grass, and as we sat down, I reached my hand out to formally shake his. "Why thank you,sir, this here picnic is the cat's meow." I burst out laughing. I couldn't contain it anymore.

Eli's face broke into an amused grin as he tackled me in the grass, but I retaliated against his tickling attack tenfold. We rolled back and forth in the grass laughing, but our wrestling turned intimate when our faces were inches apart. He kissed me sweetly, tenderly, and laid me in the grass, our lips still intertwined. He lowered himself on top of me, and his hand rested on my cheek, stroking my hair out of the way. I felt myself wanting more, but I knew I wasn't ready. I pulled away hesitantly, but Eli took the hint, rolled off, and opened my pizza box for me.

We sat and talked animatedly about nothing in particular while we ate. I was beginning to love our freedom at that park—it was like our own little paradise where we were never disturbed. While I almost felt normal again, it hit me that things with Eli would never be particularly "normal." I tried not to let those thoughts enter my mind, but sometimes I couldn't help it. I was a worry-wart, just like my mom, and it seemed to get the better of me when things were out of my hands. However, there was nowhere else in the world I wanted to be at that moment instead of with Eli. I tried to focus on enjoying the present because I knew it would be over all too soon.

It wasn't until we pulled up in front of my house that Eli touched on the Pete ordeal at all. "I hate the thought of leaving you behind. The elders have assured me you will be safe while I'm gone," he said. "That makes me feel a little better."

While our concerns stemmed from two different places, we both knew our minds were consumed by the issue. He was, I assumed, worried for my safety. I hated the idea of being away from him even just for the night. After seeing him in action with Pete and his goons, I knew he would be safe. He was capable, to say the least, and had Ren to back him up. I knew Ren would never let anything happen to him. He was almost like a second dad to Eli.

"The elders are right, you know. I'll be fine. I'll miss you, but I'll be fine nonetheless," I reassured him.

He looked into my eyes. I knew I had to get inside before I made a fool of myself. I wanted him, more of him, more than I had ever experienced. I knew it with certainty. His hand brushed the back of mine, and my breath hitched in my throat. It made him smile awkwardly.

"Glad to know I'm not the only one feeling that way," he breathed in my ear, sending fire down my spine. He kissed me lightly on the cheek. "Bye Abby. I love you." He strolled away, leaving me standing on my doorstep. Before he hopped back in his car, he looked at me once more and winked before driving away. My stomach leaped. *What was it that made him so irresistible?*

He was toying with me, and I wasn't sure I liked how much fun he was having with it. I recovered, went inside, and locked the door.

"Hi, honey! How was work?" my mom called from the living room.

"Good. I'm going to take a shower. I smell like pizza!" I said, laughing it off as I jogged up the stairs. I hoped she didn't notice I was brushing her off once again.

The steamy water felt glorious streaming down my body. It immediately relaxed my aching muscles.

I knew I couldn't hide my feelings from Eli, so, of course, he had known exactly what I was feeling. It shouldn't have surprised me that he knew. That was how our bond worked. I wouldn't have it any other way, but I wished I could hide *some* things. It sure didn't leave any mystery in our relationship—at least on my end. Then again, I had a sense about him that I didn't quite understand yet. There were senses I felt when I was with him that I couldn't explain. I would have to ask Eli about it in the future, or maybe Ren instead. He might have more knowledge about it than Eli. After all, Eli was new at it too.

Eli wouldn't be able to go home like I did, and I felt bad for the position he was in. He would be at the house with Pete until morning when Ren took over again. At least with Pete locked in the room, he could still sleep.

When I checked my messages, I found one from Kelly. I was relieved to hear from her after so long. I was beginning to worry about her.

Abby,

I'm so sorry I haven't been better at keeping in touch! I've been super busy with school and work and CHEER! Yep, that's right. I'm a cheerleader! I know we always said we would never do that, but I couldn't help it. And the crazier part? I LOVE it! It's so much fun! So I might have been avoiding your emails because I wasn't sure if you would be upset . . . I hope not. I have a boyfriend, too! He's a quarterback on the football team! His name is Justin. We've only been dating a couple weeks. I guess you could say it's a little cliché, but I don't care! He makes me happy!

> Oh Abby, I hope things are going great for you there. I miss you! When are you coming to visit me and your dad? I saw him the other day by the way. He's looking thin. I think he misses you a lot. Well, I should go.Homework—you know the drill!
> Love you,
> Kelly

My heart ached to be back in California. I was supposed to be a part of all of the things she was doing! I felt a stab of jealousy. I didn't mean to, but I couldn't help it. Her life was so *normal.* There was that word again. How many times did I used to say that my life was too normal and boring?And now all Ilonged for was normalcy. She didn't have to worry about things like crazy, troublemaking immortals. Her biggest worry was homework, as it should be. I craved a little of the lightheartedness that radiated from her message.

I thought of her comment about my dad looking thin. I had noticed it the last time I had seen him. I wondered if it was because he missed me, or my mom, or if it was because there wasn't anyone to cook for him. He sounded like he'd been pretty busy at the store since we left. Maybe he didn't have the time to cook. Either way, it made me sad.

I couldn't find the courage to write her back. I had to digest her words first. I was happy for her, and I couldn't be more grateful that she had found someone that made her happy for the moment, but I needed some time.

Bing! A little box popped up on my screen.

Eli: Hey, You okay? I'm sensing some weird feelings from you.

Man! He was too in tune with me. I grumbled a bit as I typed a response.

Abby: I'm fine. Just feeling a little regret after reading a message from my friend in California.
Eli: Regret? Why?
Abby: That I'm not there. I miss her.
Eli: Oh . . .
Abby: I wouldn't change moving here. I wouldn't have met you if I hadn't. I guess I'm just missing Kelly. We're growing apart.
Eli: Oh, I get it.
Abby: Wait, you didn't think I regretted meeting you, did you?
Eli: I should have known better . . .
Abby: I would never regret meeting you. You're my everything, Eli. Don't ever think anything but that.
Eli: I guess I still need to fine-tune these feelings. I thought I was feeling jealousy.

I felt a surge of frustration. How could I explain the situation without making Eli feel responsible?

> **Abby: Well . . . I was feeling a little jealous, but not in the way you might have been thinking. I'm jealous that our relationship is . . .complicated, and Kelly's relationship with her boyfriend is normal. She doesn't have to worry about their future. I love you, Eli, and I would never leave you, but I worry about our future.**

It took a few minutes for him to respond. I didn't blame him. I was sure those thoughts had crossed his mind though.

> **Eli: I worry too. I'm sorry. I love you.**
> **Eli signed off.**

Before I could respond, he signed off. Why did this have to be so complicated? I never meant to make Eli feel bad. I was sorry I had even said anything. *Time to go to bed.* It had been a long day, and I was ready for it to be over. 'Stressed-out' didn't even begin to cover what I felt. I was drained.

CHAPTER SEVENTEEN

Eli's trip to Colorado was scheduled for the very next night—sooner than I had anticipated. I guess the elders didn't need as much time to discuss their options as they had originally thought. Eli and Ren were given eight hours of notice before they had to leave, and they were set to meet with the elders at six in the evening on Thursday.

I was sad that Eli was leaving but glad to be getting the whole thing over with sooner rather than later. We would finally be able to move on. Maybe then we could get a taste of our new normal.

They were taking Ren's car and leaving an hour after school got out.

The uneventful day sped by, but I was on the verge of a breakdown thinking of Eli's departure. *One more problem could very well send me toppling over the edge.* I tried to think that once he left, the countdown would end, and I could start anticipating his return.

I helped Eli pack before he left. It was the first time I had been in his bedroom since I became his girlfriend. I was nervous. My eyes first went to the picture on his nightstand, and I wondered where his dad was. What would he think of what his son was going through? What would he think of me, since I started it all? I couldn't help but worry his dad wouldn't like me, and now that things were going in a new direction for Eli and me, I wondered what his mom thought of me.

My eyes kept darting to the bed, and it made my stomach feel fluttery. After that, I couldn't stop. Finally, I walked over and nervously plopped down it. At least that way I wouldn't have to look at it anymore. I had sat on that bed countless times before.*What was the problem?* I folded my hands in my lap and watched Eli pack. He caught my eye and smirked at me.

"What?" I asked, blushing.

"Nothing."He chuckled, breaking eye contact as he reached into another drawer.

I threw a pillow at him, knowing exactly what he was smirking at. He caught the pillow and threw it back as he launched himself at me. I fell back against his bed, and he landed on top of me with a thud. He kissed me playfully, but his kiss slowed, growing more sensual, more heated, more needy. A fire smoldered deep inside of me. I had to extinguish it before it took over. I pushed him away and sat up, feeling childish.

I wouldn't look at him.

"Abby, as much as I want you—and believe me, it's hard for me to stop, too—I would never do anything that made you uncomfortable." He sat next to me on the bed and put his arm around me. "The best thing about our bond is that I can always tell exactly how you're feeling. If you start to feel like we're going too far, I can sense that. You get anxious and nervous. It definitely gives me an advantage."He winked. "You can trust me. I promise."

I hadn't thought about it like that before, and I knew he was right the minute he said it. I trusted him with anything and everything. Why hadn't I trusted him with this? I kissed him and rested my head on his shoulder.

"Thanks," I whispered.

"All packed," he said.

"Already?"

"Chin up! I'll be back before you know it." He held me close for a minute before he took a deep breath and stood up. "Ren is picking me up at your house in ten minutes."

We sauntered out of his house and to Eli's car hand-in-hand. My feet felt heavy and didn't seem to want to move. I shuffled them all the way to the car.

Ren was waiting for us when we got to my house. I could see Pete in the back seat. He didn't even look at me. Maybe he was ashamed, but I was glad. I didn't want my eyes to meet his. I would be thrilled if I never had to see him again for the rest of my life.

They left as quickly as they had come, and I was alone once again. Unfortunately, I didn't have to work, but Bailey did. When I talked to her at school earlier, she was very apologetic that she wouldn't be able to come over later. In fact, she was scheduled to work every day for the next five, so our plans for lots of girl time were stomped out. Fortunately, I was scheduled to work two of the four days that Eli would be gone. Eli was supposed to be home late Sunday night, possibly sooner depending on what the elders had to say. I was keeping my heart set on sooner, and I hoped it wouldn't be broken.

I went inside and started a dinner of cheese tortellini with Alfredo sauce and broccoli and threw together a salad. It felt like it had been a long time since my mom and I had eaten dinner together, so that was something to look forward to.

Mom walked in the door just as I finished setting the table. We sat down at the very same time and started dishing up. We ate quietly, savoring the food in front of us.

I had to admit; it was hard not to think about Eli, but it was easier with my mom there. She helped distract me as she talked animatedly about work and her friends. She had finally found a place where she thoroughly enjoyed working.

We finished dinner, and I decided I would tell her that Eli and I had officially become a couple. I knew she would be thrilled.

"Eli and I are together . . ." I blurted out, but I got nervous mid-sentence and trailed off. I let it sink in and waited for her excitement.

She squealed. "I knew it!"

I couldn't help but laugh. "Mom!"

"So, when did you two make it official?" she asked.

"Monday."

I felt like my mom was just as excited as I was about Eli being my boyfriend.

We plopped in front of the TV to relax together for a while until I decided I should get my homework done. Before I headed upstairs, I checked my phone. There were two new messages, both from Eli.

I miss you already.

I love you. I'll text you when we get there.

I texted him back. *I miss and love you too. I'll be waiting for your text. Xoxo.*

As I thought about him, I felt a pull on my heart. It amazed me how much he had become a piece in the puzzle of my life. I felt incomplete without him, and I wasn't sure if it was normal for it to be so serious so soon. I had never been in a serious relationship before. But then again, there was nothing about us that was normal anyway.

I went to bed exhausted. I hadn't heard from Eli, but I knew I would have a text waiting from him in the morning. I was looking forward to it.

It worried me when I had no new messages when I awoke. I sent Eli a quick text to make sure he was okay.

Are you okay? I haven't heard from you. I'm worried. Text me.

I showered and was downstairs eating when I finally got his response.

Sorry sweetie, I was so tired when we got here I forgot. We made it, and we're doing fine. Have a good day at school. Be careful. I love you.

Thank goodness! I felt so much better. I could breathe again.

That day was only the second time I had walked by myself to school. The other days Eli had driven me or followed behind me in his car. I wished I had a car already and decided on that lonely walk to school that it was time to start looking. I had almost $2,000, and with my parents' contribution, I would have a total of $4,000 for a new car. My parents had made me a deal some time ago that they would match whatever money I saved for a car. I figured $4000 could buy a decent first car. It seemed like more than some had. I would talk to them about it, and once Eli was home, I'd get his advice. It certainly gave me something else to look forward to.

Walking into first hour, I was engulfed in a whirlwind of Bailey excitement. It seemed like she was trying to compensate for not being available the night before. I couldn't help but laugh. She wasn't going to let me feel down.

Before first hour began, I told her that about my annoyingly boring walk to school and how I had decided it was time I bought a car. She was so happy for me, and we began gushing about what kind of cars we wanted and the colors we liked.

Then Bailey surprised me with her own exciting news. It turned out when her dad was out of town, he didn't like the fact that he couldn't get in touch with her. We all knew the real reason, but her dad thought it was because she had been working or sleeping each and every time he called. So he bought her a cell phone! The rest of the day we texted almost non-stop. It was a good thing we both had unlimited text messaging, or we would have been in big trouble when the bills came.

As I walked home from school, I was lost in thought until I heard someone walking behind me. Suddenly alert, I spun around. *Randy.* I was stunned speechless.

"Well, hello there." His voice dripped with sarcasm.

"What are you doing here?" I asked, trying not to show that I was scared.

I tried to take deep breaths to calm myself. I needed to keep a level head to try to outsmart, or possibly outrun, this thug.

My phone started ringing, and I knew it had to be Eli. My fear must have been pouring into himat that very moment. But I couldn't think about that; I pushed it from my head so I could focus.

"I have some unfinished business," he said.

I took a step back to put a gap between us, but he grabbed my wrists before I could get any further and shoved me into the nearest car. *So much for outrunning him.* My phone was ringing again, and I fought through my backpack to find it. Before I could grasp it, Randy pulled it out of my hand. He threw my bag into the backseat and clamped a pair of handcuffs on my wrists, binding them together. I stifled a sob as the metal bit into the tender skin of my wrists. I wasn't sure how this was supposed to stop me from getting away, but I guess it made him feel more secure. I felt claustrophobic in his car—the roof seemed to close in on me. I took deep breaths to steady my mind, hoping to prevent myself from hyperventilating. He screeched away from the curb.

"This isn't your battle," I whispered as I stared down at my shackled hands.

"Not my battle? You made it my battle when you and your little boyfriend made me go in front of the elders!" he shouted. "You can't just split up friends and walk away like nothing happened! When you crossed Pete, you crossed me!"

"Where are we going?" I asked.

"Colorado. When Pete is done with his meeting with the elders, the real fun begins."

I tried to calm myself so I didn't upset Eli even more, but it was no use. It was happening all over again. I had been kidnapped for a third time. I braced myself on the dashboard and stuck my head between my knees in an attempt to keep my lunch down. I didn't know what to do. If Eli were here, nothing like this would have happened, and I felt guilty for even allowing that thought to go through my head. I should be able to take care of myself. I always had, but I was suddenly a walking target.

"You're going to drive me, by yourself, to Colorado?"

"That's the plan," he said snidely.

I sat back against the seat. I had to think. Colorado was more than fifteen hours away. This plan was obviously not very well thought out. How was he going to drive fifteen hours without a second person to help carry the load? I wouldn't be surprised if he fell asleep at the wheel.

Eventually, I would have the opportunity to get away; at least I hoped I would. When he turned his back or stopped for gas, his guard would go down eventually, wouldn't it? It calmed me that he was alone. It would be me against him this time, and I knew I was smarter.

Since Eli said he got my pictures clearly last time, I decided I would send him a few now to give him a clue about what was happening. I didn't know if it would make him feel better or worse, but I had to do something. I obviously wasn't going to be able to call him. I focused my thoughts and looked at Randy, pushing the image out with everything I had. Then I repeated the same with the dashboard. I figured that would be enough to give him the message that I was with Randy. A minute or so passed, and my phone rang again. It killed me that I couldn't ease his worry. I knew he had to be going crazy, maybe even as crazy as I was. At least he had Ren there to help him calm down.

The next thing I knew, a different ringtone filled the car. It was coming from Randy's phone this time. He pulled it from his pocket and answered it right away.

"Pete?" he said into the phone.

I couldn't hear who was on the other end. It was quiet for a moment.

"How'd you . . ."He stopped mid-sentence and looked at me. I knew it had to be Eli. He must have taken Pete's phone and called Randy's number, and I couldn't help but smile. My message had gotten to him loud and clear. I felt proud. The bond we shared was truly amazing. I was so grateful for it. I didn't know what I would have done without it.

"Wouldn't you like to know?" I heard Randy laughing into the phone just before he hung up.

"Eli, huh? Guessing he's not too happy with you," I said.

"I don't know how he knew I had you, but you better quit it!"

"I don't know what you're talking about. I've haven't done anything." I lifted my confined hands to emphasize my point.

He planned on surprising Eli with my disappearance, but apparently he was never informed of our bond. When it came to me, there was no way to surprise Eli.

"What did he have to say?" I wanted any connection with him I could get.

"He wants me to release you, obviously, but he's not getting his way."

"Can I at least call my mom so she doesn't worry?" I asked. "I'll lie and ask to spend the night somewhere. I just don't need to bring her into this too. There are too many people involved already."

He thought for a moment before he sighed and reached for my bag. He handed it to me. "One call."

It was all I needed. Holding the phone to my ear was a lot more cumbersome than I would have imagined with my hands held tightly together.

"Hey,Mom!"

"Hi, honey!Everything okay?"

"Oh yeah, fine.Can I spend the night at Bailey's tonight? We have a project we're working on for school that's due tomorrow, and we want to get it just right." I waited.

"Uh, I guess so, honey.But call me before you go to bed and in the morning before school, okay?"

That would be more difficult than she knew. "Okay,Mom! I'll talk to you later! Bye!" I hit *end* and looked at Randy. "She's expecting a call before I go to bed and before I go to school tomorrow," I said. "If you want me to play nice, I'll be making those phone calls."

I sent a text to Bailey so she knew to play along.

Bump in the road, can't explain.My mom thinks I'm spending the night, play along, please??

I didn't wait for a response, and Randy had been so preoccupied driving that he hadn't even realized what I had done. I checked to see if I had any messages from Eli, but sadly there were none.

"Fine," he said.

I handed my phone back to him to show I was playing along, and he put it right back into my bag. I was glad he didn't hold it. That might make any getaway attempt impossible.

We were at the edge of town. We had been driving for over an hour already. "Are you planning on stopping anywhere to rest?" I asked.

"Nope."

Dang! We were starting to get out into the middle of nowhere. It was getting dark. I wasn't sure where we were, but desert surrounded us. It scared me that I was alone with a guy I didn't know. He didn't seem all that bad the last time, but boy had I been wrong. I had tried to be nice by making sure Eli knew that it wasn't him that had cut my arm, but now I regretted it. He had proved to me that he never deserved my protection in the first place.

"I don't know why you're doing this. I don't know what you're planning, but I was wrong about you," I said to make him feel guilty. I had to try something.

He huffed and gripped the steering wheel tighter. I had obviously hit a nerve.*Might as well keep poking it.*

"Would you mind telling me what you plan to do with me?" I asked.

He still didn't answer.

"You don't know, do you?" I asked.

No answer.

"Wow." I hoped I was getting through to him. He had to know how stupid he was being.

I sulked after that. I didn't feel like I was making any headway. I glanced over at the gas gauge, hoping we would have to stop soon, but I was disappointed again: half full. He noticed me looking, and I saw his jaw clench. Maybe he knew what I was planning. I guess it would be anyone's plan of escape.

A car sped by us at an unmentionable speed. I looked at our speedometer:eighty mph. The other car must have been going at least a hundred. *Wow, must have somewhere to be*, I thought. I looked at Randy and figured he was thinking the same thing because he kept looking in his rearview mirror, like he was worried.

I rested my head on the window and watched the shrubs go by. It was lulling me to sleep. I found myself fighting hard not to fall asleep. I didn't think it was a good idea. There was no telling what I would miss. It wasn't long until I couldn't fight it anymore, and my body succumbed to sleep.

The next thing I knew, there was a loud bang, and the car swerved. My head jerked sideways, then back again, slamming into the window. *Ow!* I had no idea how much time had passed or where we were. It was so stupid to have fallen asleep—we could be anywhere by now. As I looked around, all I could see was darkness. There wasn't a car in sight.

"What happened?" I stammered. Blood pumped through my body at an alarming rate.

"We hit something in the road. It's fine."

The car started bumping, and we heard the flapping sound of a flat tire.We, in fact, had pierced the tire, in the middle of nowhere, at night. It couldn't get much worse than that. I only hoped he was smart enough to have a spare.

He pulled to the side of the road. In the distance ahead of us, I could barely make out another car on the shoulder. I wondered if they, too, hit whatever was in the road. We came to a stop, and he shut the car off. I could tell he was unsure of what to do with me. He acted as though he feared I would run.

"Where am I going to go?" I asked him sarcastically.

His eyes darted around. That seemed to satisfy him enough, and he climbed out of the car. I don't know why I reassured him I wouldn't escape, but the truth was I didn't want to escape there. Who knew what was lurking out in the desert? It terrified me. He opened the trunk and got to work.

I took the opportunity to grab my backpack from the back seat, which was quite a feat with handcuffs on. First, I found my cell phone, and the light from the screen lit up the car. I hoped Randy didn't see it, but I figured he was preoccupied. There was one text message from Bailey and one from Eli. Eli's said,*I'm so worried about you right now.I love you. I hope you get this. Randy will not get away with this! I'm so sorry I wasn't there.*

He was blaming himself more than anything for it. It was his nature. At the moment he felt like a failure in his job as a Protector, and I could totally understand that. I only hoped Ren was helping calm him. I wished I had Eli's abilities. Then maybe I could help him for once.

Bailey's text said, *Okay . . . I hope everything is okay. See you tomorrow, right?*

I didn't answer either of them for fear that Randy would catch me with the phone, but I put it in my pocket so I had it. I peeked out the window and saw Randy standing there with a dumbfounded look on his face. Geez, he must not know how to change a tire. At least my dad had prepared me for that before I moved. I clutched my backpack, pushed my door open, and climbed out. I dropped my bag with a thud on the ground next to the car.

"Do you know how to change a tire?" I asked flatly.

"Uh, no. But I'll figure it out. Get back in the car."

I could tell he was embarrassed, as he should be. Nothing about him was organized. I almost felt bad for him. *Almost.*

"I'll change it," I said as I rolled up the sleeves of my shirt. "Get me the jack, spare tire, and tire iron and stand back."

He stared at me for a minute before he finally retreated and did as I asked.

I motioned for him to remove the handcuffs. "Think you could take these off?"

He hesitated once more.

"What am I going to do? Run out into the desert in the middle of the night without a clue where I am?"

He reluctantly unfastened one cuff but left the other dangling from my arm. *Great! That would make it so much easier for me to change a tire.*

"Take notes," I said. "I think bailing you out earns me the right to be let go. Just saying." It didn't hurt to try.

He didn't say anything in return. I heard a noise off in the distance behind me. It scared me thinking about what it could be.

"What was that?" I asked Randy, looking around cautiously.

"I don't know," he answered, looking spooked himself.

Could I have been kidnapped by a less manly guy? The noise got louder. It sounded like someone was walking through the desert. Someone who didn't care how much noise they made. Whatever or whoever it was seemed to be getting closer. I stood up to watch and wait, knowing any second I would be able to see it. A second later, a man stepped out from behind a bush, illuminated by the headlights of the car. His dark hair and icy eyes stared us down. He was tall and lean but very muscular. I instinctively took a step back. I didn't want to cross him. I hoped he was friendly, but being in the desert at that time of night in the middle of nowhere didn't bode well. The profile was more fit for a psychopath than a nice, normal person.

"Hi." The words tumbled from my mouth. Where they came from, I didn't have a clue. I certainly wouldn't have been so bold normally.

The man chuckled. I held tight to the tire iron in my hand with the handcuff still dangling there like the hottest new fashion accessory. I shifted the iron across my body from one hand to the other as I stood there feeling helpless.

"Well, Randy, you can't seem to keep your nose out of business it doesn't belong in, can you?" the man asked.

I looked at Randy, shocked that the man knew him. I couldn't fathom what he wanted or how he knew we would be there. I hoped I wouldn't get caught in the middle of some stupid feud between people I didn't even know. That was precisely what had happened to Bailey, and I didn't envy the position she had been in.

"What are you doing here, Vince?"

Vince? Where had I heard that name before? I couldn't put my finger on it.

"What do you think I'm doing here?"

"You aren't taking her," Randy said.

The man smirked. "Oh yeah? Well, it looks like you're stranded, and she's the one holding a tire iron. I think she'll be the judge of that."

Randy looked at me with a frightened expression and took a step back like I was holding a gun to his head. I had no idea what was happening. *What had I missed?* I didn't know whom I should trust, but at the moment, it seemed that I was the only one holding a weapon. I took a step back from Randy and the man called Vince.

"Who says I'm going with either of you," I spat, finally finding my backbone.

"Trust me, you'll want to come with me,"Vince said. And with that, he lunged at Randy.

Instead of trying to fight back, Randy just stood there with a dumbfounded look on his face. Vince's fist connected with Randy's face hard and sent him to the ground in an unmoving heap. I looked at the man and took another step backward. He started toward me and held out his hand.

"Sorry, I didn't introduce myself before. I'm Vince," he said kindly in a gruff voice.

I refused to take his outstretched hand. "I'd introduce myself, but it appears you already know who I am." I could hear the blood pumping in my ears. "What do you want from me?"

"Whoa, I don't want anything from you. I think you have the wrong idea."

"Oh yeah? Show me how I can get a different idea. You show up in the middle of the night, in the middle of nowhere, after I've been kidnapped, and I'm just supposed to think you don't want anything. Sorry—I'm not buying." I had more venomin my voice than I ever had before. It felt good to stand my ground. I could only imagine the range of emotions Eli must be feeling, but I could say for myself that it wasn't a fun roller coaster! I was breaking down, mentally and physically. I just wanted to go home.

"I'm Eli's dad," he said quietly.

Eli's dad. I dropped the tire iron and fell to my knees. The uncontrollable sobs that followed sent tremors throughout my body. I didn't realize I'd been holding back so much emotion. Whether it was to guard myself or Eli, I didn't know, but it all surfaced in that moment. Weeks of pent-up emotion spilled out.

Why had I not recognized him? In the dark, I faintly recognized his face from the picture on Eli's nightstand. Though, to be fair, his stubble was longer, which masked the outline of his face.

Eli's dad had come to save me. *How did he even know about me?* It felt like I would never get used to the new world that had been thrust upon me.

I heard Vince rummaging around for a bit before he scooped me up and carried me all the way to his car. By the time he placed me in the passenger seat, my sobbing had subsided a bit. I had been in a complete daze, and I wasn't sure how much time had passed. He unlocked the handcuffs that were still attached to my wrist and tossed them into the back seat. Then he walked around the car and threw in my bag. I hadn't seen him grab it, but I was relieved he had made the effort. After he had got in the driver's seat, he started driving in the direction Randy had been headed.

"I'm sorry," I started to say, but he put his hand up to stop me.

"Don't be.You had a right to be cautious.Like you said, it's not as if I approached in a manner that made me look trustworthy. If you hadn't questioned me, I might have wondered what was going on in that pretty little head."

"Thanks," I said.

"You're my son's girlfriend. You've become his world, and that makes you mine as well."

"But how did you even know? Eli said he hasn't seen you for a long time."

"I've been away, but I always come back to check on him. He's my son. When he left town and left you behind, I knew where I was needed. I could see the worry in his face when he left. Pete is a tricky son-of-a-gun to get involved with. I'm not sure what all went down with you guys, but I knew as soon as I saw Pete that I'd better stick around."

"Tell me about it," I said.

He laughed.

"Give me your cell phone," he said.

I pulled it out of my pocket and handed it to him. "How did you know I had it?"

"I saw you using it in the car. I'd been watching num-nuts try to figure out how to change that tire. I have to say, it was hard to hold back my laughter when you got out to change it for him. My son has good taste in women."

I felt proud that I had shown up Randy, and Vince's comment made me blush.

He dialed Eli.

"Hey son," he said.

I couldn't hear Eli, but I wished I could. He had to be ecstatic to not only hear from his dad but to hear that he had rescued me.

"She's fine.She's with me now.Where are you?" He waited a moment."Okay, we're about thirty minutes outside of Holbrook. We'll meet you there in an hour. Drive safe, son."

He hung up the phone and handed it back to me.

"He's a dedicated scoundrel, that one. He jumped on the first flight he could to Albuquerque and got a rental car from there. I'm not sure how he made such record time, but he's only about an hour and a half from us."

I could hear the fondness in his dad's voice as he spoke of Eli. He seemed to really miss him, and I could relate. I couldn't wait to see Eli. I needed him and the strength and comfort he gave me.

Vince seemed relaxed as he drove. I don't know why I hadn't noticed before, but as I gazed at him from the passenger seat, I realized he looked a heck of a lot like Eli. They shared the same dark hair, right down to the hairstyle. Their eyes were even the same shade of blue.

"Thank you," I whispered as I drifted off to sleep.

I faintly heard him say, "You're welcome."

The next thing I knew, I was waking up in the car. Wewere in the parking lot of a grocery store, and Eli and Vince were standing just outside the car, talking. I watched them catch up. I could see how happy Eli was to see his dad. I didn't want to intrude on his moment, so I didn't move.

While I sat there, I couldn't help but think that it was refreshing to see Eli so uninhibited. Even when it was just the two of us alone, he had never been quite that carefree. I felt a pang of regret that being around me made him so guarded. I knew he had to be, but it just reiterated the fact that our relationship would never be normal.

Slowly, I opened the car door and popped my head out. The sound of the door caught their attention. In an instant, Eli was at my side, helping me out of the car. I flung myself into his arms, and he almost fell over. He held me tight and didn't let go.

"Are you okay?" he asked.

"I am now," I answered, smiling.

At that moment, I knew everything would be fine. We had an understanding, a bond. A bond I knew I'd never again have with anyone else. Nothing else mattered because we could get through it together. We could make it through anything. As long as we had each other, we could conquer the world.

If you enjoyed Obscured, consider leaving a review on Amazon, Goodreads, and/or the retailer of your choice to help other readers discover this book.

Stay in touch with C. M. Boers to find
out about upcoming releases, giveaways, and chats!
Website: www.cmboers.com
Twitter: @CM_Boers
Facebook: https://www.facebook.com/boerscm
Instagram: CM_Boers

Keep reading for a sneak peek of
Divulge
Book Two

<u>CHAPTER ONE</u>

A deep sense of dread filled me as I gave chase. I can't stop. I have to catch them. I have to. I don't know what I will do if I can't. I gasped for air and cursed myself for not being in better shape.

The vacant streets of this sleepy town lay eerily quiet, sending shivers down my spine. Rain was not far off. The fragrant must of an impending downpour filled my nose. I could see the threatening bolts of lightning in the distance coming so close to the ground that I wondered if something had been struck.

The sound of my footsteps bounced off the red brick walls and echoed around me, giving the effect of countless people surrounding me. I pressed forward toward the figure in front of me. Just ahead I spotted a flash rounding the corner and vanishing from sight. I sprinted faster. The corner seemed to be miles away. My side ached and my steps faltered as the ache intensified, engulfing my entire side in fire, fire that burned unseen deep in my muscles.

Finally I made it there. I peered around the edge of the building...

I jolted from my sleep and was met by Eli's masculine scent. It filled the air, bringing me back to reality. I felt the coolness of sweat on my forehead. I was in Eli's room. It was a surreal feeling, waking up in his bed. But it was the only way I knew the night before had been real. My nightmare, on the other hand, I could only hope was just a dream. I had a sinking feeling that was not the case. After the last nightmare came true, I hoped it had been a fluke one-time thing. The last thing I needed was another complication in my already complicated life. I couldn't keep up.

After my psycho ex-boyfriend Pete kidnapped me and Bailey, he was sentenced to appear before the elders. As it turns out, Pete's family had an axe to grind with Eli's dad, and I guess if you're friends with someone who has enemies you automatically become a target. Unfortunately, the elders asked Eli and Ren to bring Pete to Colorado for the meeting, leaving me behind. The elders had assured Eli that I would be safe, and that was the one and only reason Eli, my assigned Protector and boyfriend, had left me in the first place. But it appeared that one of Pete's buffoons had other plans, and I was kidnapped once again. It was one big fiasco after another. Eli's dad, Vince, came to my rescue that time and brought me back to Eli safely. When Eli and I drove back to Phoenix late that night, I got the privilege of sleeping in Eli's bed. Of course Eli slept on the floor, but his bed smelled of him. It was intoxicating, a scent I couldn't get enough of.

I didn't want to open my eyes. If I did, that would mean this moment here, curled up in his bed, would have to end, and I would once again have to face reality. Reality was uncertain and confusing. I wasn't ready for that. I needed just a few more moments of bliss.

"How long are you going to lay there pretending to sleep?" Eli asked, startling me from my thoughts.

Dang! I had hoped he was still sleeping. I could never pull anything over on him; because of our connection he was able to sense my every emotion, my every feeling, my every desire. I opened my eyes to find him sitting across the room in a chair, watching me with a smirk on his face. He was fully dressed and his jet-black hair was wet like he had just gotten out of the shower.

I gave him a sleepy smile as he made his way over to me. Sitting down on the bed, he laced his hand into mine. It was moments like these that made my heart feel like it would burst. Our love was a breathtaking feeling, unlike anything I had ever experienced before. It made me feel like I was floating on air, like I could do anything.

He leaned down to place a kiss on my forehead. "Good morning. It's getting late. You need to get up."

"I don't want to."

"Come on," he said, pulling up on my hand and throwing the covers off me. "You can't be late for school."

Cool air filter through the sweatpants and a t-shirt Eli had given me to wear late last night. I was so comfy that it was almost painful to get up.

I sat on the edge, giving myself a few more moments of complete relaxation before I rose. Eli pulled me into his arms and held me tight. A girl could get used to waking up to this delightful welcome, in spite of my bed head and morning breath.

"Thank god you're safe. I don't know what I would have done." His hushed voice trembled.

I knew he would blame himself for what happened, but the truth was that nobody could have predicted that Randy, Pete's buffoon, was still a threat, let alone that he would attack me while Eli was gone.

"There was nothing you could have done. No one could have

known what was going to happen," I said as I tugged his chin, making him look me in the eye.

The sadness in his icy blue eyes tugged at me. He pulled away and ran his hands through his hair. "Dang it Abby, if I had been there he never would have gotten within five feet of you." He would no longer look at me. "I should never have left you. I won't make that mistake again."

"It's okay, Eli," I said, hoping to convince him it wasn't his fault. "Besides, you can't be with me all the time."

He had already made up his mind, and there was no way I could change it now.

"No, it's not. It's my job to protect you, and last night I didn't do that."

I didn't say more, knowing there was nothing I could say that would make him feel better. He would have to work this one out on his own. Instead, I stared at the floor, unsure of what to do or say next.

"I bought some clothes for you to wear. They're in the bathroom," he said.

I kissed his cheek and wandered through the door of Eli's adjoining bathroom. He occupied the smaller of the two master suites of his parents' large, three-bedroom house.

I showered, toweled off, and looked at the clothes Eli had picked out for me, surprised to find that they were just the right size. The outfit was simple and exactly to my taste. I wondered how Eli knew me so well, but then I felt silly. Of course he knew me well—he could feel everything I felt, everything I liked or disliked.

I slipped into the clothes and combed out my hair with what I assumed was Eli's comb. I found a brand-new toothbrush lying on the counter and smiled, thinking about how good he was at making me feel comfortable and at home here.

I found Eli waiting for me in the same chair as before, reading a magazine. We went into the kitchen and found his mom and dad at the table eating breakfast together. I don't know what I had expected to find, but their coziness surprised me. I guess I figured that since his dad had been gone, his parents were no longer together, but based on what I was seeing pass between them, that wasn't the case. They seemed so happy to be together.

"Good morning guys," Vince said as we sat down at the table.

"Morning," Eli and I said in unison. We looked at each other, surprised, and I felt my cheeks warm.

We each poured our cereal and ate as quickly as we could.

"How are you doing, Abby?" Vince asked me, his voice filled

with concern.

"I guess I'm doing okay. It's been a bit of a roller coaster. Being kidnapped once sucks, but twice in less than a week is overwhelming to say the least. But I'm managing," I said, trying to sound lighthearted when that was the last thing I felt.

He looked at me sympathetically but didn't say more.

"I'm glad you're holding up," Eli's mom, Elizabeth, said.

I hadn't noticed before how radiant she was. She glowed. Maybe it was because the love of her life was back home with her. Her straight black hair hung just past her shoulders, and her bright hazel eyes sparkled. I could tell Eli got quite a few of his amazing features from her.

I wondered what life must be like for her. Her husband was a Protector, assigned to protect others at the elders' discretion. She couldn't follow him either, at least not all the time. It was the same life I was inevitably facing with Eli, and I wasn't sure how I could do it. It saddened me to think I would live much of my life without him.

When we met Bailey in the courtyard at school, she swept me up in a whirlwind of Bailey enthusiasm and immediately began firing questions.

"What in the world happened last night?"

"Hello to you too," I said, sticking my tongue out at her.

"Don't laugh at me! I was so worried about you!"

"I'm sorry, Randy kidnapped me." It came out of my mouth as a fact, as if I were detached from it, like we were talking about the weather.

Bailey's eyes grew round and for a moment she was speechless. "Oh my gosh Abby! That's awful. But how did you get away?"

"Well, he drove me to the middle of nowhere. We ended up getting a flat tire, that as it turns out, Eli's dad, Vince, caused." I grinned at Eli. "Then Vince came out of nowhere. Literally, he came out from behind a bush in the middle of the desert to confront Randy and rescue me. Eli, with our connection being what it is, knew something was wrong. He jumped on the first flight he could and drove the rest of the way out to meet us. We got back to Eli's house around one o'clock in the morning. I stayed the night, and here we are." I was breathless when I finished.

Bailey didn't seem to know what to say.

"Wow."

"We have to get to class, we're going to be late," Eli cut in.

The last thing I wanted was to go to class. I had so many questions that needed answers I wouldn't get in class. I couldn't wait to drill Eli when we were alone again.

I pushed all my troubles away for the time being and tried my hardest to focus on school. By lunchtime, I felt like my efforts were just beginning to pay off. I sat there, taking in the surrounding conversations without adding anything of my own.

I felt a little like a double agent living a secret life apart from our friends at school. Their biggest concern was their next test or why their parents were on their case this time. Mine was whether I would make it through the day without yet another person coming out of the woodwork to do Eli or me harm. To top it all off, I was having a new nightmare that had a good chance of coming true. We were worlds apart, yet here we sat, all together as if nothing was separating us at all. I longed to be like my friends again, to lead a normal life with normal problems. But then again, I wouldn't have Eli. Some things were worth the sacrifice.

I continued to push through the day with my curiosity picking and pulling its way through the web of happy thoughts I created, casting dark shadows on even the good.

When the final bell of the day rang, I felt nothing but relief. I meandered my way through the halls to meet Eli, and my heart leapt at the sight of him waiting for me. His striking good looks captivated my attention first; then he flashed a huge smile just for me. It was enough to make me melt.

He drove us to my house and, for the first time in over twenty-four stress-filled hours, I stepped past the threshold. My house waited for us, empty, perfect for our upcoming conversation. I had been both dreading and anticipating it. I grabbed us drinks before plopping down on the couch.

"Okay, what's going on with Pete?" I asked without wasting another second.

"They are proceeding as planned. They held the meeting last night; obviously, I wasn't able to be there. I talked to Ren this morning before you woke up, and the elders decided that Pete will be stripped of his immortality, which in my opinion should have been done long ago, as his dad and uncle were. He has been told to leave the United States and find a new place to live." He paused, "If he doesn't, they will be forced to take further action."

"What does that even mean?"

"I don't know."

I frowned.

"Now what?"

"Ren is holding Pete until they can carry out the punishment, and then they are trusting him to leave on his own."

"And they expect him to just do what they want?"

"I guess."

"I can't believe this! He's just going to walk away like nothing happened!"

"Well, not completely," Eli said.

I shot him a dirty look.

"Okay, okay. I understand why you're angry. I am too. But what choice do we have? There's nothing we can do."

I shrugged.

"He won't be stupid enough to come back here again," Eli said.

"Where did that kind of assumption get us last time?"

He laughed and wrapped his arm around me. We sat with our sides glued to each other, enjoying our time together. As much as I didn't want Pete to walk free, I was glad he was at least being punished. I hoped it would be enough of a deterrent for him to leave us alone. It was about time Eli and I got to relax and just have fun together.

"I should go. I have a lot of homework to catch up on."

I shot him a pouty face.

Reluctantly, I walked him to the door and kissed him goodbye, waiting until he drove away before closing the door. I already missed him. I had it bad. Really bad.

The next day I felt like an ordinary high school student, enjoying my day at school with my boyfriend by my side. We didn't discuss anything other than school and weekend plans. After so much craziness, it was nice to feel the same as everyone else. I never thought I would crave normalcy so much. Today was the day our troubles would end, the day we had waited for: Pete would be stripped of his immunity to peril and sent packing.

Eli was talking to Ren as we walked to lunch. From the sound of it, everything was progressing on schedule. He would take Pete to the elders at 1 p.m., just a short two hours away. I couldn't wait for the call that the deed was done.

When I met with Eli after school, he informed methat Ren still hadn't called. He seemed more worried than I expected him to be. It had been nearly two hours since the meeting had been set to begin.

I dialed Ren from my phone, and the call went straight to voicemail. A sick feeling bubbled up in my stomach. *What could have happened?*

Instead of wasting time waiting for him to call back, we went straight to Vince.

About the Author

Obscured was C. M.'s debut novel. What began as a way to spend her free time slowly transitioned into a passion for writing. The best is yet to come!

C. M. is a mother of three. She grew up in the sunshine state of Arizona with a love of reading and an ambition to write. But she never took her writing seriously until after the birth of her first child. After that she took up writing more seriously in her spare time and hasn't stopped since.